THE QUEEN'S TRIUMPH

ALSO BY JESSIE MIHALIK

The Rogue Queen Series

The Queen's Gambit

The Queen's Advantage

The Queen's Triumph

The Consortium Rebellion Series

Polaris Rising

Aurora Blazing

Chaos Reigning

THE QUEEN'S TRIUMPH

JESSIE MIHALIK

THE QUEEN'S TRIUMPH

NYLA Publishing
121 W 27th Street, Suite 1201, NY 10001, New York.
http://www.nyliterary.com

ACKNOWLEDGMENTS

I'd like to thank the following people for their help and support.

Thanks to my fabulous agent, Sarah E. Younger, whose insightful comments made this a stronger story. I'm delighted to have you in my corner!

Thank you to Kelsey, NYLA intern extraordinaire, who helped refine the cover. And thank you to Natanya Wheeler, Kate Ward, and everyone else at NYLA who helped bring the book into the world!

Thanks to Patrick Ferguson and Tracy Smith for listening to me gripe about writing in, this, the longest year on record. We've almost made it through!

My deepest gratitude to Chi-An Chien who graciously volunteered to beta read and offered fantastic feedback. The story is better because of you!

As always, all my love to my husband, Dustin, who reads my stories before anyone else and continually cheers me on. I love you, darling.

Finally, thanks to all of the readers who followed along as the story was posted on my website, www.jessiemihalik.com.

Writing has been as difficult as everything else this year, but I appreciate every one of you who offered encouragement and understanding when the deadline slipped further than I would've liked. I hope you enjoy Samara and Valentin's happily ever after!

1

The trick to meeting an enemy at a time and location set by a traitor was this: *don't.* I stalked through Arx trying to find a way around such a universal truth, but the plain white halls of the Rogue Coalition's capital did not offer up any suggestions.

Two weeks ago, I'd been in the Kos Empire's capital city, helping Valentin Kos find the traitors in his court. Before she'd been arrested, Advisor Hannah Perkins had set up a meeting for me with Commander Adams of the Quint Confederacy. She had probably hoped that the two of us would take each other out while she continued to undermine Valentin's authority.

It hadn't quite worked out that way for her, but the meeting still stood, and it was just two weeks from now.

Hannah and Adams had secretly worked together, so the meeting would undoubtedly be a trap. Skipping it entirely was the only way to guarantee safety, but that wasn't an option. Commander Adams had attacked my people, destroyed my ship, and now he threatened the tentative peace treaty in the works between the universe's two superpowers.

He needed to die—*slowly.*

I just had to figure out how to go to the meeting and survive. And, ideally, how to go alone.

I mulled over the problem as I moved through the familiar halls. Moving helped me think, and being out and about also gave people a chance to air their grievances before they became problems. My frequent availability was one of the reasons I was still queen after five years, despite ruling a group of people who took grave exception to rules.

I stopped in the market, and Zita shouted from her bakery, "Samara! If you don't kill Eddie, I'm going to do it for you."

She poked her head out of the building and scowled at me. She was in her forties, with pale skin and curly red hair. I was happy to see that her cheeks were returning to their usual cherubic fullness thanks to the new food supply.

Zita was Arx's main baker, and Eddie was our main chef. They'd been locked in a fierce competition to produce the best pastry, and Zita was kicking his ass. She had years of experience on him, so it didn't surprise me that he'd tried a new tactic.

"What has he done now?" I asked.

"He's been in my supplies! As if I wouldn't notice that salt and sugar aren't the same thing."

"Did you catch it before you used them?"

She looked mortally offended. "Of course!"

I laughed and raised a placating hand. "Okay, I'll talk to him. Don't start a murder spree just yet."

She harrumphed at me, but finally inclined her head and went back to work. I stayed and chatted with a few other people before moving on, but as soon as I was alone again, my mind returned to the problem of the meeting.

No matter how far I walked, I couldn't figure out a solution because Arietta Mueller, my best friend and head of security, would never allow me to track Adams solo, no matter how well suited to the task I was.

I'd tried to leave my bloody past behind, but it kept coming back. Still, I'd use every skill I'd ever learned if it meant keeping those close to me safe.

And keeping them safe sometimes meant keeping them in the dark.

I sighed and rubbed my forehead. I wasn't stupid enough to hie off after Adams without a word to anyone, so I had to figure out how to include Ari in my plans without putting her in danger.

She already knew about the meeting, so unless I was exceedingly careful, she would see through me like glass. And she wasn't exactly a shrinking violet. She would get her wife Stella involved, and then, before I knew it, everyone I cared about would be charging into danger with me.

Including Valentin Kos, emperor of half of the known universe.

At the thought of Valentin, my steps faltered. When I was in Koan, he'd all but declared he loved me. Just remembering it sent electric shocks skating along my nerves—half terror, half excitement.

In Koan, I'd felt so hopeful about our future. But now that I'd returned to Arx, I kept waiting for the other shoe to drop, for the universe to pull back the curtain and laugh at how gullible I'd been to believe such a thing, but Valentin showed no signs of deception. He didn't press, but he didn't back off, either. And now that he'd fully recovered from his injuries, I was desperate to see him in person. He was due to arrive tomorrow. Butterflies danced in my belly.

We'd both been busy lately taking care of our people. My citizens had finally lost some of the hard, hungry edge they'd been sporting for months. Cheeks were filling in and smiles were more common. We had food again, and I'd be damned if I let Adams and his crew ruin that.

The Rogue Coalition was the last resort for most of the people here. If I couldn't protect them, no one would, and that was unacceptable. I had two weeks to figure out how to kill an enemy surrounded by true believers and then speed up the truce between the universe's two superpowers.

I laughed to myself. Sure, no problem.

At least I could be reasonably certain that Adams would show at the meeting. Like me, he would expect a trap, but his arrogance would ensure his arrival. He wouldn't want to waste an opportunity to rub his success in Koan in my face. The loss of *Invictia* still ached like a lost limb.

Eddie Tarlowski stepped into the hall from a storage room. When he caught sight of me, he asked, "Hey, boss, you okay?"

"Just trying to solve all of the universe's problems," I said with a wry grin. "You need something?"

He shook his head, sending his shaggy blond hair flying. Eddie had been one of the best thieves alive before he'd been conscripted by the Quint Confederacy and wounded in battle. He'd turned up in Arx with a mechanical arm and leg and a galaxy-sized chip on his shoulder. It'd taken months and months before he'd found peace in the kitchen.

"Nah, just wondering if I needed to kick that fancy emperor's ass because he put that look on your face."

Warmth bubbled in my chest as I realized Eddie was serious. My citizens tolerated Valentin, but they didn't exactly love him. Many of them had fled from Kos territory once the war got too close, and the resulting bitterness wouldn't be overcome anytime soon, no matter how much discounted food the Kos Empire shipped in.

I smiled gently. "Thank you, but it's not Valentin. It's Adams."

Eddie bared his teeth in a quick, edged smile and spread his arms in an inviting gesture. "I'd be happy to kick his ass, too, all you need to do is ask."

"You'll have to get in line."

"Seriously, though, if you need someone to get you in, let me know. There isn't a door built that I can't crack." A sly grin pulled at the corner of his mouth. "And I'll give you my best friends-and-family discount."

I laughed. "So I'll only have to mortgage *half* of the Coalition's assets to afford you, then? You're a gem, Eddie. And I'll take my knife back."

"I'll get you sooner or later," he grumbled good-naturedly.

My combat knife appeared in his hand, seemingly pulled from thin air. He handed it back with a flourish. Eddie talked with his hands, a clever visual distraction that worked even when he appeared to be too far away to steal. He never stole for keeps, now, more for the thrill of it. The knife would've turned up later somewhere obvious in my quarters—my *locked* quarters.

The knife had been clipped in a holster on my utility belt. I hadn't felt him lift it, but I'd felt the balance of the belt shift slightly once it was gone. If I'd been less attuned to my weapons, he would've gotten away with it.

I waited, staring him down, but he had innocent down to an art. I raised an eyebrow and his mouth turned down into a pout. He handed me the magazine of plasma rounds he'd lifted while returning the knife.

"You're no fun at all."

I had to fight to keep my expression stern and suppress the grin that wanted to escape. "I haven't murdered you, yet, despite an impassioned plea from your most recent victim. Did you really think that Zita wouldn't notice that you'd switched her salt and sugar?"

The innocent look was back. "I have no idea what you're talking about."

"I am fine with pranks," I said, "but if Zita *hadn't* noticed, then food would've been wasted. You know better." We all shared the recent memory of gnawing hunger and months of PRiMeR, the cheap meal replacement that was only a half step up from animal slop.

Eddie nodded once, sharply, something fragile in his expression. "I got carried away. It won't happen again."

I squeezed his shoulder. He froze slightly at the contact but didn't pull away. "We all get carried away once in a while. Apologize to Zita. And if you need to talk, you know where my quarters are."

When I didn't say anything else, he blinked at me. "That's it?"

"That's it." Justice in Arx was swift and brutal, when warranted. Harsh consequences were necessary when a good percentage of the population remained outlaws and rogues. But small pranks allowed people to keep their skills sharp and reduced unrest. There were only a few rules—no damage, stolen items must be returned promptly, and if the subject of the prank asked you to stop, you did.

"I figured you'd slap me back to peeling potatoes for a month," Eddie said with a faint grimace. He'd peeled mountains of potatoes when he'd first arrived.

"Zita caught it, so no harm done. And apologizing to her is going to be harder than peeling potatoes anyway."

He groaned when he realized I was correct. "You're evil, boss."

I grinned at him. "Don't forget it."

———

I WAS NEARLY BACK to my quarters when I received a neural link connection request from Valentin. The butterflies came back armed with knives.

When I accepted the link, his voice filled my head, warm and familiar. *Would it be okay with you if I arrived a day early?*

A day early meant *today*. It was just a single transit to tunnel here from his home on Achentsev Prime, so if he left now, he could arrive in an hour or two. He could be here before dinner.

I swallowed my nerves and gave him the truth. *Of course. You are always welcome here.*

Good, he said with a smile in his voice, *because I'm in orbit. Permission to land?*

Shock stole my breath for a moment. *You're here?*

Yes. I haven't contacted ground control yet because I'm testing out some new stealth tech and it appears to be working. His tone turned rueful. *I'm hoping you'll smooth it over with Ari before I get on-planet and she murders me.*

Letting Ari at you would serve you right, but I'll talk to her and get you approval to land. You might as well use my hangar unless you're in your flagship.

Your hangar is perfect, thank you. See you soon.

I murmured my farewell and disconnected the link. Valentin was here. *Now.*

And he'd bypassed our security and made it to orbit without anyone knowing. Ari really *was* going to kill him.

I opened a neural link to Ari and updated her on the situation. She was displeased—to put it mildly—but she agreed not to murder him straight away. She did, however, refuse to let me meet him alone. She wanted to be there when he landed, just in case he'd decided to turn traitor. Ari's paranoia kept us safe, so I agreed, even though I really didn't think it was necessary.

Ten minutes later, she knocked on my door. When I opened it immediately, she laughed at me. I could've waited a few moments so it wouldn't seem as if I had been waiting for her, but Ari knew me too well for that. "Anxious, are you?" she asked.

"Terrified," I admitted quietly.

She nodded sagely. "When we first met, Stella thought I had heart problems because while I appeared calm, my pulse was always sky high." Ari laughed and shook her head. "She wanted me to do a bunch of tests. I didn't have the courage to tell her that it was because I was totally gone for her until much later."

"How did she react?"

"She knew, of course. I wasn't as smooth as I thought. But she was delighted when I finally admitted it because she felt the same." A secret smile touched Ari's mouth. "The rest is history."

Ari was tall and blonde and beautiful. Stella was petite and dark-haired and lovely. Together they were a stunning couple, made even more so by their obvious love. Longing tugged at my heart. I wanted what Ari and Stella had—someone who always had your back and felt like home. And the more I thought about it, the more that image looked like Valentin Kos.

I followed Ari to my private hangar. The main hangar was much bigger, designed for large military ships, but I'd taken over the base commander's quarters, and they came with an attached hangar designed to house a smaller, personal ship. I'd avoided it since my return from Koan. The empty space just twisted the knife of *Invictia*'s loss.

A ship was already on the ground, but it wasn't *Korax*, Valentin's personal ship. This ship was the same jet black as *Korax,* but it was all smooth curves and sweeping lines. It was beautiful, and I'd never seen a ship quite like it. I itched to see if the inside was as unusual as the outside.

The cargo ramp lowered and Valentin emerged, trailed by his guard, Luka. Valentin had a lean build that belied just how strong he was. Today he'd skipped the formal regalia and wore black pants and a lightweight, cream-colored sweater. His tousled dark hair, sharp cheekbones, and strong jaw completed the picture. He was, in a word, *gorgeous.*

Behind Valentin, Luka hovered with his trademark scowl in place. He was built like a muscled mountain topped with ice-blond hair. When he glanced over my shoulder and his scowl got worse, I had to suppress a smile. Not only was Ari not Luka's favorite person—not after she'd stolen his prototype armor—but she also wasn't Imogen.

Imogen had accompanied me to Koan as my personal guard.

She and Luka had butted heads many times, but Imogen was far tougher than she looked, and I was pretty sure she had Luka wrapped around her finger.

I made a mental note to ask her to come to the official meetings. I didn't need another guard, but I wanted to see the sparks fly.

I met Valentin halfway across the hangar. I was afraid our meeting would be awkward, but he smoothly took my hands and kissed the air next to my cheek. "I missed you," he murmured into my ear.

His rich voice was even better in person, and my worry melted away. "I missed you, too. I'm glad you're here."

He stepped back with a secret smile. "I brought you a present."

I glanced at his empty hands uneasily. Whatever he'd brought had to be small. Was it a ring? Terror and longing fought for dominance.

Valentin's smile turned into a laugh. "It's not what you're thinking," he assured me with a wink. "Not yet."

"Then what is it?"

"I left it in the ship. Come with me and I'll show you."

I couldn't help the grin. "You know that sounds like a bad pickup line, right?"

His smile turned wicked. "That wasn't what I meant, but I could show you *that,* too, if you'd like."

Heat spiraled through me. I *would* like that. I let myself imagine it for a second before returning to responsibility. "Later," I promised. "For now, I want to see the inside of this ship. Is it a prototype?"

"Something like that." He turned to Luka. "Stay here and keep Ari company."

Luka's scowl got fiercer and a muscle flexed in his jaw, but he remained silent and nodded curtly. I figured this wasn't the first time Valentin had run this plan by him.

Ari was more vocal. "I'm not staying behind while you take Queen Rani on a foreign ship—especially not one capable of defeating our sensors." She was being excruciatingly formal and her tone had a chilly bite. She hadn't forgiven Valentin for his little stunt earlier.

Valentin swept his arm toward the ship. "You're welcome aboard, of course."

Ari grunted her agreement, and I hid a smile. That grunt meant she wanted to argue, but Valentin had taken all of the wind out of her sails with his easy acquiescence.

Valentin guided me toward the ship. Luka and Ari fell in behind us, silent, grumpy shadows. We climbed the ramp and entered the cargo bay.

"Welcome to *Ardia*," Valentin said.

The inside of the ship was as beautifully built as the outside, even here where most ships were bare and utilitarian. The walls were sculpted metal and the floor had been etched to resemble wooden planks. A staircase with a banister of what looked like real wood led to the upper levels of the ship. The understated elegance on display meant this ship was *ridiculously* expensive.

"Are you replacing *Korax*?" I asked. "Did Asmo's family bribe you with this ship to lighten his sentence?" Asmo Copley was one of Valentin's former advisors—one who'd betrayed him. Copley Heavy Industries was one of the largest shipbuilding companies in the Kos Empire. If anyone could build this ship, they could.

Valentin's expression hardened at the mention of Asmo. "No, I'm not replacing *Korax* and if the Copleys tried it, I'd lock up the whole family. They know they're on thin ice." He glanced at Ari. "Would you mind waiting here? I promise I'm not going to harm Samara, but I'd like to give her the present in private, please."

Ari looked set to argue until I glared at her. She linked me instead. *Shout the second anything seems strange.*

Do you really believe Valentin is going to try anything, after all we've been through?

She wrinkled her nose at me. *No,* she admitted, *but caution is prudent.*

Noted. Don't kill Luka before I get back.

No promises.

I closed the link just as Ari said, in her grumpiest voice, "Fine, but don't be too long."

Valentin inclined his head in agreement and offered me his hand. I slipped my hand into his, and the butterflies took wing once again.

He led me upstairs to *Ardia*'s main level. In the corridor, the walls and ceiling were lined with color-changing panels—another incredible expense. The panels currently displayed a soft gradient that started with yellows and oranges at the bottom and transitioned through to pale blue at the ceiling. The effect made the hallway seem like it was bathed in sunset. A fraction more color and it would've been too much, but the soft pastels worked perfectly.

This wasn't a random computer generation; this had been designed by an artist with an excellent eye.

Valentin had stopped and turned to watch me as I stared at the panels, mesmerized. I couldn't be sure, but I thought the colors were ever-so-slowly changing, like a real sunset.

"This is lovely," I murmured. "Completely unnecessary, but lovely."

"I thought you might like it." He tilted his head, considering me. "May I kiss you?"

The simmering desire I'd been feeling blazed brighter. He waited with quiet patience as my gaze tracked across his face. If not for the heat in his eyes and the tense line of his jaw, I'd think he was completely uninterested in my answer.

Rather than answer, I wrapped my hand around the back of his neck and gently pulled his face down to mine. Our lips met and my eyes slid closed. His lips were warm and firm as they ghosted across mine, once, twice. He made a low sound in the back of his throat, and the kiss changed from light and teasing to hot and heavy. Fiery pleasure sent my blood fizzing through my veins.

Valentin was warm and solid and *here*. There hadn't been another attack after I'd left Koan, a worry I'd carried every day for two weeks. I put all of the feelings I couldn't yet admit into the kiss and he groaned again.

This felt like home.

By the time we pulled apart, I had forgotten all worries about awkwardness. His expression was fierce with desire, and I wanted nothing more than to drag him into the nearest bedroom and have my way with him. But Luka and Ari were waiting in the cargo bay.

I thumped my head against his shoulder in frustration and breathed in the warm smell of cloth heated by his body. "Do you think Ari and Luka would leave if we asked them?"

Valentin wrapped his arms around me and ran a soothing hand down my back. "Thanks to my entrance, I feel like maybe I'm not Ari's favorite person right now, so, no, I don't think so." His tone was rueful, but I could hear the smile.

"Then I suppose the personal tour of the bedroom will have to wait."

Valentin's arms tightened as I straightened. "On second thought," he said with a grin, "Ari and Luka will definitely leave."

I laughed and brushed a light kiss across his mouth. "Show me my present."

"Do you want to see the rest of the ship first?" At my nod, his grin turned sly. "The captain's quarters are nearby. Should we start there?"

My grin matched his. "Perhaps we should leave the best for last."

Valentin's hands flexed against my back, but he drew away

and swept an arm toward a door on the port side of the hallway. "Then let's start in the guest quarters."

We toured the rest of the ship, and the more I saw, the more I wondered why he had acquired it if he wasn't planning to replace *Korax*. Every detail was exquisitely perfect. *Ardia* had been lovingly designed by someone with piles of money and excellent taste. I started making mental notes for the ship I still needed to order to replace *Invictia*. I couldn't afford a fraction of the elegance of this ship, but there were a few things I could do to get a similar effect for less money.

By the time we stopped outside the captain's quarters, I was desperate to see the design. So when Valentin opened the door, I immediately swept past him into the room, only to freeze in place.

The walls were a familiar pale gold, and a big bed dominated a room that was strikingly, heartbreakingly familiar. This room was a near perfect—but larger—replica of my quarters on *Invictia*.

2

"Do you like it?" Valentin asked quietly from somewhere behind me.

It took two tries before I could swallow past the lump in my throat and force the words out. "What is this?"

I heard him shift. "It's not perfect, but I tried to get it as close as I could remember. I know nothing will ever replace *Invictia*, and I'm so fucking sorry you lost your ship because of me. But I'm hoping that you'll accept *Ardia* as a poor replacement." He paused, then tacked on, "Surprise."

That did surprise a half laugh, half sob out of me. I looked around the room with vision gone watery. It wasn't an exact replica, but it was such a close match that Valentin must've personally specified every detail from memory—and he'd only been on my ship once.

In the soft sunset light still streaming in through the open door to the hall, it was incredibly, unimaginably perfect, and I wanted it more than I'd ever wanted almost anything.

But it was far, *far* too much.

This ship would easily buy four or five ships of *Invictia's* caliber—and that was before you added whatever special stealth technology the ship had.

The door swished closed as Valentin moved farther into the room. He stopped in front of me, expression shuttered. He gently touched my damp cheek. "I apologize. I just thought…" He shook his head. "It doesn't matter. You're welcome to pick whatever ship you like, of course. It doesn't have to be this one."

"It's perfect," I admitted softly. "I love everything about it. But I can't possibly acc—"

Valentin interrupted me. "If you don't accept, then *Ardia* will sit, unused, in a berth somewhere. I already told you that I'm not replacing *Korax,* and I won't sell *Ardia*. I had this ship trimmed out just for you, so you'd be doing me—and the ship— a favor by accepting."

I arched an eyebrow, back on firmer ground and glad that he hadn't made a big deal of my tears. "Are you trying to *guilt* me into accepting a ship?"

He grinned at me. "Yes. Is it working?"

I had to laugh at his shameless honesty. "Maybe."

"Do you want to see the bridge before you decide to mothball poor *Ardia* for the foreseeable future?"

I wavered, torn. If I saw the bridge, the ship would be as good as mine. My ability to be selfless only extended so far, and the rest of the ship, plus this room, had already stretched it to the breaking point.

"It's got all of the latest technology, plus a few surprises," Valentin tempted.

I paced across the plush rug—an upgrade from the worn one I'd had on *Invictia*. "You're not playing fair."

"No, I'm playing to win. You deserve a ship even nicer than this one, but I worked with what I could on a limited timeline."

"When did you order it?" I asked, looking at him.

"Right after the attack on *Invictia*," he admitted.

"That was before I left Koan!"

"I did tell you that I had some ship designs in mind."

"You also told me that it was my choice."

"It absolutely is. If you truly don't like *Ardia,* I'll buy you whatever you want. But if you're just declining because you think it's *too* nice, then I'm going to try to persuade you to keep it, by whatever means necessary. One benefit of being emperor is plenty of money. I've started giving it away fast enough to give my advisors gray hair, but let me be selfish and do this for you."

His expression told me that he was deadly serious. If I didn't like *this* ship, he would buy me something else. At the height of my career as the Golden Dahlia, I'd made very good money. Death was an expensive business, and I'd used my proceeds to buy *Invictia.* But even after I'd had the money, I'd agonized for months over the design, sometimes going so far as to price out individual parts.

Being able to buy multiple ships at the drop of a hat, one of them *marvelously* expensive, was a level of wealth that was so far out of my normal that I couldn't wrap my head around it. Even when the Rogue Coalition was running at peak performance we couldn't just buy ships willy-nilly.

Valentin frowned. "What?"

"What are you doing with me?"

His frown deepened. "What do you mean?"

"You can buy all of this," I waved an arm around to indicate everything in the ship, "and I'm a former assassin turned rebel queen who almost let her people starve to death. We could not be more different. Why me? Why not some princess or the daughter of an industry titan. Someone more suited to your life."

I had plenty of self-confidence in most areas of my life, thanks to hard lessons learned well and a driving need for self-reliance, but relationships were not one. I knew I had many amazing qualities, but I had even more glaring flaws and liabilities. *I* wouldn't date me.

Valentin's expression smoothed out into a blank mask. It was somehow worse than the frown. "Do you really think I'm that shallow?"

I'd hurt him. I hadn't meant to, but that was irrelevant. "No, of course not. I didn't choose my words with care. I apologize. I'm the one who's lacking here, not you."

"I wasn't raised to be Emperor. If anyone is lacking, it's me, but do you know what I see when I look at you?" he asked, mask still firmly in place.

I shook my head and refused to drop my eyes, even though I didn't want to look at him while he laid me bare.

"I see strength, resilience. Caring, self-sacrifice, and love." My lips parted in surprise, but he wasn't done. "I also see cunning intelligence and fierce protectiveness." He cupped my face and smoothed a thumb across my cheekbone. "Your life wasn't easy, but it shaped you into the woman you are now, and I like you just as you are."

His words pierced me, not with the hurt I'd feared, but with the strength of his care. Standing in this room, on this ship, the enormity of that care crashed into me. Valentin Kos, emperor of half the known universe, was here for *me*—and he wasn't leaving.

I tipped my face up to his, and he met me halfway. His lips ghosted over mine, and I lost myself in the pleasure of the kiss. The pieces fell into place. Valentin had already slipped past my emotional defenses.

He was *mine*.

I drew back with a surprised inhale. For the last couple of weeks, I'd been subconsciously holding back, waiting for him to come to his senses, waiting for his interest to be revealed as a huge cosmic joke. But I was half of this relationship, and if I wanted it to work, I had to fight for it.

I *always* fought for what was mine.

My doubts settled as they always did when I had a plan and a path forward. There would still be occasional issues—no plan was perfect—but I felt more grounded. And I excelled at modifying plans in motion.

I kissed Valentin again, a quick brush of my lips against his.

"What was that for?"

"That was an apology for being an ass. Thank you for the ship. I love it more than you could possibly know. Show me the bridge before I forget Ari and Luka are waiting for us in the cargo bay."

Valentin's eyes softened before a playful grin tilted up one corner of his mouth. "If we take long enough, maybe they'll get bored and leave."

"Or barge in and interrupt."

His laugh echoed around the room. "Yeah, you're probably right."

———

THE BRIDGE WAS JUST as amazing as the rest of the ship. Glass and metal surfaces gleamed under the soft lighting. At Valentin's urging, I sank into the deeply padded captain's chair, and the console in front of me lit with a beautiful blue glow.

"Welcome, Captain Rani," the ship greeted in the best impersonation of a masculine human voice I'd ever heard. It was uncanny.

"Thank you," I murmured instinctively.

"You're welcome. Please let me know if you need anything. I currently answer to Ardia. Would you like to change my name?"

"No, thank you."

The ship chimed an acceptance and fell silent.

"That's not a normal ship computer."

Valentin laughed. "No, it's not. I did tell you that I had a few more surprises for you. Ardia—the ship's computer—is one of them. It's the latest artificial intelligence assistant. The more you use it, the more it will learn your habits and preferences. It also has a full Kos military module and can control the ship's offenses, defenses, and flight during hostile maneuvers."

"Is it any good?"

Valentin's teeth flashed in a fierce smile. "Yes."

My fingers itched to launch the ship into the sky, to see how well it handled, but I resisted the temptation. I wanted my first flight to be when Valentin and I could be alone—then we could christen the ship properly.

I stood and wrapped my arms around Valentin, drawing him into a tight hug. "Thank you," I whispered into his chest.

His arms settled around me, returning my embrace. "You're welcome."

I enjoyed the simple pleasure of the hug before I pulled back enough that I could see Valentin's face. "Should we see if Luka and Ari are still alive?"

He reluctantly let me go. "If we must."

"We must. But nothing's stopping us from returning later tonight for a private flight. Just the two of us. Assuming you can get away from your overprotective shadow."

"I'll make it happen," Valentin promised, his eyes full of heat.

I nodded in silent agreement and led him back to the cargo bay. Despite my concern, Ari and Luka were chatting comfortably. Well, Ari was chatting and Luka was listening. Once I got close, I realized Ari was telling him about how Imogen had waded into a drunken fistfight between two men twice her size and came out without so much as a single bruise.

I couldn't decide if the story was designed to be a warning or an enticement, but Luka was listening avidly—or as avid as I'd ever seen him, which meant his scowl was barely visible.

A mischievous smile tipped up the corner of Ari's mouth. "Imogen has an undefeated record against all opponents in friendly bouts. Even our illustrious queen gave it a go and Imogen didn't break a sweat."

In a friendly match, Imogen could—and did—kick my ass. We were evenly matched in strength and speed, and I couldn't put her down without seriously hurting her. So I'd lost our bout, much to everyone's delight. But in a true fight, the odds shifted. I had more experience fighting dirty and enough moral gray area to use every advantage available. If I'd been fighting for my life, the fight would've been over in seconds with a very different outcome.

"You lost?" Valentin asked with a grin.

"Badly," I agreed. "Imogen looks all cute and harmless but get her in a ring, and she's a force of nature. Don't let her con you into a match unless you like eating floor."

Ari's expression turned angelic, a sure sign she was up to something. "I bet Luka here could hold his own." She turned to him. "Care to try?"

Imogen had apparently sparred with Luka in Koan and said he moved like liquid, which was high praise coming from her, but I had a feeling she'd like a much more private round with him.

"I've seen her in action," Luka said. "She's undefeated for a reason."

I smiled at the diplomatic response and headed Ari off before she could press him further. "We're done on the ship. Let's show Luka and Valentin to the guest suite."

Ari nodded and headed down the ramp, then she linked me privately. *You're no fun.*

It was the second time today that someone had reminded me that I was a stick-in-the-mud. I tried not to take it too person-ally—professional stick-in-the-mud was basically my job as queen. And *that* cosmic joke would never get old. If my younger self could see me now, she'd think I'd been replaced by an alien.

I doubt Imogen wants their reunion to be a public spectacle, I said over the link. *Invite her to the planning meetings. In fact, invite her to meet us at the guest suite. She can be the official security liaison while they're here.*

And what am I? Ari grumbled.

Busy.

Ari had no argument for that, so she dropped the link without a response.

3

Imogen waited for us at the door to the guest suite. She had deep brown skin, striking cheekbones, and short, curly black hair. She must've been on duty because she had on a long-sleeved purple shirt, black utility pants, and heavy boots. Even in her work clothes, she looked gorgeous and harmless, which led people to assume she *was* harmless—much to their regret.

If I hadn't been paying attention, I wouldn't have noticed the tiny change in her expression when she spotted Luka. She was playing it very cool, as was he, but her eyes were just a bit brighter when she smiled at us in greeting.

"Imogen, you remember Valentin and Luka?" I asked. When she nodded, I continued, "I'm assigning you as their security liaison while they're here. If you need anything, contact me or Ari directly."

"Will do." She turned to the two men. "It's nice to see you again."

"You, too," Valentin said.

Luka grunted in acknowledgment, and Imogen rolled her eyes. "I see you haven't learned how to use your words, yet." She gave him a smile edged with mischievousness. "Let me show you the suite's security features so you can prevent your principal from being murdered while you sleep."

If Luka realized she was tossing his words from Koan back at him, he didn't show it. But he eased closer to her and inclined his head in agreement.

After a brief tour of the suite, which we'd cleaned out after Valentin's first visit, we went to meet up with the rest of my advisory council. Ari had *helpfully* called them together to discuss our strategy for dealing with Adams, and by the smug look on her face, she'd done it so I would be forced to include her—and everyone else—in my plans.

That was the problem with a best friend who was too damn smart and observant.

On the way to the council chamber, I desperately tried to come up with a plan that wouldn't get anyone I cared about killed. My initial meeting location had been discarded, as I'd known it would be. It had been deep in Kos territory, an opening gambit designed to fail. I'd given Hannah a list of acceptable locations, and she and Adams had eventually settled on Caldwell Prime 57.

It wasn't my first choice, but it wasn't as bad as it could've been, either. CP57 was a space station in the disputed zone between the Quint Confederacy and the Kos Empire. They'd gotten tired of the perpetual war, so they'd declared themselves independent, something they could do because a majority of the universe's information and black market goods moved through the station.

They had the money and power that the Rogue Coalition lacked.

The space station was a huge, sprawling complex that continually grew. There were no habitable planets nearby, so for ships on long journeys, CP57 became a natural layover stop. More than half a million people called it home and ten times that many transited through it every year. It was both the best and worst type of place to meet.

On the positive side, there were plenty of places to hide, and it was easy to get lost in a crowd. Setting up an ambush would be tricky but possible in some areas where station security wasn't as diligent as they should be. However, the same was true for Adams. Everything that benefitted us, benefitted him, too.

In addition, one of the best information brokers in the universe called CP57 home. We would have to be very, very careful or they would know what we were up to before we even arrived.

The council chamber—a glorified meeting room with a large rectangular table—was nearly full when we arrived. Ari, my security and military advisor, went to greet her wife, Stella Mueller, my medical advisor and top doctor. Zita, my food and nutrition advisor, no longer scowled at me, so I hoped that meant Eddie had already apologized to her.

On the far side of the table, Robert Brown, my mercenary and trade advisor, sat next to Tasha Rizak, my fleet advisor. Robert was in his sixties, his tan skin grizzled and scarred, with white hair and a build that remained thick with muscle. Next to him, Tasha seemed especially young and tiny, even though she was in her early thirties and of average height and build.

Tasha was beautiful, with deep ebony skin and a dazzling smile. She would rather be elbow deep in a ship's internals than in a council meeting, but she'd reluctantly agreed to advise me on how we should spend our relatively tiny ship-purchasing budget. No one knew more about our existing ships and their capabilities.

Rounding out the table were three elected officials representing the public—two dark-haired women and a blond man, all in their thirties. If my advisors couldn't agree on an issue, the public votes were given more sway. As queen, I technically had the final say, but I had only broken from my advisors' counsel a handful of times.

Valentin was met with polite smiles and cool nods. When I seated him beside me at the head of the table, a quiet ripple ran through the room. "Problem?" I asked sweetly.

No one was fooled by my saccharine tone and the murmur subsided.

"What do we know about CP57?" I asked the table.

"We have people on the station," Robert said. "Most of our information comes from long-term residents who are family to our citizens, but I sent a pair of teams over last week to establish better connections. If Adams is doing the same, he's keeping it quiet."

I had also sent people, but I'd done it before Hannah had contacted Adams. My team reported much the same: if Adams was establishing connections, he was being very careful, and that wasn't good for us. We needed him to make a mistake.

"He won't be able to blockade the station," Ari said. "As far as we know, he doesn't have the ships, firepower, or political clout. So his best bet is to attack or abduct you on-station and then fall back to a more powerful position."

"For the record, we don't have the ships to blockade the station, either," Tasha said. "We barely have enough working ships to *get* to the station."

"We could do it," Valentin said.

The whole table side-eyed him.

"I'm not saying we *will*, I'm just saying the Kos Empire is capable, if that's something we need to consider."

"While I appreciate the offer, we're trying to get you out of a war, not start another one," I said. "So we need to be prepared for Adams to run, which means we need to tag his ship. Do we have anyone with access to the docking database?"

"I might have someone," Robert said. "I'll have to check with my contacts."

Ships needed permission to dock anywhere on CP57, but it was relatively easy to fake a ship's registration data. If we didn't have anyone on the inside with enough access, I'd have to use one of my outside contacts, which carried a risk. I trusted them, but as my former security specialist had proven, even trust and years of working together wasn't always enough to prevent betrayal.

"How many people are you planning to take with you?" Ari asked, a hard gleam in her eye.

"As few as possible. We can't leave the Rogue Coalition unprotected while I'm away. It would be best if I went alone."

Half of my advisors made unhappy noises while the other half just glared at me. Ari and Stella were firmly in the glaring half.

Valentin turned to me, his expression grave. "Please don't go alone."

"I worked alone for years. I know what I'm doing."

He shook his head. "That's not what I meant. I don't doubt your skill. But you don't *have* to work alone. You have a team. Use them. Use me. You have plenty of people ready and willing to help."

"He's right," Ari agreed quietly. The rest of the table nodded.

I *knew* he was right, but I couldn't live with myself if anyone got hurt because of my plan. It was one thing to risk myself and something entirely different to risk those I cared about.

"Okay," I agreed at last, "I will agree to a very small team—six or eight only. Maybe another one or two to tag Adams's ship in case he slips through our net. And if anyone is going to play bait, it will be me." I slashed my hand through the air when Stella looked ready to argue. "Or I will go alone."

No one looked particularly happy, but we got down to the work of planning. We talked through various options and weighed the pros and cons. Ideally, we would separate Adams from his team and take him alive for questioning, but that was the least likely scenario.

By the time we were done, it was dinnertime and we had the beginnings of a working plan: draw Adams out, capture or kill him, and ensure his crew didn't escape. It sounded so easy, but there were a million points where things could go wrong—and would. Worry gnawed at me, especially because the team consisted of people I held dear: Ari, Stella, Imogen, Eddie, Valentin, Luka, and myself.

I stood and stretched, ending the meeting. My body was locked in fight-or-flight mode, and I needed to burn off some adrenaline before I gave myself an ulcer.

Stella stopped beside me on her way out, her voice pitched for my ears only. "We know what we're doing, too. You don't always have to put yourself between us and danger."

"But I will."

She nodded. "I know. It makes you a good queen and a terrible patient." Her dark eyes were clear and solemn. "We've all seen war. We know the risks. But more than that, we're your friends. Everything you feel when we're in danger, we feel that for *you*. It hurts when you throw yourself into danger for us. You're saving yourself pain by making us feel it. Don't be that selfish."

I sucked in a quiet breath and bit off the defensive replies I wanted to give. *It was my job. I was best equipped. They could survive without me.*

And the whole time I was away, my friends would worry about me. I *was* selfish.

I nodded, once, sharply, without saying anything. Stella pulled me into a gentle hug. "We love you, Samara. Don't forget that."

"Thank you," I murmured.

"Will we see you at dinner?"

"No. I asked Eddie to send us a meal in the guest suite."

Stella's grin turned sly. "In that case, I'll see you tomorrow. Sleep well. Don't stay up *too* late." She didn't wink, but her meaning was clear enough.

I snuck a glance at Valentin, who waited patiently with Luka and Imogen. When he caught me looking, his smile warmed. Nerves fluttered in my belly. Soon, soon I would have him to myself.

Stella chuckled and excused herself, leaving us alone with our guards. I had a plan to ditch them, but I needed Valentin's agreement.

I sent him a neural link request. He accepted immediately. *Are you okay?*

Warmth bloomed at the concern in his tone. *Yes. Stella only told me a truth I should've realized on my own.*

Just because it's true doesn't mean it isn't painful.

I inclined my head in silent agreement but turned the conversation to why I'd contacted him privately in the first place. *Can you shake your shadow for the evening?*

Valentin's eyes lit. *Depends,* he teased. *Are you planning to murder me?*

I kept my expression serious, though my eyes kept trying to crinkle in amusement. *If you're very good, it'll only be a little death.*

He laughed aloud and pulled me into his arms. *I adore you.*

The feeling was entirely mutual.

VALENTIN DID MANAGE to shake his shadow, but only because he had ordered Luka to accompany Imogen to the mess hall for dinner and not come back until given permission. Luka had glared grumpily at me, but he'd gone without as much of a fuss as I'd expected. Maybe he was starting to trust me.

And maybe unicorns would wing into our airspace at any moment.

Eddie had outdone himself, with an elegant, three-course meal. And someone had laid the guest suite table with real linens, a pair of candles, and fancy china and cutlery. I didn't know we even *owned* fancy china.

Valentin opened the bottle of wine that had been left to accompany dinner and poured us each a generous serving. He raised his glass. "To success. And to us."

I repeated the toast and gently touched my glass to his. The first sip of wine exploded on my tongue, bold and sharp. I hummed in appreciation and Valentin's gaze snapped to my mouth. My belly tightened in anticipation. Feeling daring, I took another sip and then slowly licked the wine from my lips.

Valentin's fingers went white around his glass.

Unfortunately, my stomach rumbled and the moment was broken. I covered my face and laughed. "Sorry. I forgot to eat lunch."

"Then let's see what your chef has prepared for us. You need to keep your strength up."

I raised an eyebrow. "Oh?"

Valentin's expression was innocent, but his smile had a wicked edge. "Yes. Don't you want to test your new ship? We can't have you passing out at the controls from low blood sugar."

I pursed my lips to suppress the smile. "I thought you might have more... *vigorous...* activities in mind to christen my new ship."

Valentin stared at me with naked desire, his wine glass forgotten. I clenched my muscles against the impulse to crawl into his lap and lose myself in his mouth and body. Soon, *soon.*

"Such as?" he demanded, his voice rough.

It took me a second to pick up the thread of the conversation. I gave him a coy glance through my lashes. "Hot, sweaty, dirty sex."

He hadn't expected me to actually say it and my words hit

him like a blow. He reached for me, then aborted the move and clenched the edge of the table. "Eat, now."

I squirmed in place, on the edge already. "The food can wait."

He shook his head, his face carved into granite lines of self-control. "No. You didn't eat lunch. And once I have you, I'm not going to let you go for *hours*. Eat."

I felt the shiver all the way to my toes, but I dutifully turned my attention to the food. It was exquisite, but I barely tasted it. I needed a distraction or I wouldn't make it through dinner. And I was very much looking forward to dessert.

"Do you think Adams will show?"

Valentin considered it for a moment, then nodded. "Like us, he'll be expecting a trap, but I still think he'll show. His hubris demands it."

It did not escape me that the same could be said about me.

I poked at the vegetables on my plate. A month ago, fresh vegetables had been few and far between. If Adams succeeded in pushing Kos and Quint back into war, then my people would suffer along with everyone else.

"We have to stop him," I murmured. "The peace treaty won't survive with someone actively working against it, especially if he still has the Quint Chairwoman's ear."

"He is well connected," Valentin confirmed. "He's been attempting to sow doubt about my sincerity since his time in Koan. So far it appears that Chairwoman Soteras is ignoring him, but that might not last if her council starts pressuring her."

We lapsed into silence. I knew what I had to do. Selfish or not, I would keep my friends safe, no matter what the cost. Because if I didn't, so many more people would be hurt.

Adams could not be allowed to escape.

4

Valentin and I spent the rest of dinner on more pleasant topics. As the meal ended, anticipation pushed my pulse faster. Finally, Valentin stood and offered me a hand. I slid my fingers into his and sparks danced up my arm. He helped me to my feet but made no move to pull me closer, despite the heat in his gaze.

"Would you like to check out your ship now?"

I nodded wordlessly. Truth be told, my ship wasn't the only thing I hoped to check out tonight. I sent Ari a message explaining that I was taking Valentin for a private flight in *Ardia,* so ground control wouldn't try to stop us when I took off.

"Should you let Luka know?"

"Already done."

We headed for my private hangar. On the way, I reached out and threaded my fingers through Valentin's. He smiled at me and my stomach flipped over. Giddy excitement mixed with nervousness, but as soon as I set foot on the ship, my nerves settled. Proof of Valentin's care surrounded me, an unmistakable statement.

And I would show him exactly how much I cared, too.

But first, I had to get us in the air. I was dying to get a feel for the ship that would become my home away from home. I led him to the bridge. Instead of letting him go, I pulled him closer. "Thank you," I whispered, trying to put the enormity of my feelings into those two words.

Valentin's mouth curved into a tender smile. "You're welcome."

"If I kiss you right now, I'm not going to stop at a kiss. And then we won't take off, and Ari and Luka will interrupt us to figure out what's going on."

Heat blazed in Valentin's eyes, and his hand flexed against mine. "Get us in the air," he demanded, his voice low and rough.

I shivered as the sound washed over me. I reluctantly let go of his hand and stepped away from him. Moving away felt impossible, but the faster I got us in the air, the faster I could stop worrying about interruptions.

I slid into the captain's chair and the console lit up. After a final, heated glance that caused my stomach to clench, Valentin dropped into the navigator's chair and shrugged into the harness. I did the same.

The console was an update on the familiar controls of *Invictia*. Everything was just a little easier, a little nicer. I let ground control know that we were about to take off, then went through the launch precheck. *Ardia* passed all of the checks with flying colors.

I opened the hangar roof and a slate gray sky slowly appeared on the screens that lined the front of the bridge. Looking at the screens, it was as if the front of the ship didn't exist and I could see directly outside. The images were piped in from the cameras embedded on the hull.

Once the roof was fully open, I initiated the liftoff under fully manual control. I wanted to see how the ship handled before I put the autopilot through its paces. The ship rose, and the ground dropped away in a dizzying rush. The engine barely hummed, not taxed at all.

"Oh, you're a beauty," I murmured appreciatively. "Hold on," I warned Valentin.

At his nod, I jerked the controls hard to port. The ship slid sideways through the air, as smooth as butter. I felt a very slight pull against the harness holding me in the chair, but the compensators were the best I'd ever experienced.

I flew a crazy pattern, just because I could. The ship kept up beautifully without so much as a single warning beep.

I laughed in pure delight.

A few minutes later, we broke atmosphere and entered into the vast openness of space. I plotted a course to a distant planet. The stardrive's recharge time was listed as just under three hours, which was unbelievable. I looked at Valentin, who had turned his chair so he could see me. "Is this recharge time correct?"

He nodded, a smile hovering on his lips. "But I would prefer if you kept it to yourself."

"You should've been destroying Quint," I murmured.

Valentin nodded. "Maybe not destroying, but we certainly would've been doing better if they hadn't known our every move before we made it." His tone took on a dangerous edge. "And now that the traitors have been removed, Quint will find us a much more difficult opponent if they decide to back out of the treaty talks."

"Is that a concern?"

He shook his head. "Not currently."

I looked at the plotted route again. "I told Ari not to expect me back tonight. Is Luka going to freak out if I tunnel us somewhere?"

The corner of Valentin's mouth curled up into a wicked grin. "Probably. Where are you taking me?"

"Somewhere where we won't be bothered for a while. Is that okay?"

I froze as Valentin's attention morphed. Before, he'd been contained. Now languorous heat filled his eyes and smile. He watched me with the still, quiet patience of a large predator.

"Are you planning to take advantage of me?" he asked, his voice rough.

Desired blazed bright, bringing with it the urge to play. I grinned at him. "Very much so."

He made a low sound, and his fists clenched against his thighs.

I changed our destination to Trigon Seven, a local planet. It was still technically in the Rogue Coalition's loose boundaries, but the planet was uninhabitable, so that part of space was empty.

The planet was also very pretty, bathed in brilliant colors that swirled through the gaseous atmosphere.

I tweaked the route to ensure we were on the sunny side of the planet and plotted a distant orbit that put us well outside of any danger from the planet itself.

As fun as it was to tease Valentin, I needed an honest answer. "Would you prefer to stay here in case something comes up?"

His mouth quirked, but he resisted making the joke I'd inadvertently set up for him. "No, I'd prefer to go somewhere. That way you won't be able to escape for at least three hours." The predatory look returned. "If only *Ardia* had a worse stardrive."

I focused on him completely, as if he were one of my targets. He stilled, recognizing the danger. I let desire bleed into my expression and warned, "If we transit, *you* won't be able to escape *me*."

"Tunnel now," he demanded.

I hit the confirmation button without looking. *Ardia* easily slid through space with barely any vibration. The stardrive truly was exceptional.

Trigon Seven had barely appeared on the screens before Valentin was on his feet, muscles tense.

Anticipation tightened my stomach, but I checked our course to ensure we wouldn't accidentally find ourselves in a moon in the next few hours. That done, I slowly unclipped my harness and stood. Now it was finally time to play.

Valentin lunged towards me, only to pause when I mirrored his movement, keeping the captain's chair between us. He frowned and took a purposeful step around the chair. I matched the step with a grin. I wouldn't be caught so easily.

Before he could cut off my escape, I dashed for the door with a laugh. It took a heartbeat, but then his steps echoed mine. The ship was too small to truly provide much challenge, but I sprinted down the main hallway and vaulted over the railing into the cargo bay. I landed in a roll, using my momentum to bring me back to my feet. I turned to dash down the lower hallway, but Valentin landed in front of me, absorbing the fall with his legs.

He had me, and he knew it. A feral, victorious smile transformed him into the hottest thing I'd ever seen. I trembled as my desire blazed out of control, but I couldn't give up quite so easily.

I moved to dart around him, but Valentin snagged my waist in a lightning fast move that would've been hard to counter—had I wanted to, which I didn't. He pivoted so that we ended up chest to chest, with his arms wrapped around me. I tipped my head back to meet his eyes, and my breath caught at the blatant desire carved into his face.

Then his mouth crashed down on mine and static filled my thoughts. There was only heat and lust and the slick slide of his tongue.

I buried my hands in his hair and arched into him. After several moments, I broke the kiss long enough to gasp, "Bed!" I wasn't too particular about the location, as long as he started losing clothes and soon.

He bent and swept my legs out from under me as he lifted me against his chest. I kissed the strong column of his neck and his steps faltered. Pleased, I did it again, and he growled something unintelligible.

We made it to the master suite, and Valentin set me on my feet. With proof of his care and devotion surrounding me, I strategized the fastest way to get him out of his clothes. He beat me to it, though, peeling himself out of his sweater with such slow deliberation that it had to have been intentional.

I watched, mesmerized, as lean muscles encased in golden skin were revealed a centimeter at a time. Once the sweater hit the floor, I pressed my hands to the hard ridges of his abdomen, and his breath caught.

He drew me closer, and I met his mouth halfway. The kiss was a sweet exploration, a homecoming, and a roaring fire all rolled into one.

I wanted him. *Now.*

I pulled back and dipped one finger under the waistband of his pants. At his nod, I popped the button open. Together, we freed him from the last of his clothes.

He stood, naked and proud, his desire obvious and unmistakable—and deliciously thick.

"Can I touch you?" I whispered.

"Yes, anywhere you like." He flashed a crooked grin. "I have some suggestions if you need ideas."

I stepped closer and closed my hand around his length, giving him a single stroke from base to tip. His breath hissed out, and his head tipped back. "That's an excellent start," he said.

I chuckled. "I thought so."

He met my gaze, his gray eyes both hot and tender. "You're wearing far too many clothes."

I loved my body, with all of its strengths and flaws, but next to Valentin's golden perfection, I felt the flaws more than usual. But the heat in his expression burned away the anxiety.

I slowly peeled off my clothes, and as each new piece fell away, Valentin's eyes darkened. When I was bare, he reached out a reverent hand, not touching. At my nod, he cupped the curve of my waist, his hand hot against my skin.

Now it was my turn for my breath to catch. And when he slid that hand up, slowly, slowly, over my ribs and to the underside of my breast, I bit my lip against the urge to climb him right where he stood. His palm lifted the weight of my breast while his thumb smoothed across the pebbled nipple.

I moaned, my muscles clenched tight. This was exquisite torture.

Then his head dipped and a hot mouth replaced his thumb. I arched and buried my hands in his hair, desperate to hold him in place.

"You are so beautiful," he whispered against my skin. "I'm afraid this is only a dream and it'll evaporate when I wake."

Tender affection swept through me. I pulled his face up to mine and stared into his eyes. "Then we should make it the best dream possible." I kissed him, slow and deep. "But I'm not going anywhere."

We eventually stumbled our way to the bed. I pivoted at the last second so Valentin ended up below me, spread out like a feast. I pressed tiny, heated kisses to his neck, shoulder, chest, and abs, working my way down with endless patience, even as desire turned my blood molten.

When I licked him, his whole body shuddered. When I enveloped him in the heat of my mouth, his back bowed and he groaned, "Fuck."

I drew it out as long as I could, but eventually desire won. I climbed up until he pressed exactly where I needed him. "Yes?" I confirmed. He nodded and watched with hooded eyes as I slowly sank down on his length.

My nerves lit with pleasure as he stretched me, and I let my head fall back at the sheer delight. Beneath me, Valentin groaned. His hands wrapped around my waist, and he effortlessly lifted me a few centimeters then pulled me back with a flex of his hips.

Stars exploded behind my eyes. I braced my hands on his shoulders and found my rhythm. I set a brutal pace, past teasing. I drove our pleasure higher and higher, until I didn't think I could survive it. Then with a twist of his hips and a thumb pressing exactly where I needed it, Valentin catapulted me into bliss.

He rolled us over and drove into me, prolonging the pleasure. When I raked my nails down his back, he shuddered and joined me in ecstasy.

We were both breathing hard and sweat glistened on our skin. Valentin collapsed to the side, pulling me with him until we were pressed together in a tangle of limbs. He kissed me, slowly, tenderly.

I drifted with my head on his chest, listening to the beat of his heart. I was happy, content, boneless with pleasure, and willing to stay here for as long as possible.

Valentin seemingly shared my thoughts. "If this is a dream, I don't want to wake up," he whispered.

I leaned up and kissed the corner of his mouth. "Me, either." Then I gave him a sultry glance from under my lashes. "But whatever are we going to do for the next couple of hours until we can return to Arx?"

He rolled over and braced himself above me with a growl. "I can think of a few things."

I gave him a brilliant smile. "So can I."

5

Valentin and I returned to Arx in the early hours after midnight. I'd planned to stay away all night, but responsibility and worry kept nipping at me in quiet moments. *Ardia* settled into the hangar with a gentle bump. It truly was a lovely ship.

We walked back to my suite. At the door, Valentin paused, looking uncertain.

I held out a hand. "Join me?" I invited.

He slid his hand into mine and pulled me close. "Always. But I didn't want to assume or cause trouble for you with your people."

I laughed. "Our relationship isn't exactly a secret. There's a betting pool for when we'll seal the deal, so to speak. Ari is running it."

Valentin blinked in shock for a second before a grin tipped up the corner of his mouth. "Did we ruin her chances at fabulous wealth?"

I matched his grin. "Probably."

I opened the door, and we took the private stairs up to my rooms. I hadn't moved back to the top floor yet, even though we could afford to heat it again. Maybe I would once Adams was no longer a concern.

"Does Luka know that you're back?"

Valentin nodded, and his grin deepened. "He seemed somewhat distracted when I linked him earlier. And less enthused about my early return than I thought he would be."

My eyebrows rose. "Him and Imogen?"

Valentin lifted one shoulder. "I didn't ask, but I told him I'd be sleeping somewhere else tonight."

"And if I hadn't invited you?"

"I would've circled back and slept on the ship." Valentin pulled me close, his hands on my hips. "But I was hoping for an invite," he murmured.

"I sleep naked," I warned. "And steal the covers."

He nuzzled my cheek. "So do I," he whispered into my ear, "and I'll risk it."

———

I WOKE with Valentin spooning me from behind, his arm wrapped around my waist and the covers tucked around us both. I was pleasantly sore in all the best ways. I mentally checked my messages, but nothing urgent had come in overnight. In fact, my inbox was suspiciously light, and I wondered if Ari had warned people to leave me alone.

When I stretched, Valentin hugged me close and pressed a kiss to the back of my neck. His lips weren't the only thing pressing against me.

"Did you have good dreams?" I asked with a hidden grin.

"Mmm," he agreed sleepily. "I dreamed of you."

Bright, sparkling happiness spread through me like the sweetest honey. "Was dream me nice?"

"Very." He shifted his hips, rubbing against me. "Shall I show you what we were doing?"

I moaned as desire ignited. "Please."

———

BY THE TIME we emerged from my suite, it was nearly lunchtime. We'd showered twice because the first time had led to more distraction. When we stopped by the guest suite to pick up Luka, we also found Imogen. They both looked coolly professional, but they were standing just a little closer together.

I pressed my lips together to stop the smile. "Have you eaten?" I asked.

Imogen shook her head. "Not yet. We were waiting for you. Of course, we waited for breakfast, too, until it became clear you wouldn't be making an appearance." She said it with a straight face, but her eyes danced. She looked happy and relaxed, so whatever had happened—if anything—had been good for her.

"Well, I'm starving, so let's eat, and then we'll see what needs to be done today."

When everyone agreed, I slipped my arm through Valentin's and led the way to the mess hall. Eddie was on duty behind the counter, and he took one look at our faces, then our linked arms, and scowled playfully. "I owe Stella twenty credits," he grumbled. "I—"

I shook my head. "I don't even want to know," I said before he could elaborate.

His grin was sly. "Maybe you can make it up to me. Did you f—"

"Not one more word, Eddie, or you really will be peeling potatoes until the end of time."

He held up his hands in surrender. "Fine, fine. Did you at least enjoy dinner first?"

"Eddie," I warned. When he gave me an unrepentant grin that couldn't quite hide his eagerness to know what I thought of the meal, I relented. "Dinner was exceptional. You outdid yourself. Thank you."

"Dinner was delicious," Valentin agreed. "You have incredible talent."

Eddie's grin softened into a smile that made him look younger. "I'm glad, and you're welcome. It's nice to flex my culinary skills occasionally."

I took a deep breath, trying to figure out what was for lunch. The air was rich with spices and garlic. "What smells so good?"

"Pasta with vegetables and garlic bread."

"Is that lunch or dinner? Because it smells amazing." My stomach growled in agreement.

"It's lunch. You all eating?"

At my nod, Eddie served up four plates of pasta and vegetables topped with cheese. A thick slice of bread slathered with butter and roasted garlic accompanied each plate. For the past month, Eddie had slowly been increasing the richness of the meals he prepared so that the transition from PRiMeR wasn't as jarring to the system.

Clearly the transition period was over.

The food was as delicious as it smelled, and conversation was light as we all focused on our meal. I made a mental note to check with Eddie to ensure his assistants could handle the kitchen while he was in CP57 with us.

I had so many things to do to prepare and so little time to do them. The meeting was supposed to be in two weeks, which meant I needed to be in CP57 already. I trusted my team, but nothing beat being there in person. And Adams would be a fool if he waited until the meeting date to arrive. Best case, I'd catch him early and unprepared. Worst case, he'd do the same to me.

And I'd had enough of worst-case scenarios where that asshole was concerned.

After lunch, I visited medical with Valentin and our ever-present shadows. It was a whirlwind of activity. Stella stood in the eye of the storm, directing the chaos. Two large duffels were slowly being filled with supplies for every conceivable injury.

"Make sure you leave enough for everyone here," I advised mildly.

Stella scowled at me. "If you're just here to cause trouble, go bother someone else."

"Will you be ready to go tomorrow?"

"I'll be ready by dinner," she said. Her expression turned forbidding as one of her assistants nearly dropped an expensive trauma-doc. The man ducked his head with a muttered apology, his pale cheeks bright red. Stella turned back to me. "Is it tomorrow then?"

"I don't know. I'm checking in with everyone. I would like to go tomorrow, even if a second wave has to follow later."

Stella nodded. "I'll be ready. The new schedule is approved and everyone knows when their shifts are. If anything happens here, we'll have enough doctors and nurses to cover it."

"Let's hope it doesn't come to that," I murmured. But it was another worry I carried around. What if Adams decided to attack Arx while I was twiddling my thumbs waiting for him on CP57?

Valentin had offered to move several ships into close patrols around Trigon Three as a precaution. I hated that we needed the help, but I wasn't stupid enough to turn it down. The same would be happening around Koan on Achentsev Prime. As far as we knew, Adams was on his own, no longer supported by the Quint Confederacy—at least not openly. That meant his access to new ships and weapons should be limited.

"I'll check in later and let you know if we're on for departure tomorrow," I said.

Stella waved me off, already back in the controlled chaos that was packing for a trip where you didn't know how many—or how badly—people would be injured. We hoped for none and planned for the opposite.

I tracked Ari to the main hangar, where she was looking over the available ships with Tasha. The Rogue Coalition didn't have a huge number of ships—we weren't a military power. Both Quint and Kos had left us alone because we were small and not sitting on anything valuable, not because we could fight them off.

When Ari caught sight of me, she smiled. "Stella warned me you were on the way. You want to leave tomorrow?"

"Yes. Stella said she'd be ready by tonight. How's it going here?"

"Our options are limited," Ari said with a grimace.

Tasha jumped in. "Most of our ships were, umm, *acquired*." She sent a meaningful glance Valentin's way, and I pressed my lips together to contain the laugh. She continued, "Sending one of them to CP57 is asking for trouble."

"Last I knew, we have a few ships that should work. Are they all out of commission?"

"A couple of them are undergoing routine maintenance, and the ships with the best offensive capabilities are probably too big. Plus, we need to ensure we leave enough ships behind to protect Arx."

"I'm going to take *Ardia*. Does that help?"

Ari gave me her hard stare, but I refused to back down. After a long moment, she sighed. "Fine. We were planning to take multiple ships anyway, so that will work. But you're not going by yourself."

"I wouldn't dream of it," I lied with a sly smile.

Ari barked out a laugh. "I know you better than that." Her gaze cut to Valentin. "But I feel like I'm going to have backup this time." When he nodded, she beamed at him.

"Spoilsports," I grumbled at them. I looked at both Ari and Tasha. "Do you think you'll be ready by tomorrow?"

"Should be," Ari said. "We've almost agreed on the ships, but I think I'm going to need a crew."

"Volunteers only. And keep the key details to yourself."

Ari rolled her eyes at me. "It's not my first day on the job." Before I could apologize, she grinned. "But I know you turn into a tiny tyrant when you're worried. I don't hold it against you."

She wasn't wrong, but I mock glared at her anyway. "Watch it. I'll lock you in a tower guarded by a dragon and lose the key."

"Stella will rescue me," Ari said breezily. "I'll be out before dinner."

"You *do* have formidable allies," I conceded with an exaggerated grimace. "I suppose I must reconsider. And I will see what I can do about my tyrannical tendencies."

Ari's answering smile was kind. "Don't worry about it. You keep us safe. If you get too overbearing, we'll rein you in."

I *would* keep them safe.

No matter what.

6

In the end, we took three ships. Valentin, Luka, Imogen, and I were in *Ardia*. Stella and Ari were in a small corvette with a crew of four who would stay on the ship. Eddie was in a tiny little ship that was best for stealth missions. He'd claimed that he could slip through CP57's defenses and dock without permission, but I made him promise to approach the space station legally—sort of.

All of our ships were using faked registrations that were tied to dummy companies with information trails that led to even deeper lies. It would take an information specialist at least a month to sort everything out, and even then, it would never lead back to the Rogue Coalition or Kos Empire, which was exactly the point. If Adams wanted to find us, he was going to have to work for it.

Each ship took a different route to get to CP57. Eddie had two tunnel transits, so he would be the last to arrive. Ari and Stella's route only had one transit, but they were aiming for a tunnel endpoint several hours away from the station.

Our group tunneled as close to CP57 as we legally could. The exclusion zone around the space station was only twenty minutes in a reasonably fast ship, and *Ardia* proved to be exactly that. By the time we had docking authorization, we were only a few minutes away.

CP57 loomed huge in front of us. The already massive structure of the central station had been expanded so much that it had been swallowed up by the new sections built around it. Open flight paths cut swaths through the outer sections of the station, allowing well-heeled guests to dock close to the popular central district. I didn't want to draw quite that much attention, but I had paid for a dock in one of the better areas not too far from the inner hub. Flight control guided us in.

The arrival timing had been another fight. No one thought Valentin and I should arrive first, which was exactly why I'd pushed for it. If Adams was already on-station, he would expect my team to arrive before me, which might allow Stella, Ari, and Eddie to slip in unnoticed.

And the only way Adams could take Valentin, Imogen, Luka, and me would be if he'd bribed CP57 to assist him, which meant that three more people wouldn't help anyway—and it would be even more important for them to be free to come to our rescue.

The berthing clamps attached to *Ardia* with a brief jolt. Once the ship was secure, the docking port extended and fastened onto *Ardia*'s starboard hatch. A series of pressure tests came back green, indicating the seal was secure.

An external berth offered a faster escape than a landing bay because once the clamps were released, the ship was free to move. A landing bay had to be depressurized, which could take thirty minutes or more, depending on the size.

Eddie also planned to dock at an external berth, but Ari and Stella would dock in a landing bay. Their ship carried most of our supplies and offloading them through the larger landing bay doors was far easier and less suspicious than trying to maneuver them through the smaller external docking port.

I unclipped from the captain's chair, and my nerves settled, as they always did when I was on a job. Valentin, Imogen, and Luka were already standing. I looked them over with a critical eye. All three wore simple, dark clothes, but Luka's height and breadth gave him a distinctive silhouette. Even with a hooded coat, he would stand out.

This was one area where being petite helped quite a bit. It was much easier for me to disappear into a crowd than it was for Luka. But even if Adams was already on-station, he wouldn't have the resources to watch every dock. As long as we kept our faces hidden, we would just be four random people here for private business.

And private business had built CP57. My money was good, and that was all that mattered. No one would ask any inconvenient questions.

"I've booked us rooms for a month. We hopefully won't be here that long, but I'm going to let it slip that I'm working on a sensitive deal with multiple parties. That will explain the rest of the team coming and going. As far as anyone else is aware, you're all my guards."

They all nodded. We'd discussed this previously, but as Ari had pointed out, I tended to get bossy when I was worried. And going over the plan one more time before we left the relative safety of the ship was never a bad idea.

Valentin slid his hand into mine, and my heart fluttered. He met my eyes. "We're prepared. We have a solid plan. That asshole won't know what hit him."

Luka and Imogen silently slipped out of the bridge, leaving us alone. "I hope you're right," I murmured.

Valentin drew me close and pressed my hand to his chest. "I'm always right," he said with a perfectly straight face.

"Must be nice," I whispered. I could feel his heart beating under my palm. It took so little for that fragile organ to be silenced forever. I vowed it wouldn't happen to anyone I cared about on this trip.

Valentin tipped my face up and brushed his lips over mine, softly, gently. When I responded, he deepened the kiss until we were both breathing hard.

He pressed his forehead to mine. "Don't put yourself in danger. Trust your team. Trust *me*."

"I do, never doubt that." I pulled back so I could see his face. "But you need to trust me, too. This was my job for many years. I know what I'm doing. If I see a way to save lives, I'm going to take it, even if it wasn't in the plan."

His mouth flattened. "Promise me that you won't take unnecessary risks."

I agreed easily. The risks I would be taking were entirely necessary.

———

We found Imogen and Luka in the cargo bay, drawn by Luka's low rumbling voice and Imogen's light laughter. Imogen sat on a crate while Luka lounged against the wall nearby, as relaxed as I'd ever seen him.

"You think Ari's got a pool going on them?" I asked under my breath.

Valentin laughed. "I'm sure."

I thought so, too. But anyone who bet too early was going to lose their money. Luka and Imogen might have a strong attraction, but they were both too honorable to act on it when it might affect their jobs. It was a good reminder that more than my and Valentin's happiness rode on this mission.

Imogen hopped off the box. "All set?" she asked.

"Yes. Let's do it."

We each had a large pack with essential supplies. On the off chance that Stella and Ari were denied entrance, we had enough gear to keep us safe until we could locate a trustworthy supplier on the station. And we left a few surprises behind on the ship, just in case things went *really* sideways.

My pack included a few sets of clothing, emergency medical supplies, and a wide array of weapons. It weighed almost as much as I did, and I wouldn't have been able to carry it without my strength augments.

I'd designed the pack myself. In addition to the weapons I'd be wearing visibly, I could grab two hidden plasma pistols and a quartet of knives from the pack without removing it from my back. If I needed more firepower, it took less than ten seconds to swing the pack down and draw a plasma rifle.

If I needed more firepower than *that,* I'd be looking for an escape route.

We donned our packs and lightweight hooded coats and left the ship. I counted while the airlock cycled us through into the station's docking tunnel. It took twenty seconds for the hatch to open and that was when the airlock itself was already pressurized.

We stepped through into the tunnel and the airlock's hatch sealed closed behind us. It would take at least another twenty seconds for it to open again. If we needed to leave in a hurry, then getting to the ship would not be a fast process.

I started a group link with Valentin, Imogen, and Luka. *Keep your eyes open. Look for places where we may run into trouble if we need to leave quickly.*

Everyone agreed, and we delved deeper into the station. Our short private docking tunnel soon dumped us into a large shared hallway dotted with the entrances to the berths next to ours.

The station's time ran about six hours earlier than the local time on Arx, so it was either very early morning or late night, depending on your perspective. A few people hurried by even at this hour. CP57 never truly slept. Most of the others in the hallway had hats pulled low or hooded coats or cloaks covering them from head to toe. At least that much hadn't changed since the last time I was here.

I checked that the door to our private docking tunnel was closed and locked. We each had a virtual key that would open the door, and the keys were tied to the ship's registration rather than our personal IDs. The ship wouldn't open for anyone outside of our group, but in the privacy of the docking tunnel, someone could get up to no good far easier than out here in the public hallway, and there was no reason to make ourselves easy marks.

For the same reason, our coats hid whether or not we were armed, making us less interesting targets. CP57 cracked down on major crimes, but in parts of the station, a friendly robbery or two was the cost of doing business—at least for the unwary.

I mentally accessed the station map and headed left down the hallway. Imogen, Valentin, and Luka silently fell in behind me. Nothing to see here, just a businesswoman with three well-trained guards. The fact that I carried my own pack made me even less of a target, the guards notwithstanding. It meant I was used to getting my hands dirty and doing my own work. I wouldn't roll easily.

We crossed through the first emergency airlock—left open until said emergency—and entered the main part of the station.

CP57 was divided into numbered blocks. Each block was separated from the others with thick firewalls and airlocks built to contain any loss of pressure, because hull breaches, while extremely rare, were the worst-case scenario on a space station, right up there with explosions and uncontrolled fires. If an emergency was detected, an automated system would lock down the affected blocks, essentially sacrificing everyone inside who hadn't made it to a shelter.

Blocks varied in size, and some of the inner blocks were huge, with soaring ceilings that felt almost like a sky stretching overhead. Others were small and closed-in, with every square centimeter used so the pathways felt narrow and dangerous. Each block operated like an independent city within the station itself, and while public transit crisscrossed the station, many full-time residents rarely traveled farther than a block or two from their home.

The block numbers had started out sequentially from the interior, but as the station had grown, the numbering system had fallen apart. So while it was a good bet that blocks less than fifty were near each other, after that, the numbers no longer indicated relative position. We'd entered in Block 83 and would travel through Blocks 68 and 61 before reaching our destination in Block 48.

Block 83 was a fairly typical dock block. The ceiling was low, less than three stories, and it hunkered over a space filled to the brim with shops that offered every conceivable vice—and some I'd never heard of. Bright signs, beautiful bodies, and slick sales pitches drew in the unwary. I'd heard stories of people who had visited CP57 and never made it more than ten meters inside before losing all of their money, some willingly, some not.

The overhead lights were dim, signaling that it was still night, but it was hard to tell with all of the shops lit up like stars. I sliced through the crowd with a bold, determined stride. Most of the merchants recognized I wasn't worth their time, but there were always one or two who had to try their luck.

A tall woman in a sheer gown stepped into my path. She was beautiful, with long, curly blond hair and a curvy figure. Her makeup was flawless, accentuating her cheekbones and lips. When I moved to step around her, she darted into my path, fast and smooth. I stopped and held up a hand when the group behind me would've moved closer.

"Hello," the woman purred, her voice a lovely contralto. "See something you like?"

That pulled a grin from me. Most of my face was in shadow,

thanks to the hood, but she must've caught sight of my mouth, because her lips tilted up, too. "You're gorgeous," I agreed, "but I have business in 48."

"That's a long walk. You should rest first." Her smile turned sly. "I know just the place."

"I'm sure you do, but sadly business must come before pleasure."

"Perhaps you just haven't found the right pleasure yet." She snapped her fingers. An incredibly handsome man stepped up next to her, muscled chest bare and low-slung pants barely clinging to his hips. He gave me a smoldering glance. Behind me, Valentin growled something under his breath and Imogen smothered a laugh.

When I didn't immediately accept, the man's smolder turned into a pretty pout. The woman, however, wasn't so easily deterred. "Perhaps I could help you with your business. No need to go all the way to 48. Whatever you need, I can get it for you here, and you can relax while you wait."

You know, now that I think about it, I am *tired,* Imogen said on our group link, a grin in her mental voice. *It was such a long walk from our ship.*

It was five minutes, Luka growled.

As much as I would like to poke them both, I had to answer the woman or she'd think I was considering her offer, and I didn't want to waste her time. The faster she was done with me, the faster she could move on to more lucrative clients.

"Unfortunately, I must go, but good hunting."

The woman sighed and stepped aside. "Remember me when your business is complete. I'll be here." She pointed at the man next to her. "So will he." Her eyes glinted in the light. "But I'm the best you've ever had, guaranteed."

I smiled at her easy confidence. She was a professional and a successful one based on what I could see. But she wasn't Valentin. Still, I inclined my head to her. "I'll keep it in mind."

7

The madam wasn't wrong—it *was* a long walk from Block 83 to 48. It took nearly an hour to work our way through the intervening blocks. By the time we stepped through the Block 48 airlock, I was ready to drop my pack and stretch the muscles of my back and shoulders, even with my strength augments.

We could've taken an automated taxi or public transit, but I'd wanted to get a feel for the blocks between us and the ship. The path back wasn't straight, and even at a run, it would take twenty minutes, depending on the crowds.

Stepping into Block 48 was like stepping into a shady back alley market planetside. It was far larger than the previous blocks we'd visited, with a soaring ceiling that had to be at least twenty stories tall. However, the block still managed to feel cramped thanks to the profusion of tall, tightly packed buildings. It was one of the more populated blocks, which was one reason I'd chosen it as our meeting point.

Watch your pockets, I warned the group.

And your kidneys, Imogen muttered back. *I'll be surprised if we aren't attacked before we get to our rooms.* She'd closed the distance between us until I could practically feel her breathing down my neck.

I looked around. It wasn't *that* bad. I'd been to far shadier places and had emerged unscathed. The trick was to be aware of your surroundings and not to do anything stupid.

The streets were thick with people, even at this hour. We hadn't made it more than a hundred meters before I stopped and caught the small hand that had darted into my coat, aiming for my pocket. When jerking away didn't free her, a young girl stared up at me with wide, innocent eyes.

I didn't believe it for a second.

I pressed a credit stick into the hand I held. "Spread the word: leave me and mine alone, and I'll make it worth your while."

Her mouth turned down into a mutinous frown.

I shrugged and made to remove the stick, but her fist clenched tight around it, and she nodded once, sullenly. I stared at her for a few more seconds and then let her go. She slid away and vanished into the crowd with the ease of experience. A hundred credits was a small price to pay. It wouldn't buy me loyalty, exactly, but it was a start.

Told you, Imogen said.

I'll have you know that I still have both kidneys. And that was hardly an attack.

There's still time, she grumbled sourly.

I smiled, though she couldn't see it. Imogen had never delved much into the shady side of the law, so this trip was going to be an eye-opener for her, in more ways than one. I just hoped she'd still be talking to me once everything was said and done.

I led our group deeper into Block 48's warren of narrow alleys and winding pathways. Our house was in Sector G, near the heart of the block. I'd rented the first three stories of a long, narrow building with ground-level access on both sides and upper-level access to a pair of skybridges. More entrances meant more places to keep watch, but it also meant that we were less likely to be trapped inside.

The door opened with the virtual key I'd been sent after my payment went through. *Stay alert,* I linked to the group. I drew my pistol and eased through the door. I didn't *think* Adams could've already made my safe house, but assuming was a good way to get dead.

I silently dropped my pack and coat in the first room, which appeared to be a cross between a sitting room and a waiting room. *We need to sweep the building.*

The others dropped their gear as well, and we split into two teams. Imogen and I took the ground floor while Valentin and Luka started on the third. We met in the middle, sweeping for anything suspicious or any unexpected surprises.

We didn't find anything.

A scan for camera or audio recording devices also came up empty. After ensuring that all the access doors were closed and locked, we headed back to the sitting room.

"I knew CP57 was big, but I'd forgotten just *how* big," Imogen said. "How are we ever going to find Adams in this mess?"

"Luck and skill. Barring that, we'll let him find us."

She shot me a troubled look, but I waved it away. I wasn't going to play bait quite yet.

I picked up my pack. "There should be enough bedrooms for everyone, so no one needs to double up unless they want to." At my raised eyebrow, Imogen found the far wall incredibly interesting.

Valentin moved toward me, his mask firmly in place. He linked me privately. *What will we do?*

I frowned. *I thought we'd share a room,* I said slowly, *but we don't have to.*

His expression heated. *I want you in my bed.* He grinned. *Or me in yours. Take your pick.*

I shook off the tension that had tightened my muscles. Silly man. As if I was going to let him go now that I'd caught him. Everyone already knew we were sleeping together. We might as well find enjoyment where we could because the rest of the trip would be severely lacking in fun.

Luka and Imogen were either linking privately or ignoring each other as we climbed the stairs to the second story. Most of the bedrooms were on this level, with public rooms on the ground floor and private spaces—like the kitchen—on the third.

I'd already viewed all of the rooms, both in the original listing and when we'd done the earlier sweep. The bedroom at the end of the hallway that overlooked the front of the building was the nicest, but only because of the window. Otherwise, the room looked just like the others, with a bed big enough for two and a single nightstand. A built-in wardrobe had a few shelves for clothes and gear.

Everything looked worn but clean.

I dropped my pack on the bed. "Does this work for you?" I asked Valentin.

He nodded and set his pack next to mine.

"You'd be safer in an internal room," Imogen said from the doorway.

"I'd be safest on Arx, and yet, here we are. I like the light." Being able to see out was just an additional bonus.

"Is the window reflective outside?"

"Yes. It'll shield us from view during the day, but it won't be enough when it's dark outside and light in here. We'll draw the curtains when we leave the room and leave them closed overnight."

Imogen knew a losing battle when she saw one. She pointed at the closest door on her left. "I'll be there."

Without a word, Luka entered the room across the hall from hers.

"Unpack," I told her. "We'll head back out in a little bit. I want to get a feel for the area. And we need to pick up some food."

Imogen couldn't quite hide her grimace at the thought of returning to the neighborhood, but she nodded and entered the room she'd chosen.

Once we were alone, Valentin shut our door and pulled me into his arms. "I hate that you are involved in this," he murmured. He held on when I tried to pull back. "I know you're more than capable, but I can still hate it."

I relaxed. "I hate it, too. I'd much rather we were still on *Ardia.*"

His arms tightened. "Me, too." His hot gaze roved over my face. "How long until the others arrive?"

"It'll be at least a few hours before Stella and Ari arrive. Eddie will be longer than that. Why?"

The corner of his mouth tipped up in a wicked temptation. "I was just thinking that the house was going to be full of people with very sharp hearing pretty soon. Maybe we should take advantage of the relative emptiness while we have a chance."

I rolled my eyes but couldn't help the grin. "I'm pretty sure Luka and Imogen both have excellent hearing." I pulled his face down to mine. "But I can be quiet if you can," I whispered against his lips.

He made a low sound deep in his chest and fused his mouth to mine.

———

VALENTIN and I both proved ourselves liars, but when we reappeared a while later, neither Imogen nor Luka made any comment. Of course, we found them in the upstairs living room with a vid blaring in the background, so they really didn't need to say anything at all. I didn't even try to fight the hot rush of color that bloomed on my cheeks.

"Did you have trouble unpacking?" Imogen asked with a perfectly straight face. "I heard banging."

Luka made a strangled sound halfway between a cough and a laugh.

Ah, so she'd just been waiting for an opening. Good for her. There was a time not so long ago that she wouldn't have been comfortable enough to tease me. And the double entendre was sheer perfection.

I grinned at her. "Unpacking was very relaxing, as a matter of fact. What about you? Did you have any trouble settling in? If you need a hand, I'm sure we can find someone to help."

She tipped her head in thought. "There was that gorgeous shirtless man back in 83," she said with an odd bite in her voice. "I wonder if he's still available."

Out of the corner of my eye, I saw Luka's fists clench. I linked Imogen. *Is everything okay between you two?*

Yes. Mostly. He hurt my feelings. I know he didn't mean to, but he hasn't apologized, and I'm not over it yet.

Do you want to talk about it?

No, she said with a minute shake of her head.

Want me to kick his ass?

Imogen laughed aloud. *No. He'll figure it out soon enough. If not, I'll kick his ass.*

I didn't know what he'd said, but for all of her physical strength, Imogen's heart bruised easily. If Luka was playing with her, I would make him regret it. Luka caught my glare, and his expression iced over. He glanced at Imogen and whatever he saw on her face caused his expression to chill even further.

Stop glaring like you're going to murder him, Imogen said across the link.

Nothing so dire as murder. But maybe a broken bone or ten would teach him some manners. Think he's dumb enough to spar with me?

Imogen snorted. *Not when you're wearing that expression.*

Let me know if it becomes a problem or if you just want to talk. I'm serious. I don't want you to be uncomfortable.

I'm not uncomfortable, Imogen assured me. *Just a little upset. I will let you know if it becomes a problem.*

She dropped the link, and I let her go.

Valentin brushed a hand against my back. I met his eyes and shook my head slightly. I might tell him later, if it became a problem—or if I needed to knock some sense into Luka—but for now, we needed to head out.

Which was going to be its own drama.

"We need food, I want to scout the neighborhood, and someone needs to stay here to keep an eye on our stuff so it doesn't walk off."

"I thought this block was safe," Imogen said.

"It is, but we don't know who else might have keys to the building. Until the rest of our supplies get here and we can secure the doors by alternate means, someone needs to stay and keep an eye on things. If we split up, we can meet back here in an hour."

My statement met a wall of resistance, but I refused to be swayed.

After ten minutes of arguing about who should stay and who should go, we split up. Imogen remained behind to watch the building. Luka and Valentin went to buy enough food to last us for a week. And I slipped out the door into the shadows between buildings.

I'd lost the pack but kept the hooded coat, and I still had my weapons. I didn't expect trouble, but I was prepared to meet it if it decided to find me anyway. Imogen had insisted on an active link, so she rode along with me, a quiet connection in the back of my mind.

The connection would allow me to keep an ear on her, too.

I wasn't looking for anything in particular, I was mostly making a mental map of the area, but I did keep an eye out for shops that might sell useful—and illegal—items. Shadowy doorways guarded by people who looked like they fought for fun were as familiar as my own reflection, and they looked the same across the universe.

I'd spent years in places just like this. Imogen might be uncomfortable in Block 48, but to me, it felt like my natural habitat.

8

I'd been out for half an hour when I picked up a shadow. They were good, but not good enough to avoid detection. The odds of it being someone who worked for Adams were astronomically low, but no matter who it was, I wanted to send a clear message that I was off-limits.

Someone is following me, I told Imogen over the link. *Do not leave the house. I will deal with it.* I enabled location sharing, just in case. It gave Imogen access to my real-time location data.

I've got a lock on you. Be careful, she said.

It took me another five minutes to find the right spot. I slipped into an alley that was too narrow for shops—I didn't need any witnesses. A few steps down the corridor, there was a decorative ledge between the first and second story.

The person tailing me had been staying about five seconds behind, which gave me just enough time to jump and haul myself up. I flattened myself onto the ledge, which was conveniently dirty enough to match the color of my coat.

I held myself utterly still. Many people wouldn't look up at all, and even those who did were mostly scanning for movement. Still and shadowed by the buildings around me, I would be hard to spot even for a trained professional.

A second later, a slightly-built person wearing a hat pulled low strolled around the corner. When they saw the empty alley, they glanced around in panic, but their eyes passed over me without stopping. They focused on the intersection farther down the alley and hurried toward it.

When they were just below my hiding place, I rolled off the ledge and landed on my feet. The sound was impossible to cover and they whirled around in surprise. That was a mistake. If they'd ran instead, they might've escaped.

A young man with pale skin stared at me in shock from under the brim of his hat. I hadn't stopped moving, and I caught him before he could draw the weapon at his waist. I slammed the front of his body up against the wall with his arms behind him. "Why are you following me?"

"I wasn't!" he whined. I adjusted his age down a few years. He was a teenager, all lanky limbs and false bravado.

It's a kid, I told Imogen. I squeezed his captured wrists hard enough to sting, and he hissed out a low curse. "Want to try again?" I asked.

"I ain't telling you shit," he growled. Or he tried. It came out with a faint whine.

"I suppose I'll have to take it up with your boss, then. Who do you work for?"

He remained mutinously silent.

I sighed. "Look, kid, I don't want to hurt you, but people following me around is bad for business. If you're not going to talk, I'm going to have to ensure you won't be able to follow me again." I let the threat hang in silence.

He broke in less than ten seconds.

"I'm not working for anyone. I saw you give something to Mo when she tried to dip you. I don't want her getting mixed up in trouble."

"So you decided to get mixed up in my trouble instead?"

"Better me than her," he spat with fierce protectiveness.

I patted him down with my free hand and removed the knife from his hip. "If I let you go, are you going to run?"

"No," he said, a little too quickly.

I chuckled. "You're a bad liar, kid."

"I'm not a kid," he growled.

"How old are you? Sixteen?"

His jaw jutted out, even though his cheek was pressed against the wall. "Old enough."

"Says the sixteen-year-old." I sighed. "I'm looking for info and willing to pay for it. And if you run, I'm keeping your blade. So decide." I let him go and backed up, his knife held loosely in my left hand.

He spun to face me but didn't immediately bolt. He eyed the knife warily. "What do you want?"

I decided to start with something easy. If he proved himself trustworthy, then I might ask him more interesting questions. "Where's the best place to find information?"

"What kind of information?" He peered at me, trying to see my face through the shadow of the hood.

I smiled at him. "The kind one doesn't blurt out to sixteen-year-olds on the street."

He huffed out a breath. "I'm eighteen." At my skeptical expression, he grumbled, "Seventeen and a half."

"You got a name, Mr. Seventeen-and-a-half?"

"You can call me Ran. The best place to find information depends on if you mean in Block 48 or in general. Both answers will cost you."

"I'll pay you a hundred credits each."

His eyes narrowed. "Five hundred. Each."

"One hundred each, and I'll forget that you were following me with a knife." I flipped said knife and caught it without looking. His face paled.

I didn't get any satisfaction from scaring a kid, but if he stuck his nose where it didn't belong at the wrong time, he would get hurt far worse than a little scare. And if he'd been watching me earlier, then he knew where I was staying. That wasn't good for either of us.

His mouth set in a mutinous line. "Fine. Let's see the money."

I withdrew two credits sticks with a hundred credits each and held them up.

Ran eyed the knife and decided lunging for the credits was not a wise choice. He was getting smarter. "In Block 48, you want old man Flack. He's in Sector J. Tell him I sent you and he'll help you."

My initial research had turned up Flack as a potential source of information, so I tossed Ran the first chip.

"In general, the most connected person on CP57 is Sawya, but they are in Block 1, and you'll need an invitation to set foot in there." His expression turned sly. "I can get you one—for a price."

Sawya and I went way back. They had originally introduced me to Jax, the traitorous little shit who'd decided that Quint money was better than mine. I didn't think Sawya had sold me out because Jax and I had worked together many times before he'd betrayed me, but caution would be wise.

I tossed Ran the second credit chip. "I'll let you know if I need help getting an invite." I didn't tell him that an invite wouldn't be a problem if I wanted to go as myself—I had a standing invitation. Or, rather, the Golden Dahlia did. But if I used those credentials, then I'd potentially be revealing far more than a simple invite warranted.

"What about my knife?" he demanded.

I threw it before he could react. The tip embedded into the composite wall a half meter from his head. I could've landed it close enough to cut his hair, but he was a kid and jumpy, so I took the cautious route. I didn't want to accidentally stab him in the face because he'd startled. Still, I'd thrown it hard enough that the hilt vibrated from the impact, and he stared at it with wide eyes.

"Watch your back, Ran. I don't want to catch you following me or my people again. And if you try it, I will."

I turned to leave, but his voice stopped me. "Are you going to leave Mo alone?"

"That depends on how good your information is."

His expression turned mulish. "It's good. And if you need more, find me in Sector B."

I nodded and slipped from the alley. Once I was out of sight, I stepped into a shadowed alcove and waited for Ran to leave. He did, heading toward Sector B and away from the building I'd rented. Hopefully, that meant he was done following me.

I circled back toward our home base. My hour of exploring was nearly up. If I stayed out too long, Imogen would come hunt me down, as long as Valentin didn't beat her to it.

———

BY AFTERNOON LOCAL TIME, the house was full. Ari, Stella, and Eddie had all arrived safely, and as far as anyone knew, they hadn't attracted any suspicion. Their ships were on other parts of the station, giving us multiple fallback points.

In the ideal case, none of our preparations would be needed. But the universe was rarely ideal.

Imogen and Luka were talking again, which I took to mean that Luka had pulled his head out of his ass and apologized. I silently wished them both luck.

Valentin volunteered to make dinner while the others got unpacked and settled. I went with him.

"Can I help?" I asked. I wasn't the best cook, but I could follow directions.

"No need." He handed me a drink that smelled citrusy. "But you can sit at the bar and keep me company."

I climbed onto a barstool and looked around. I conceded that he'd made the right call. The kitchen was small enough that I would've just been in his way. He pulled out ingredients with the ease of practice.

"Where did you learn to cook?" I asked as I tasted my drink. It was deliciously cool and refreshing.

A grin turned up the corner of his mouth. "I didn't always have people waiting on me. Until last year, I had to feed myself."

I rolled my eyes. "Weren't you an officer in the military? Didn't they feed you?"

The grin transformed into an abashed smile. "They did, and I'm sure that my food was better than most. But I wasn't always on a fancy ship with staff. So when I had time, I taught myself to cook. I enjoy it."

I sipped my drink and watched him move around the space. My heart twisted. The simple domesticity called to everything in me. I imagined the days we'd spend together: Valentin would cook, I would clean up, and then we'd retire to bed early. I knew it was an illusion—he was an emperor, and I was a queen, albeit of a rag-tag group of rogues and refugees. We had far too many responsibilities to just walk away. But I enjoyed the fantasy.

The meal wasn't gourmet, but it was hearty and delicious. Everyone was a little subdued, and conversation was light. We were all focused on finding Adams and getting home safely.

After dinner, we moved down to the ground floor. We'd designated the large office as our on-station command center. The room had plenty of seating, a big desk, and multiple displays on the walls.

Ari and Stella sat close together in a pair of padded chairs. I sat on the edge of the desk and Valentin joined me. Luka and Imogen leaned against opposite walls while Eddie prowled around the room, repeatedly revealing and vanishing a coin with sleight of hand. He was equally skilled with either hand, despite one being mechanical. It had taken him many long hours of practice to get the calibration just right.

Ari took charge of contacting the teams that Robert had sent. The mercenary advisor had been clever. He'd sent two teams, one as a smoke screen for the other. The first group didn't have any apparent ties to Arx, but someone who went digging would find threads that led back to the Rogue Coalition fairly quickly.

The second group was in deep cover, and they were professionals. It would take weeks to tie them to the Rogue Coalition.

It was too dangerous to meet in person, but neural links were almost as good and didn't risk exposure.

"Dammit," Ari said a few minutes later.

"No luck?" Stella asked gently.

She shook her head in disgust. "Either Adams and his people aren't here or he's a fucking ghost. Neither team has heard anything."

I'd contacted my own team, with similar results. One of my contacts had worked her way into the docking department since the last time I'd talked to her, and her careful searches had turned up nothing but dead-ends. I was still convinced that Adams would show for the meeting, but I started making mental contingency plans in case he didn't.

"Are we wrong?" Eddie asked. "What are we missing?"

"We still have almost two weeks until the meeting," Ari said. "Maybe we're giving him too much credit. Just because we're here early doesn't mean he will be."

I instinctively shook my head, dismissing the thought, but then I stopped. "Adams isn't dumb, and he's able to plan complicated attacks that require a lot of coordination. If he's not here, it's a choice. Why make that choice?"

"He suspects a trap," Valentin said.

"Of course, but so do we, and we're still here."

"He wants to force you to tip your hand," Eddie said.

"Which means he had *some* way of knowing what's happening on CP57, even if he's not here. That would usually mean a team, but maybe he's paying for information another way."

"We don't have the resources to track information flow," Ari said. "Not on a station this big."

I sighed. "I might have an option for that, but it'll be very expensive and should be saved for a last resort. Let's see what the rest of this week brings, first."

"Well, that's not ominous or anything," Stella grumbled.

"It's one of my old contacts," I said.

Her eyes widened in understanding. "No wonder it sounded ominous." She waved her hands. "No reason to rush into that. There's still time. Let's see what happens."

"We'll stick to the plan for now," I agreed. "Now that we're here, we can do our own recon. The meeting was set for a building in Block 20, which is two blocks over. If Adams picks a similar location, he'll likely be within a ten-block area."

"That's still a lot of ground to cover," Imogen said.

"It beats the whole station."

She conceded the point with a shrug.

Stella yawned. "Today started early, and station time is messing with my internal clock. I say we all get some sleep and reconvene in the morning. Everything looks better in the morning."

"I don't," I said drily.

She rolled her eyes at me. "You know what I meant."

I stood from the desk. Stella was right. I could use some sleep because today had been long. It was still relatively early by station time, but I'd been up for nearly twenty hours. "The doors are secured from the inside, so we shouldn't have any surprises tonight. If you need to go out for something, make sure you disable the alarm. And let someone know where you're going."

Imogen pointed a finger at me. "Don't go out without me."

I gave her my most innocent expression. "I wouldn't dream of it."

9

Imogen didn't have to worry about me creeping out because I crashed as soon as my head hit the pillow. Even the temptation of Valentin in my bed—still a delightful novelty—wasn't enough to prop my eyes open.

I slept hard and woke refreshed. The dim light spilling around the edges of the curtains meant that it was still very early. The station never went truly dark, but the overhead lights were lowered at night.

Next to me, Valentin's breathing was deep and even. Rather than moving and possibly waking him, I stayed where I was and checked the local news on the net, including the latest rumors and gossip. There were no splashy headlines announcing the arrival of the Rogue Queen or the Kos Emperor, so I figured we were still incognito.

For now.

Eventually, Valentin would be missed in Koan. When that happened and the news leaked, it wouldn't take a genius to figure out where he was. Adams would know I had backup.

I checked my messages, but none of my team had found anything new in the few hours since I'd last talked to them. It was so easy to expect instant results and forget the days and weeks and occasionally *months* of patience that had been required on my previous hunts.

Sooner or later, Adams would fuck up, and I would be there to catch him when he did. I just had to remember to be patient.

Valentin drew a deep breath and rolled over, sleepily nuzzling my shoulder. "Good morning," he whispered.

"Good morning. Did I wake you?"

"No. I've been drifting in and out for an hour." He pulled me closer, pressing his body against mine. "But I'm glad that you're awake now." He idly caressed the curve of my waist.

I couldn't help the grin. "Oh, yeah? Why is that?"

"Because now you can be my pillow."

"You already have a pillow."

I caught the flash of his smile. "You're better. Let me show you."

He pillowed his head on my shoulder and pressed a soft kiss against my neck. When I hummed in appreciation, he did it again, then he trailed kisses over my collarbone and up the slope of my breast.

His tongue touched my skin, and my breath caught. "You must really like your pillows," I breathed.

His eyes crinkled with his smile, but rather than replying, his mouth closed over my nipple, and the wet heat spiked lust straight into my bloodstream. I buried my hands in his hair, holding him in place, though he showed no inclination to leave.

His hand slid down my body, over my belly and lower. I parted my legs, and it was his turn to hum when he found me slick and hot.

And still, he didn't rush.

He leisurely moved to my other breast before nibbling his way down my stomach. All while his clever fingers drove me to the edge of sanity. No amount of desperate pleading altered his pace, and when he finally reached his destination and licked me, my back arched off the bed as pleasure whited out everything else.

"Now," I demanded as soon as I could breathe.

He surged up, his face set in hard lines of desire and restraint.

But still, he didn't rush.

He slid into me a centimeter at a time, as if he had all day. The delicious feel of him so soon after my last orgasm nearly pushed me into another one. I clenched around him, and he hissed out a breath. I just needed the slightest nudge.

I tried to move, to find the right angle, but he had my hips firmly pinned against his. I pulled his face down to mine and growled, "If you do not move *this instant*, I'm going to murder you."

He laughed and pressed a quick kiss to my mouth.

Then—*finally*—he rushed, moving with sure, hard strokes that drove us both off the edge of the world.

———

AFTER THE MORNING'S delicious delayed start, Valentin and I got ready to go see Flack. I applied heavy makeup that would help disguise my features. Valentin was too recognizable, even with a hooded coat, so he was painting his face with a geometric black and white pattern used to foil face recognition. Imogen and Luka would do the same so Valentin wouldn't stand out.

I watched him smear the paint across his cheek with steady fingers. He caught my gaze. "What is it?"

"Will you be able to tell if Flack makes a neural link connection to someone else while we're there?"

Valentin nodded, his handsome face half covered in paint. "As long as I'm relatively close." He stared at me for a long moment. "You haven't asked how I can intercept neural links."

I hadn't asked, but I *had* hunted for the information after the first time I saw him use the ability. I was pretty sure it was experimental Kos tech, but unlike their armor, this secret was much better kept, and I hadn't found much. "I figured you would tell me when you were ready. Or if you could."

His grin turned teasing. "What did you find when you searched?"

I laughed and pressed a quick kiss to his lips. "You know me too well. I didn't find much. Your secret is safe."

"I have an upgraded neural link implant that has additional chips and is more deeply integrated with my brain," Valentin said. "It's a benefit of being part of the imperial family."

"Wait, Margie has one, too? Why didn't you warn me?" I demanded. I tried to remember if I'd linked anything embarrassing in front of Valentin's mother while I was in Koan.

Valentin smiled. "Mother rarely uses the ability. It gives her blinding headaches."

"What about you?"

Valentin shook his head. "Mine is a newer model. If I use it too much I'll get headaches, nausea, double vision, and nosebleeds. But that's rare or when I overextend myself. Mostly it just makes me tired."

"Your nose bled when I rescued you from Adams."

He had the grace to look sheepish. "I might've overextended myself a bit."

I pointed a finger at him. "Don't do it again."

"I will do everything in my power to keep you safe," he said, expression hard. "You would do the same for me, so don't even try to deny it. But I won't be reckless, I can promise you that."

I kissed him again. "Thank you."

***

By the time the lights reached the daylight brightness, Valentin, Luka, Imogen, and I were already deep in the heart of Block 48.

We all wore our hooded coats, and the three of them flanked me like guards.

I skirted around a busy early market. Mo worked the crowd, her small form flitting between unsuspecting targets. She caught sight of me and dipped her chin, letting me pass without trying to empty my pockets.

It was a moment's work to find Ran, hidden in the shadows, watching the scene with a feigned nonchalance that did nothing to disguise his sharp attention. His eyes narrowed on my face, then flickered over my shoulder to the others, but he didn't move from his post.

I mentally wished them both luck and moved on.

A little digging had turned up Flack's exact address in Sector J, but rather than going there directly, I meandered my way through a dozen other Sectors first. Not only did it help my mental map, but it also made us harder to track. And as far as I could tell, we weren't being followed and no one had tried to pickpocket us.

Flack ran a tiny little store that sold antique books. Inside, the air smelled of dust and musty paper. It looked like a volume hadn't moved from the shelves in forty years. The man himself was stooped and wizened with age, with snow-white hair and light brown skin that was wrinkled and papery thin. But his eyes were sharp and his smile was full of secrets.

He stepped out from behind his counter with a surprisingly sprightly gait. "Welcome, welcome. How may I help you?"

"I'm looking for a particular item and a young man who called himself Ran said you might be able to help."

"I hope that boy didn't give you any trouble. He's full of the impetuousness of youth." Flack shook his head with a fond smile.

"We came to an understanding," I said mildly.

"You must have, if he sent you to me. What are you looking

for?" He waved his arms at the jam-packed bookcases. "I have a little of everything."

"I'm looking for information."

Flack's expression gave nothing away. "What sort of information? My books cover every topic."

Some information brokers preferred a roundabout conversation, but I didn't have time for that. Either Flack would be able to help me or he wouldn't, and it was best to figure out which it was as soon as possible—while giving away as little as I could.

I met his eyes. "I'm brokering a very sensitive deal, one that several parties would enjoy seeing fail. I would like to know if any of their agents land on CP57, so I'll have time to prepare the appropriate countermeasures." The lie slid from my tongue as smoothly as truth.

His gaze traveled over my three bodyguards, weighing exactly what those countermeasures might be. He remained unruffled. "Do you know which ships they are traveling on?"

I let a grin tug at the corner of my mouth. "If I knew that, I wouldn't need you."

He chuckled. "You'd be surprised, my dear." He rubbed his chin in thought. "Many people, especially those who don't want to be found, come to CP57 with a numerical ID tied to their ship. They don't use their real names or identifiers."

He gave me and the rest of my team a significant look. I met it with an even stare of my own.

When I didn't rise to the bait, he continued, "Finding someone who doesn't want to be found is delicate, difficult, *expensive* work."

I inclined my head. He wasn't telling me anything I didn't already know. "I am aware of the value of said work, but I don't need them found, I just need information on the likely ships coming in." My smile sharpened. "I can find them myself."

"Thousands of ships dock every day, and that information is

heavily protected. I can find a few specific ships for you, but getting information on every ship, or even a large number of ships, is impossible." He shook his head. "No amount of money could make that happen."

There was very little that a vast amount of money couldn't make happen, but since I didn't have coffers that deep, I let it go.

He spread his hands in an inviting gesture. "Tell me what you are looking for, and I will have my people find it for you. You won't find better information outside of Block 1."

That's what I was afraid of. I already had someone in the docking department who could run careful searches. I needed someone with better access, and it appeared that Flack didn't have it.

I suppressed my disappointment and pulled out a credit stick with five hundred credits on it. "Thank you for your time. I was never here. If someone questionable starts asking about me, I'll pay you ten times that much to bring me the information on them." It was a decent amount of money, but not so much that it would be suspicious all on its own.

He accepted the stick with a calculating smile. "Do you need help getting in to Block 1? No one is allowed inside without explicit permission."

"I don't know if that's where my travels will take me yet or not. But if I need help, I'll let you know."

"Until next time."

I echoed the farewell and then left the shop, leading the others on a roundabout route back toward our rooms. As soon as we rounded the first corner, I linked Valentin. *Anything?*

No, he didn't make any links while we were there.

That could be good news, or it could just mean he was waiting until we left. Only time would tell. I thanked Valentin and closed the link.

Once we were well away from the shop, Imogen created a group link and asked, *Why didn't you hire him?*

Because he doesn't know more than we do, and information is a blade that cuts both ways, I responded. *He now knows that someone is looking for us. The more information I give him, the more valuable it becomes.*

Are you going to try to find someone else?

I silently shook my head. According to my research, Flack was the best option in this block, and no one in the surrounding blocks was any better. And the more people I approached, the more interesting I became.

We will see what our teams find, I said.

I hoped it would be enough.

10

By the end of the sixth day with no new information, I was done with every person in the house except Valentin. He remained safe only because he was smart enough to let the others ask, for the millionth time, if I had any updates.

No, no I did not.

But even Valentin had started wearing a worried expression when he thought I wasn't looking.

In the past, I'd enjoyed the information-gathering part of any mission, but I had been working alone without pressing deadlines. The dynamic changed when I had a team of people counting on me to deliver crucial information in a timely fashion. The continued failure pressed on me, sharpening my temper. After the latest report, Stella had taken one look at my face and ordered me to spend some time alone "for everyone's sake."

I'd taken her advice and buried myself in the downstairs office while Eddie cooked dinner. I was as far away from everyone as I could get without physically leaving the building —which remained an option.

One that was becoming more likely. I'd promised Valentin that I wouldn't take any unnecessary risks, but all risks were becoming more necessary as time wore on.

I muttered a curse under my breath when the office door opened. "What now?" I demanded.

Valentin stuck his head in and held up a bottle of whisky and two glasses. "I come in peace."

"I'm not good company today," I warned.

His smile lit up the room. I desperately wanted him to stay, even if I was going to end up growling at him. "I won't hold it against you," he promised.

He entered, closing the door behind him. I watched as he crossed the room. His posture was relaxed, so at least he wasn't here to deliver more bad news. *Probably.*

Valentin reached across the desk and set a glass in front of me. He held up the bottle. "How much?"

I held my fingers a couple of centimeters apart. I'd like for him to fill the glass to the brim, but I needed to remain alert in case Adams decided now was the perfect time to show his face.

Not that I had much hope of that happening.

Valentin splashed whisky into my glass, then gave himself the same amount. He sat on the edge of the desk and raised his glass in a toast. "We'll get him."

I touched the rim of my glass to his, then took a sip. The alcohol had a smooth burn and a delicious smoky flavor. I looked at the bottle, but I didn't recognize the brand. "Did you buy this here?"

He shook his head. "I brought it with me. For you."

Warmth fought with frustration. Valentin kept doing all of these amazing things for me, and I couldn't even catch the person who'd kidnapped him and threatened his safety. I bit my lip and stared at my glass. I vowed to do better, no matter what I had to do to make that happen.

Valentin stood and circled around to my side of the desk. He scooped me up and then sat in my chair with me held sideways in his lap. "What's wrong?" he asked quietly.

I leaned my head against his shoulder so I wouldn't have to meet his eyes. "I'm frustrated and worried. And I can't even repay all of your kindness by doing the one thing I'm supposedly good at because my target is a fucking ghost and my hands are tied trying to keep everyone safe."

He hugged me close. "Kindness isn't something that accumulates debt," he said, his voice velvety soft. "You owe me nothing. I enjoy finding ways to help you or brighten your day." His lips brushed across my forehead. "You're so capable that you make it a challenge."

We sipped our drinks in silence, and I let the comfort of his embrace and the warm buzz of the whisky loosen some of my tension. A few minutes later, I murmured, "Would you like to know a secret?"

"Always."

"My days are always brighter when you're in them." Valentin stilled under me and my cheeks heated. Was that too sappy? Not sappy enough? Why were relationships so hard?

I shifted uncomfortably, but Valentin's arms tightened around me, and he settled me more firmly on his lap. "I'm glad," he whispered, "because I feel the same."

My nerves steadied. I braced myself against Valentin's chest and pressed my lips to his. His mouth opened, and I deepened the kiss. He tasted of whisky and desire—my new favorite combination. I reluctantly pulled away before the kiss burned out my self-control. As much as I'd like to have him sprawled under me on the desk, I needed to discuss a new plan.

One that he wasn't going to like.

Sensing the shift in my mood, Valentin set his glass on the desk and waited for me to gather my thoughts. His arms loosely encircled me, offering support without making me feel trapped.

I loved the way he intuitively knew what I needed.

"The meeting is set for a week from now," I said. "And we still don't know where Adams is, or even if he's going to show. We've scouted all of the potential blocks. We have people searching the docking database. We've done all we can. We need more information."

Valentin's expression remained even. "You plan to go to Block 1."

"I do. If Adams is anywhere on the station, Sawya can find him. If he's not, they still might know where he's hiding."

"I will go with you."

I shook my head. "You can't. I appreciate the thought, but you are too tempting as a target. We don't want to draw any attention to you, and no disguise will protect you from Sawya."

"You said this was a last resort. What will it cost you?"

I glanced away. "I don't know."

It wasn't a lie, exactly, but it wasn't the full truth. If I wasn't extremely careful, Sawya would smell the desperation on me. They were cheerfully ruthless and would exploit every weakness. And I risked not only myself but Valentin and the Rogue Coalition, too.

Valentin's body turned to stone, and his mouth pressed into a flat line. His hand flexed against my hip, like he was fighting the urge to pull me close. "Are you sure it's the only option?" he asked at last.

"It's the best option."

Valentin blew out a frustrated breath and bowed his head. "I hate this," he murmured. "I want to put you in *Ardia,* fly us home, and lock you away with me in an unbreachable fortress. Everyone else go can go fuck themselves."

I gently stroked his jaw. "You don't mean it. You care about your people too much."

"I care about *you,*" he said, his expression fierce.

My heart skipped a beat. "I care about you, too," I admitted quietly. "And I would prefer it if you were already safely locked in that fortress while I dealt with Adams."

His lips twisted into a bitter smile. "Neither of us gets what we want."

I kissed him, brushing my lips across his until his mouth lost the bitter edge and softened under mine. "Not yet," I murmured against his skin. "But once Adams is caught, the rules change. And I'm overdue for an extended vacation in a remote fortress somewhere." I grinned at him. "Do you know where I might find such a place?"

Valentin pulled me close and buried his face against my neck. "I know the perfect spot. And I'm going to hold you to it, Queen Rani, so let's catch the asshole."

His soft hair tickled my nose as I leaned my head against his. "As you wish, Emperor Kos."

———

UNFORTUNATELY, trying to persuade everyone else that Sawya was the best option took the better part of two days. The scheduled meeting with Adams was less than a week away, and we still had nothing on him, so I stopped negotiating and started dictating.

I called everyone into a meeting.

As soon as they arrived, I said, "I am going to see Sawya tonight." When Ari growled something under her breath, I slashed a hand through the air. "I've already scheduled the meeting, so you can help me prepare or you can leave. Decide."

The office was deathly quiet despite being full of people. Valentin stood beside me, a silent show of support. He'd been working on convincing Ari, Stella, and Imogen, too, despite his own misgivings.

"What can I do?" Eddie asked.

I smiled at him. "You can go with me."

The room erupted as everyone started talking at once.

"You can't—"

"*Eddie?*"

"Are you out of your—"

"*I* will go—"

I let them talk themselves out. When they quieted, I raised an eyebrow. "Are you ready to listen now?"

"We just want you to be safe," Stella said quietly.

"I know. But we are running out of time, and there aren't any easy solutions left. Confronting Adams without information puts us all in danger. And if he's not coming at all, then we're just wasting time while he plots something new. I've dealt with Sawya before. I know what I'm risking."

I turned to Eddie. "Did you find a way in?"

He grinned at me. "Of course. It's full of traps, but nothing I can't handle."

"You weren't able to get an invite?" Ari asked.

"Oh, I did. I could walk through the front door. But Sawya appreciates a little theater, and I plan to deliver. An entertaining entrance will make them more likely to listen to my request."

"How do you know they aren't already working with Commander Adams?" Ari asked.

"I don't."

Ari threw up her hands in exasperation. Stella wrapped an arm around her waist and leaned into her side. Ari closed her eyes and tucked Stella close. She took a deep breath and let it out with a sigh. "What can we do to help?"

My smile had a sly edge. "I'm so glad you asked."

———

I CHOSE my clothes with care. I couldn't show up dressed for war, no matter how much I might prefer it. But just because I couldn't *look* like I was dressed for war didn't mean I wasn't ready for whatever the night might bring.

I finally decided on a tailored pair of slacks in a shade of deep charcoal gray and a loose, black, tunic-length blouse over a tight black cami. I'd had the outfit made for my trip to Koan. The technical fabric had been ridiculously expensive, but it worked as a type of lightweight armor that would block blades and deflect glancing plasma pulses. The pants had a built-in sheath in each pocket the perfect size for a slender knife.

Each ankle also sported a small sheathed knife, and I had a pair of blades built into the soles of my short boots. Finally, I had two plasma pistols: a tiny one in a waistband holster at the small of my back and a larger one in a shoulder holster tucked into the curve of my waist. The long shirt covered both.

I laid out a reversible cloak that was gold on one side and black on the other and a large, gold, dahlia-shaped filigree clasp set in onyx. Tonight was not a night for subtlety.

Valentin sat on the bed and watched me get ready with an unreadable expression. I stopped to press a kiss to his lips. "It'll be okay."

He nodded, his eyes clear. "Good. Because if anything happens to you, I'm going to tear this station apart with my bare hands."

The statement was all the more powerful for the quiet delivery.

I kissed him again. "Don't do anything rash."

I pulled back but stopped when his fingers gently closed around my wrist. "I would burn down the world for you," he said, expression as serious as I'd ever seen it. "Never doubt that. If anything happens, I *will* come for you, no matter what."

My heart tripped over itself. What would I do if someone threatened Valentin?

Burning down the world would just be the beginning.

I smiled even as tears pricked the backs of my eyes. "If that happens, I'll be sure to save a few enemies for you so you won't feel left out."

He pressed a kiss to the center of my palm. "Deal."

He let me go, and I applied my makeup with hands that weren't quite steady. It took two tries before I was calm enough to ensure the eyeliner didn't end up in my eye.

It had been a long time since I'd fully donned my Golden Dahlia guise, but memory was a funny thing. Glancing in the mirror, it felt like no time at all had passed. My eyes were transformed by the heavy liner and golden eyeshadow. My cheekbones were more pronounced thanks to careful contouring, and my lips appeared smaller and thinner.

It wouldn't hide my identity, but it was just different enough from my normal appearance that it made people question their memory.

I turned for my cloak, and Valentin's gaze traced over my face.

"Well?" I prompted when he didn't say anything.

"You're beautiful, no matter what makeup you're wearing—or not. Tonight, you look dangerous."

"You always say such nice things," I murmured without thinking. "No wonder I love you."

Valentin froze, and I did the same, looking for the threat. It took a beat before I realized exactly what I'd said. I lifted my hands and started to stammer out *something*—a joke, an apology, a reiteration—but I didn't get a chance because Valentin rose and enfolded me in his arms.

"Don't run," he pleaded, his voice whisper soft.

Valentin knew me well because my first instinct was to deflect, to hide, to *run*—if not physically, then emotionally. I swallowed the urge, but I couldn't loosen the tension that tightened my muscles. I stood stiff and still as Valentin held me gently, carefully, like I was a fragile blossom he didn't want to crush.

I took a deep breath and gathered my courage. Held this closely, I couldn't see his face, but maybe it was easier this way. "I didn't mean to tell you that," I said quietly, "but that doesn't make it untrue."

Valentin's arms flexed around me, a minute tightening that betrayed his emotions. "Are you going to run if I tell you the same?"

I froze again, and a short laugh worked its way past my tight throat. "Maybe."

Valentin's lips brushed across my temple. "I love you," he whispered into my ear. "Run if you have to. I'll be here when you get back."

Something in me unlocked, and the tension drained away. I pulled back so I could see his face. His arms briefly tightened, as if to hold me in place, before slowly falling away. His jaw clenched, but he made no move to reach for me again.

I traced my fingers over his jaw and the flat line of his mouth. "I like the company here, so I think I'll stay, if that's all right with you."

His mouth fell open, and I took advantage, pulling his face down to mine and fusing our lips. I licked his bottom lip and he shook off the shock, taking over the kiss and leaving me breathless.

A light, buoyant feeling spread through my chest, followed by hardened certainty. I would catch Adams. I would broker peace between Kos and Quint. *No one* was going to keep me from being with Valentin.

Not even the most dangerous person on the station.

11

Despite my fears that everything would change with a declaration in the open, Valentin did not try to prevent me from visiting Sawya. Instead, he sent me off with a solemn request to be careful and a lingering kiss.

Eddie and I swept through the intervening blocks with swift efficiency. I wore my cloak with the black side out so that we passed unnoticed. I would reverse it once we arrived in Block 1. Eddie wore unrelenting black from head to toe. His clothes were so dark they seemed to absorb all of the surrounding light. I wasn't sure exactly what he had on, except that it fit close to his body.

The entrance Eddie had found was in Block 8, which was diagonally adjacent to Block 1. The two blocks barely touched, and even directly adjacent blocks were only supposed to be accessible through the airlocks, but thanks to a network of service hallways, ventilation shafts, and illegal modifications, a path had opened.

I had no doubt that it remained open because of Sawya's influence.

Eddie slipped into a narrow opening between the back of a

building and the wall of Block 8. He fiddled with a tall grate for a second, and then it silently swung open on well-oiled hinges. "After you," he whispered. "Stop four steps in."

I did as he asked, and he followed me in, closing the grate behind us. The tunnel was dark, but thanks to my specialty night-vision contact lenses, I could see well enough, if only in shades of greenish gray.

Eddie passed me with a light touch on my arm. "Follow me and step where I step. Don't touch anything."

It took us nearly forty minutes to travel a couple of hundred meters. Eddie disabled the traps and alarms in front of us and then enabled them behind us. We could've left the path open—Sawya would've closed it soon enough—but it was all part of the entertainment.

Sawya had to know what was happening because for all of his skill, Eddie hadn't been able to avoid all of the cameras, and we didn't have a security specialist to remotely disable them. But no one came to drag us out.

We stopped just before the door leading into Block 1. I reversed my cloak and raised the hood while Eddie reset the last alarm behind us. Eddie paused at the door. "Ready, boss?"

I inclined my head. *We're going in,* I sent across the link to the group.

We're in position, Valentin said. *Good luck.*

Eddie opened the door, and I stepped through. My contacts automatically adjusted to the light. It was late, but Block 1 never really slept. The overhead lights were low and the towering ceiling consisted of display panels that displayed a sea of stars, but the buildings were brightly lit.

I led Eddie deeper into the block. Unlike the rest of the station, Block 1 had plenty of empty space. Every square centimeter was worth more than the entire Rogue Coalition, but wide streets and green parks nestled around the bases of tall buildings that housed every form of entertainment from casinos and shopping to live fights and sexual fantasies.

It was designed to look like a city on-planet and the illusion held up fairly well—as long as one didn't look too closely.

The streets were filled with well-dressed pedestrians. They strolled slowly, showing off the latest couture and trying to blind each other with the amount of jewelry on display. It was such a difference from the rest of the station that it felt like a dream—which was part of the appeal.

Black-clad bodyguards trailed behind their clients, shadows hinting at the darkness hiding beneath the block's pretty lights.

Eddie fell in behind me, just another guard protecting his capricious charge.

Sawya's building was impossible to miss. It was dead center and clad in silver. It glowed like a beacon.

Who do they think they are? Eddie breathed across the link.

I'd added the feed from my contacts to our group link, so the others could see what I was seeing. I let them marvel for a moment before I replied, *Sawya is the most powerful person on CP57. Who do you think funded the station's independence?*

Behind me, Eddie blew out a breath.

I approached the door. A uniformed woman with a perfect smile opened it before I could reach for the handle. "Welcome," she said.

I inclined my head and swept inside, Eddie on my heels.

The lobby was three stories tall and dripping in crystal chandeliers. They should've clashed with the sleek, simple furniture and minimalist design, but it worked. Elevators whisked clients up to whatever pleasure they desired.

I bypassed the main elevators and headed for a secluded alcove guarded by five large men in silver suits. The largest stepped in front of me as I approached. He scowled at me without speaking.

I suppressed a smile. "Dahlia."

The guard's eyes flickered as he communicated with someone. He stepped aside.

The alcove housed a single elevator that stood open. There was no call button. I entered with Eddie, close enough together that the door couldn't close between us—something I absolutely would not put past Sawya. The door slid closed behind us. There were no buttons inside, either, but after a beat, the elevator smoothly whisked us upward.

We had not been searched for weapons, which sent its own message about Sawya's confidence. They knew exactly who I was and what I carried and had determined that I wasn't a threat.

I hoped I wouldn't have to prove them wrong.

The elevator was lined with mirrors, and I took a second to check my appearance. I lowered my hood and fixed my hair. I pushed the cloak over my shoulders so it looked more like a cape, a river of gold down my back.

Showtime.

The elevator stopped, the doors opened, and my connection to the net died. The constant buzz in the back of my mind went silent. Behind me, Eddie sucked in a surprised breath. I'd warned everyone that it was possible, but even braced for it, it was a shock to the system.

"I'm okay," he murmured.

Taking him at his word, I strode from the elevator into an optical illusion as beautiful as it was dizzying. We were in the penthouse. Floor-to-ceiling windows wrapped the edges of the room, giving a glimpse of the rest of the block.

But the floor... the floor was a piece of art.

Embedded video panels under our feet made it look like we were standing on the top of a building made entirely of glass. Tiny virtual people moved on the various floors below us. In the center of the room, right where Sawya's desk sat, the display showed a long open drop straight to the ground floor. Sawya stood next to the desk and appeared to be standing on nothing but air.

Sawya was tall and sleekly muscled, with pale skin, wintry gray eyes, and short, curly blond hair that was tousled *just so*. They wore a long, silver, sleeveless dress with sharp, wide shoulders and a deep, narrow V-neck that dropped to their bellybutton. The floor-length skirt was a frothy swirl of multiple lightweight layers that flowed around their legs like a cloud. The color made their skin look even more fair, as did the smoky eyeshadow and pale lipstick.

Sawya was gorgeous and knew it.

They held out a hand, and I stepped forward and brought it to my lips with a shallow bow. "Thank you for agreeing to see me."

"Darling, it's been too long," they said and sent me a canny glance. "I heard a rumor that you went all straight and proper."

I laughed. "Does that sound like me?"

They smiled, then glanced over my shoulder. "Who is this delicious delicacy who slipped through my alarms like a spirit?"

I motioned Eddie forward. "This is Eddie. He's mine."

Sawya pouted, then waved a hand at Eddie. "Be a doll and fix us a drink, won't you? The bar is over there." They gestured toward the wall with the elevator. A half-dozen guards stood like stone sentinels in their silver suits. More would be hidden nearby.

Eddied bowed. "Of course. Do you have a preference?"

Sawya cast their eyes to the ceiling, which mirrored the stars shown outside. "Something smoky, with a bite. Fix yourself one, too."

Eddie withdrew with a nod.

Sawya sat in a bright blue wingback chair and waved me to a low black sofa. Below my feet, the tiny virtual people went about their lives. Or perhaps they weren't virtual at all. Sawya could be collecting enough data for a real-time display.

"Do you like my new floor?"

"Yes, it's incredible. Is it accurate or a simulation?"

Sawya smiled and didn't answer.

I chuckled. "Fair enough."

"Why didn't you come to see me when you arrived?"

"I was trying to keep a low profile."

Sawya hummed. "You know who *did* come to see me?" They met my eyes. "Commander Tony Adams."

I kept my posture and expression relaxed through sheer force of will. "You always did keep the most interesting company," I murmured neutrally.

They laughed. "I met him as a lark. He's quite the nasty little man, but so full of delicious information. And he had a great deal to say about *you*."

"I'm sure he did. I have plenty to say about him, too."

Eddie returned with three lowball glasses balanced on a small tray. He presented the tray to Sawya. "A spicy whisky sour with a twist," he said. "Please enjoy."

"Should I be worried about poison?" Sawya asked nonchalantly as they picked up a glass.

Eddie grinned. "Not unless you poison your own bar."

Sawya's eyes lit up.

I huffed out an amused breath as Eddie handed me one of the remaining two glasses. "Don't give them ideas, Eddie."

"He's *darling*," Sawya breathed. "Can I keep him?"

I rolled my eyes. "Not unless he wants to be kept."

Sawya turned their considerable charm on Eddie and purred, "Consider it, pet. I would blow your mind." A playful smile tipped up one corner of their mouth. "And a few other things, too."

A flush climbed Eddie's cheeks. Sawya laughed in delight and pointed at the other end of the sofa. "Sit with us."

Eddie sat, his color still high.

Sawya sipped the drink and sighed in delight. "Delicious."

I cautiously tasted my own drink. I wasn't too worried about poison, but I needed to stay clearheaded. The flavor exploded on my tongue—sweet, sour, spicy... the drink *was* delicious.

Sawya swirled the alcohol in their glass, then looked up and met my eyes. "Let's talk business, shall we? You are worth an incredible amount of money right now. So tell me why I shouldn't just hand you over and be done with it."

I feigned ease and waved a hand around the room. "You already *have* an incredible amount of money."

"You know what they say: *more is better*."

"But friends are priceless."

Sawya's head tilted. "Are we friends?"

"More than you and Adams, I'll wager."

"That is a dangerous bet," Sawya warned lightly, but their expression remained clear and calm.

I shrugged delicately. "Perhaps. But did he even *attempt* to come in some way other than the front door? Did he sidle and scheme and play, or did he demand and bully and shout? And most importantly of all, did he respect you, or did you see the truth in his eyes when he thought himself clever enough to get away with it?"

I took another tiny sip of my drink. I'd pushed as much as I could, and Sawya was right—we *weren't* exactly friends. We'd worked together often enough back in the day, but it had been more of a close business relationship than a friendship.

I still didn't know if Sawya had known that Jax was unreliable and connected us anyway, but Adams had been here, and I hadn't been picked up yet, so I had a reason to hope.

"You always were an idealist," Sawya murmured. "It's good to see that some things never change."

I wasn't sure the description was entirely accurate, but I lifted my glass in a silent toast.

"I've heard rumors that the new emperor is trying to end the war. Are they true?"

Dealing with Sawya was like walking a tightrope. There were times to deflect and times to answer honestly, and part of the dance was knowing which was which.

"Yes," I said after a moment. "And Adams threatens that peace."

Sawya's eyes narrowed. "War is very profitable." I met their gaze without flinching. They sighed. "But it's never been to my taste."

On the other end of the sofa, Eddie blew out a heavy breath. I knew exactly how he felt.

"What are your plans for Adams?" Sawya asked.

I smiled and said nothing.

Sawya laughed. "You know I love it when you play hard to get, darling, but you must know I'm not going to turn you over to that nasty little worm. We *are* friends, of a sort, and I make it a priority not to stab my friends too often. Plus, I owe you for Jax, though you took care of that little problem rather admirably."

I dipped my head in acknowledgment of the unspoken apology. Sawya rarely made promises, but when they did, their word was solid gold. I'd never heard of them going back on it.

So, for now, I was safe.

I blew out a breath and relaxed a tiny fraction. "My plans depend on what happens during capture. If we manage to catch him alive, he'll stand trial in Koan. If not, I won't shed any tears."

Sawya lifted an eyebrow. "You would let him live?"

My answering smile was dark. "It wouldn't be my first choice, no. But I also don't want to give him a chance to become a martyr."

"He's surrounded himself with zealots," Sawya agreed. "And he's planning something."

My eyebrows rose. "You don't know what?"

Sawya chuckled. "While I appreciate your faith in my being all-knowing, there are some things that even I can't easily uncover. Someone warned him about me, and he's being very careful."

Eddie shifted in place. When Sawya's attention turned to him, he asked, "Is Arx in danger?"

I'd cautioned Eddie to stay as quiet as possible, but I understood his need for reassurance. I wanted to know the answer, too.

Sawya's eyes softened. "No, I don't think so. The whispers I'm hearing indicate that it may be something here."

"Tell me where he is, and I'll find out for you," I said with studied casualness.

The corner of their mouth lifted. "It's difficult for a dead man to speak."

"If you want him alive for questioning, I'll personally deliver him wrapped in a pretty bow."

Sawya leaned forward, like a predator scenting blood. "Oh, no, you misunderstand. I want him *dead*. I want his plan stopped. And I want CP57 to lead the treaty negotiations between Kos and Quint."

I took another sip of my drink while I mulled the offer and the repercussions. "Why do you want him dead?"

Their smile was sharp and vicious. "My reasons are my own."

I didn't know what Adams had done, but whatever it was, it had monumentally pissed off Sawya. They usually didn't involve themselves quite so directly in someone's demise, instead relying on veiled hints and oblique suggestions to get the outcome they wanted. This one was personal.

"Only two of those are within my ability," I said at last. "The first two, in case it wasn't clear."

"Are you so sure?"

I nodded. "I do not have that kind of influence."

Sawya sat back, a dangerous light in their eyes. "Perhaps I should have your beau brought to me so I can ask him myself."

It took every bit of my training to sit in place, calm and placid. I tilted my drink from side to side and thought about all of the ways I could kill them before the guards noticed anything amiss. I let that knowledge seep into my expression. My tone, however, remained deceptively mild. "I would not recommend it."

Sawya threw their head back and burst into peals of laughter. After getting themselves under control, they delicately wiped at their eyes. "Your expression," they gasped before breaking into yet more laughter.

It was one of the better outcomes, all things considered.

"I would not have believed that the Golden Dahlia would fall for him of all people, but it actually raises my estimation of him. Very well. Because we are friends, I will give you the information you want on Adams. In return, you will ensure that whatever he is planning fails and that he doesn't survive. And you will do your best to persuade your beau to let CP57 negotiate the peace."

I turned the wording over in my mind, looking for pitfalls, but there were surprisingly few. "What if Adams puts his plan into motion before I get to him?"

"Then you will clean it up."

"I will do what I can, but I am only one woman. I may require your assistance again."

Sawya shot me an unreadable look but inclined their head in agreement.

"Very well," I said. "I agree."

Sawya clapped once, and my net connection came back in a noisy rush. The group link reconnected, and everyone started talking at once.

Quiet! We are fine. Don't distract me, I told the group. *I will update you in a few minutes.*

The link quieted.

Sawya studied me with a shrewd expression, like they knew

exactly how many people had just shouted in the back of my mind. And perhaps they did. I wouldn't put anything past them, not in their own tower.

"I will send you all of the information I have on Adams. That should be plenty for you to get started. If you need something else, you know how to contact me, and while I do adore seeing your lovely face in person, I will respond electronically, just this once."

I bowed my head. "Thank you."

Sawya rose, and Eddie and I stood, too.

They escorted us to the elevator, and the door opened as we approached. "I expect this mess cleaned up in the next few days. I don't like vermin running loose on my station. Especially not vermin who think they are a match for me." Sawya's mouth curved into a predatory smile. "Remind Adams and his goons why CP57 is feared."

"I will move as fast as possible," I promised.

They nodded and waved us into the elevator. Eddie and I stepped inside, then turned back to the door.

Sawya raised a hand in farewell. "Tell your team to stop lurking outside my walls."

The doors began to close, but just before they touched, Sawya added, "And I expect an invite to the wedding."

Their wink was the last thing I saw before the doors sealed and reflected my stunned expression back at me.

12

We exited the tower without any difficulty. Sawya sent me an electronic information packet, as well as instructions to exit the block via the airlock into Block 4. It was the opposite direction of Block 48, but I figured they had a good reason and weren't just trying to immediately double-cross me.

I told the rest of our team to withdraw and meet us there.

"Was it just me, or did that go better than expected?" Eddie asked once we were several streets away from Sawya's building.

"Far better," I agreed. "And we have Adams to thank for it. If he hadn't infuriated Sawya, then negotiations would've been much more painful."

Murdering someone who I was probably already going to kill and trying to persuade the universe's two superpowers to let CP57 negotiate the peace were small asks, all things considered. I'd been braced for so much worse.

"What did Adams do?"

"I don't know, but I'm sure he was his usual charming self. He either threatened them or didn't respect them."

"*You* threatened them," Eddie pointed out.

"Barely. And only after being threatened myself. It's a delicate dance, one that I'm sure Adams didn't fully understand even if it was explained to him. And it sounds like he has some sort of plan for CP57 that Sawya did not appreciate. Adams is likely trying to undermine Sawya's authority, which is a quick way to get dead."

"I thought CP57 was governed by a council."

"Technically, yes, but Sawya pulls the strings."

We lapsed into silence, and I used the time to open the information packet. Adams was indeed on-station with a team of eight and a secondary team of six. An unknown number more remained on his ship, which was docked on Block 107. Thanks to the somewhat random numbering, that block was on the other side of the station from where we'd landed.

I skimmed the info, which was plentiful. Adams had made his base in Block 14 which was on the far side of Block 4. I wondered if Sawya hoped that we'd run into him as we exited their block.

It would not surprise me, tentative friendship or no.

Be careful, I told the group. *Adams is based in Block 14. He could be traveling through Block 4.*

A chorus of agreements came across the link. I'd reversed my cloak as soon as we'd left Sawya's building, but now I pulled up the hood. I'd rather confront Adams when we were fully prepared, not randomly because of a chance meeting.

The guards at the airlock gate let us pass with a wave. The small crowd gathered on the Block 4 side tossed us envious looks. Some of them would wait days for entrance. Some of them would never make it through the gates.

I spotted Luka's massive form first. Even covered by a long coat, it was impossible to miss him. He and Valentin watched the airlock from a deep shadow between buildings. Block 4 wasn't quite as impressive as the block we'd just left. The buildings still towered overhead, but they weren't as bright. It felt like we had stepped from day to night when crossing the airlock.

There were too many people gathered around the gate, so I turned away from Valentin and Luka and led Eddie deeper into the block.

Where are you going? Valentin asked.

I'm going to see if we pick up a tail. Stay put and see if anyone peels off.

I ambled along, stopping to look in shop windows and changing direction at random. No one followed us. I waited another five minutes, then circled around to Luka and Valentin, who had moved back so they couldn't be seen from the gate. Ari, Stella, and Imogen had not arrived yet.

Valentin pulled me into a tight hug. "I'm so glad you're okay," he whispered.

I wrapped my arms around him and leaned into his chest. "Same. It went better than I thought it would." I would eventually have to tell him what I'd agreed to do, but for now, I just enjoyed the moment.

When I pulled back, Valentin reluctantly let me go. I opened a private link to Ari. When she accepted, I asked, *Where are you?*

We're in Block 6. Is something wrong?

No, but we're in the open here. We'll head your way and meet in the middle. Stay alert.

Sounds good. You, too. She dropped the link.

"We're going to meet the others on our way back. They're in Block 6 now, so we'll probably cross paths in 5."

Valentin slipped his hand into mine and squeezed my fingers. "Lead the way."

———

I DIDN'T RELAX until we were back in our rooms in Block 48. I'd held off most of the questions until we were somewhere safer, but now everyone headed to the office by unspoken agreement. I would have to tell them what I'd done.

Everyone in the room knew that I'd been an assassin in my former life. Some people, like Ari and Stella, knew more than the others, but it wouldn't entirely shock any of them that I'd agreed to murder Adams, considering the guy wasn't exactly a saint himself.

Except for maybe Imogen. I braced myself for the horror on her face when I explained what I planned to do.

I was too antsy to sit behind the desk, so I paced in front of it. I wasn't the only one too wired to sit still because everyone else stood, too, though Luka leaned against the wall, seemingly at ease.

"What happened after the connection died?" Ari asked, her voice quiet.

"Adams had already been to see Sawya. He offered them a large amount of money to deliver me. Presumably Valentin, too, but Sawya didn't say."

"How long ago?" Imogen asked.

"I don't know. Sawya knew that we'd been here for a week. They keep an eye on the station, but there are too many people traveling for them to notice us without being tipped off. However, once they found us, it wouldn't be too hard to track down when we arrived, so Adams could've visited yesterday or before we arrived."

Ari blew out a frustrated breath. "So Adams might have been here all week while we've been looking in the wrong places."

"Yes." I didn't try to sugarcoat it, though I felt the failure as sharply as anyone, like an itch under my skin.

"Why didn't Sawya turn you over?" Luka asked, his voice carefully neutral. He watched me just as carefully.

I wanted to make a joke about how I was a secret spy sent to kill Valentin in his sleep, but joking about death didn't seem so funny when I *had* agreed to kill someone. "We've worked together before, and Adams insulted them. I'm sure they were still entertaining the offer when I arrived, but for whatever reason, they decided against it."

Valentin swore under his breath.

"So Sawya just let you go with a pile of information on Adams from the goodness of their heart?" Luka asked, his skepticism clear. He looked to Eddie, but Eddie had gone still and stone-faced.

I laughed. "If Sawya has a heart, it's well hidden. It's true that we have history, but ultimately, choosing to let me go was a business decision. They think Adams is planning something for CP57, and they want me to stop it—and Adams. And they want CP57 to negotiate the peace between Kos and Quint."

Valentin slanted an unreadable glance at me. "And you agreed?"

"Partially. Sawya wants Adams dead, and I promised to see it done. I also promised that I would clean up whatever plot he hatched here on CP57. As for the peace negotiation, I said I'd try to persuade you, but I did not promise results."

"You promised to kill Adams?" Imogen asked with wide eyes. "Just like that?" When I nodded, she continued, "What about a trial?"

"He kidnapped Valentin. He attempted to beat information out of me with his fists. He attacked Arx, blew up my ship, and tried to kill me multiple times. I regret many things I've done, but I will not regret his death."

Imogen stared at the floor and said nothing.

"Did you agree to kill him yourself?" Valentin asked.

I thought back over the exact wording. "No. I promised he wouldn't survive, but I made no promises about how or when, except that it would be soon."

"So we could capture him and take him to Koan for a quick trial."

I wrinkled my nose in thought. "We *could*," I said slowly, "but that involves a lot more risk. Sawya said Adams has surrounded himself with sycophants who would try to free him. And Sawya would *not* look kindly on him escaping. I could easily find myself the subject of a kill contract of my own. And life in prison is not the same thing as death."

"Attempting to kill the emperor is a capital crime," Valentin said. "It's something to consider, that's all." He let the matter drop and changed the subject. "What is Adams planning?"

"Sawya didn't know. Apparently, someone warned Adams to be careful while he was on-station. But odds are, it won't be pleasant, so the sooner we catch him, the better."

I sent everyone the data Sawya had sent me. "This is everything I was given. Take a few minutes tonight to look through it and see if you can find anything interesting. It's already late, so let's reconvene in the morning to discuss strategy."

"You're not going to try to sneak out and take care of this yourself, are you?" Ari asked. Beside her, Stella watched my reaction with narrowed eyes.

"No. He has a large team with him. It will either need to be a coordinated attack or we'll have to draw him out. I can't afford a mistake that lets him escape. I don't want any of you trying it, either. I brought you along so that we could solve this problem together as safely as possible."

Stella nodded. "Don't forget to sleep." She looked at the rest of the group. "That goes for all of you, too. Exhaustion leads to mistakes, and I don't want to have to patch you all up."

"I'll see what I can do," I promised with a wan smile. "Goodnight, everyone."

Imogen lingered as the others left the room. Valentin met my eyes, silently asking if he should stay. I shook my head, and he brushed a kiss across my cheek. "I'll see you upstairs."

Once the room was empty, Imogen shifted nervously.

"Do you want to go back to Arx?" I asked quietly. "You don't have to stay. I won't hold it against you."

Her eyes widened. "No, no that's not what I want at all. I wanted to apologize for being hypocritical. I killed people during the war who probably deserved it far less than Adams, and I didn't blink." She shook her head. "I don't know why this feels different."

"It *is* different," I said, my tone gentle. "Taking a life isn't easy —or it *shouldn't* be, at least—but planning to murder someone is far different than killing during the heat of battle. You have to be able to look yourself in the mirror every morning. I will understand if you decide this mission is not for you."

Her expression hardened. "I was in the transport when his people attacked it. I was in the building when he blew it up. He tried to kill me, too. I will not mourn his death."

"Take tonight to think about it." When she tried to protest, I held up a hand. "I'm serious. Think about how you'll feel if the whole plan goes sideways and you're the one left who has to pull the trigger. Let me know tomorrow what you would like to do. If you don't want to return to Arx, but you don't want to be actively involved, you could stay here as our coordinator."

She nodded. "I will think about it."

13

After Imogen left, I sat at the desk and tried to order my thoughts. Valentin waited for me upstairs, but I needed a moment to decompress. I hadn't lied to Ari, I *wasn't* going to go rogue and hit Adams tonight on my own, but the temptation certainly existed.

I let Valentin know that I was going to be in the office for a little while and then started going through the data Sawya had sent me. To say it was extensive would be an understatement. There were logs of when people left the building, including who, how many, and their destination. I shivered. Sawya would have just as much information on me, and they could've easily turned it over to Adams.

According to this, Adams had arrived a day after us, but he hadn't wasted any time—he'd gone straight to Sawya. It made me feel a *little* better that he hadn't been here for weeks.

He'd chosen his building well. There was no easy way to get a team in. We would have to draw him out or at least catch him when he was outside. Unfortunately, according to the logs, he let his lackeys handle everything. He rarely left the building.

I was going to have to play bait after all. I grimaced in distaste.

A while later, Ari stuck her head in the office. "Mind some company?"

I smiled at her. "Did Stella send you to ensure that I'd go to bed?"

"I have no idea what you're talking about," she said with the worst attempt at a straight face I'd ever seen.

It worked, though, and I broke into laughter.

She dropped into the chair in front of the desk with her usual lazy grace. "Planning?"

"Thinking, mostly," I said.

"I half expected you to sneak out, promise be damned."

I tipped my head in acknowledgment. "That's because you know me." I sighed. "But it won't be that easy. Adams is holed up and breaking in is too risky."

"Nothing's ever easy," Ari grumbled. She looked me over. "How are you?"

"Worried. Worn." I paused and pursed my lips. "I accidentally told Valentin that I loved him."

Her eyes rounded and she leaned forward. "What?! How did he react?" When I didn't respond fast enough, her expression closed. "Do I need to kill him?"

I smiled. "He loves me, too."

"Of course he does," she said breezily, as if she hadn't just threatened his life. "He's a smart man."

"Do you think I'm making a mistake?"

She gave me a soft look. "No. He makes you happy." Ari wasn't my best friend for nothing—she knew all of my weaknesses. "And you *deserve* happiness."

I sidestepped the whole issue of what I deserved. "I'll feel better once Adams is taken care of. And then after the war is over."

"Do you think Quint and Kos will really be able to negotiate a lasting peace this time?"

I blew out a slow breath and leaned back in my chair. "I don't know. There are plenty of people who don't want peace, but I'm hopeful that there are more who *do*. Valentin seems convinced he can make it happen, and I wouldn't bet against him."

"I wouldn't, either," she murmured. "It would be nice to see some of my old friends, assuming they survived."

I nodded in understanding. Many of those who had chosen the Rogue Coalition had done so out of desperation, often leaving loved ones behind. While they didn't *have* to sever the relationship, it was often safer for both parties if they did. Instead of direct communication, they scoured the news and passed along rumors, hoping to hear about the people they'd left behind without giving away what they were doing.

Ari cocked her head and her eyes crinkled with her smile. "Stella says that if we don't go to bed, she's going to come down here with elephant tranquilizer and she's not going to be gentle about it."

I'd never seen an elephant in person, but it didn't surprise me that Stella had something in her bag of tricks capable of taking down one of the massive creatures.

"Now who's the tiny tyrant?" I asked as I stood.

Ari rose with me and grinned. "I'm going to refuse to answer that for fear of sleeping on the floor for all of eternity."

"Smart," I agreed with a laugh. "Very smart."

VALENTIN LOUNGED AGAINST THE HEADBOARD, with an arm resting on his bent knee. He'd changed into loose pants and a snug, short-sleeved shirt. His eyes lost their faraway look as I moved into the room. He'd either been using the net or going over the information I'd sent.

"Welcome back," he said. "Everything okay?"

"Yeah. I chatted with Ari for a while."

I turned away from the bed and started peeling off my clothes with nervous fingers. There was no reason that this had to be weird. Just because it was the first time we were alone together since I'd blurted out those three little words didn't mean anything.

Valentin's fingers closed over mine, and I jerked in surprise. I hadn't heard him move. I'd been so busy ignoring him that I'd done it a little *too* well.

"Allow me," he said quietly.

I dropped my hands as he easily unbuckled the shoulder holster that I'd been fiddling with. He left the cami and knelt, unlacing my boots. He carefully removed them and the knives strapped to my ankles. He peeled off my socks and tears welled unexpectedly at the amount of care he took.

I blinked them away.

Valentin rose and lightly rested his fingers on my waistband. He met my gaze, silently asking for permission.

I swallowed and nodded.

He removed the holster at the small of my back, then unbuttoned my slacks and carefully eased them down my legs. His fingers trailed over my skin with reverence.

He pressed a soft kiss to my thigh, and I buried my fingers in his hair. "Valentin," I whispered.

"I know," he murmured against my skin. But he didn't alter his deliberate pace.

I trembled as the last piece of clothing hit the floor. Valentin had stopped long enough to strip off his own clothes, leaving us naked in the middle of the room. He had burned out any embarrassment I might've felt with soft kisses and softer caresses.

Now I burned for a different reason.

And I was going to show him just how much I appreciated his care.

When I kissed my way down his body, sinking to my knees, he groaned deep in his chest. I grinned up at him and his fingers touched my jaw, gentle and adoring. "You don't—"

I licked him.

He bit off what he was going to say with a low curse, and his fists clenched. "Never mind," he growled. "Please continue."

I hummed in agreement, and he groaned.

It was a long time later before we finally dropped into an exhausted, sated sleep.

———

THE NEXT MORNING came too early. Everyone at the breakfast table looked like they hadn't gotten enough sleep, despite Stella's admonishment. She frowned at us and shook her head, but she didn't say anything because she wasn't exactly looking bright and perky herself.

"Thoughts?" I asked.

"I found the floor plans of the building," Eddie said. "I can get us in, but it's broken up into a bunch of rooms like this." He waved his arm around. "Seems like a good way to die."

I'd spent an hour this morning, cuddled in bed with Valentin, going over the data. Eddie wasn't wrong.

"Adams doesn't seem to leave the building on any sort of set schedule," Luka said.

"But his people do," Imogen added. "They're sweeping the surrounding blocks, same as we did. They usually go in pairs."

"We could grab them," Ari said, "but I don't know if that will be enough to draw him out."

If we had time, I would find a perch overlooking the main door to their building and wait for Adams to emerge. A single, long-range shot was far less risky than an in-person attack, but I didn't think Sawya would be happy to wait that long.

And when Sawya became unhappy, things got messy.

"We could set his building on fire," Eddie suggested. When everyone turned to glare at him, he held up his hands. "I didn't mean we *should*. It was just a suggestion. I'm thinking out loud."

I rolled my eyes. "Does anyone have a suggestion that *doesn't* involve killing a whole block?"

When no one came up with anything, Ari sighed. "Your presence could probably draw him out." Stella growled something under her breath and Ari nudged her shoulder. "You know she was *already* thinking it; I am just getting it out in the open."

"Could you get Sawya to set up another meeting with him?" Valentin asked.

I considered it, then shook my head. "Sawya doesn't want to be involved, and if Adams is murdered while on his way to see them, that's a little too connected. But luring Adams out for some sort of early meeting isn't a bad plan, and Sawya might pass the information. We know where Adams is, but he doesn't know where we are. That gives us an edge."

I turned to Eddie. "You've looked at the floor plans. Is there a way out of the building that isn't obvious?"

"No. Front and back doors only, unless they've illegally modified it."

"So we could have a spotter on each door, and then when we know which way they're going, hit them en route."

"Attacking on the move leaves a lot of room for error," Ari said.

"Which is why it won't be expected. He'll expect the trap at the meeting place, not on the way."

Ari shook her head. "Not only is it dangerous for us, but if we go around murdering people in the street, then station security is going to take an active interest."

I tapped the table while I thought. "*That* might be something Sawya can help with."

A plan began to form. I let the others continue to toss out ideas while I thought it through. It was risky, but everything was risky at this point. If we couldn't go to Adams, then making him come to us was the next best thing.

Ari and Luka got into a heated argument about who would be better bait: me or Valentin.

Finally, Imogen tossed up her hands. "None of this matters," she said. "Adams is a coward. He's not going to leave his safe house unless he thinks he can grab one of you without issue."

My plan solidified, and I smiled at her. "That's why you're going to betray me."

14

Imogen gripped my arm as we waited. "I don't like this," she muttered for the tenth time.

"I know," I said. I didn't particularly like it either, since I would *much* rather be waiting with the attack party that was focused on Adams. "But this was the best option on short notice."

We were in the corner of a small, out-of-the-way courtyard in Block 19. Sawya had picked it, assuring us that we wouldn't be disturbed. They had given us the location before Adams, so we had arrived early to choose our position.

Here, tucked away in the darkest corner, tall columns gave us some cover. I was cuffed, cloaked, and blindfolded, though I wasn't truly as helpless as I appeared. My blindfold looked good, but I could see straight through it.

"If one of Adams's goons kills you, Valentin is going to kill *me*," she said, "and I very much enjoy being alive."

"Valentin won't kill you. And even if he tries, Luka won't let him."

"Why couldn't *Luka* be the one to hand you over to Adams? That seems far more realistic."

"Maybe too realistic," I agreed with a laugh. "But he doesn't have family in Quint territory, and Adams will be rightfully wary of him. You're a woman. Adams will automatically underestimate you for that alone."

"I still don't know how you knew about my family," she grumbled.

"Don't take it personally. I looked into your background before I took you to Koan with me."

Her head tilted. "Why take me at all if you knew I might be compromised?"

"Ari vouched for you."

Imogen nodded and lapsed into silence.

We've got movement, Eddie said over the group link. *Front door. Team of four. No sign of Adams. I repeat, Adams is not with them.*

Let them pass, Ari said. *Samara's team can handle them. We wait for Adams.*

We'd had spotters in place all day. Unless Adams had spent the night somewhere else, he was still in the building. I hoped confirmation of my presence would be enough to draw him out. If not, I would take out the first squad and see if *that* did it. If nothing else, it might startle him into flight.

Tonight it was all hands on deck. The two groups sent by my council had joined Ari, Valentin, and Luka. Anyone who wasn't comfortable fighting was with Stella to provide medical support. My team was spread out on the upper floors of the buildings facing into the courtyard, with a couple of spotters farther out to let us know when Adams's group approached.

I carefully arranged myself on the ground so that my bound hands were visible and my cloak wouldn't be in my way when I stood. I didn't *love* being on the ground, even with the columns between me and the open courtyard, but Imogen had supposedly drugged me in order to capture me, and we had to sell the story.

The minutes slipped by in silence. Adams was apparently going to let his team come all the way here before he risked his own neck, just as we'd expected.

Incoming, a spotter on my team warned. *Confirmed team of four.*

I heard them before I saw them. A second later, four men in dark clothes stomped into the courtyard. I couldn't see them directly, but the tiny camera I'd installed gave me a visual. The men were armed with short plasma rifles and, for all of their excessive noise, they held the weapons like professionals.

"Imogen Weber?" the tallest one called.

Imogen peeked out from behind her column. "Who are you?"

"We're here on behalf of our commander."

"That wasn't the deal. How do I know you're not just after the money for yourselves? You're not cutting me out of this, not after what I've been through." Her voice cracked. She was a hell of an actress.

The man scowled and waved an arm at me. "We have to verify the identity."

The group wasn't acting like soldiers in hostile territory. They hadn't taken defensive positions and they continued to shift around, making noise. Something was wrong.

Team Two, report.

All of the team members reported in with nothing unusual, but I couldn't shake the feeling that we were missing something.

"If you want to verify her identity, then put your gun down and approach," Imogen said. "Only you. And don't try anything or I'll shoot you."

The man cocked his head and smiled. "Why don't *you* put *your* gun down and step away from the target."

A single, nearly soundless footstep was all the notice I got before Adams shimmered into view directly behind Imogen, the visor of his combat armor open. He clamped a hand on her shoulder a pressed a plasma pistol into her back. Around the courtyard, four more soldiers in armor appeared.

Imogen sucked in a surprised breath.

I remained limp on the ground and kept pretending to be unconscious, but I shouted across the link, *Adams is here in fucking Kos combat armor! Everyone converge—*

My connection to the net died in a blast of static. Adams's team wouldn't be able to keep it down for long, but they didn't need to. Even if Valentin and the others figured out what I meant, they had to cross three blocks to get here. Adams would be long gone before they arrived.

I'd lost access to the camera, but I could still see Imogen and Adams through my blindfold. The other soldiers didn't seem to be getting any closer.

"Dropping your gun is an excellent idea," Adams said. "Carefully now. I wouldn't want you to die before you can spend your hard-earned reward."

I mentally urged her to do as he said. I couldn't get a clear shot at him from my position and even if I could, he was liable to pull the trigger on his way down. Imogen and I both wore a flexible, lightweight armor base layer, but it wasn't guaranteed to deflect point-blank shots.

At least my team had decided to hold their fire. I had warned them not to risk Imogen, and apparently, they were listening. Or maybe they had already bailed. Adams had snuck an entire squad in combat armor right past my spotters, all of whom had thermal cameras *for just such an occasion.*

I'd thought it a bit overkill since none of Sawya's information had mentioned armor, or even large supply boxes that could *hold* armor, but I liked to prepare for all possibilities.

A lot of good that did me.

None of our spotters had reported extra soldiers, and while one or two might be compromised, Eddie *wasn't.* I knew it in my bones. Had Adams found a way to suppress the armor's thermal signature? If so, we were *fucked*.

Imogen dropped her pistol. She had at least two more on her, but she had to be free to draw them.

"Where's my money?" she demanded.

"All in good time, my dear," Adams said. "You'll forgive me if I don't completely trust your change of heart."

Imogen snorted. "For the amount of money you're offering, a saint would have a change of heart—and I'm no saint."

"Is the queen alive?" Adams asked.

Imogen lifted her free shoulder in a careless shrug. "Last I checked. I don't think you're supposed to mix alcohol and sedatives, but I didn't have much choice."

"So if I shoot her, she won't feel it?"

I kept my body relaxed and my breathing deep and even. I'd be delighted if Adams pointed his gun at me, because then it wouldn't be pointed at Imogen, and I could act.

Imogen shrugged again. "Who knows? But I'd rather have something between us before you attempt it. She's going to be mighty pissed when she wakes up."

Adams chuckled. "Oh, I'm counting on it."

Imogen's fingers twitched and her pinky curled in, leaving three fingers. After a beat, her ring finger curled. She was counting down.

I groaned and twitched. Hopefully, she would understand that I was on board.

Adams turned his attention to me. "I thought you said she was unconscious."

Imogen sighed. "I don't know how much of the sedative she actually drank before she passed out. Then I had to drag her all the way here. Pay me before she wakes up and kills us all."

She curled in her middle finger and I groaned again, louder. Adams shifted, but his gun remained pointed at Imogen's back.

Come on, you asshole.

"Beale," Adams said, "come—"

Imogen's last finger fell and she twisted away, faster than Adams expected. The gun went off, but I couldn't tell if she was hit. I surged to my feet, breaking out of the weakened cuffs and removing the blindfold. I drew a pistol on my way up.

Plasma pulses rained down from above as my team laid down suppressive fire. One of the soldiers in armor went down, but the others shimmered and disappeared. Plasma pulses appeared to come from thin air as they returned fire.

Fuck, why couldn't a single thing go right today?

Imogen and Adams were locked together, wrestling for control of the gun. Adams was strengthened by the combat armor, so even with her augments, it was all Imogen could do to hold him off.

I didn't have armor-piercing rounds in my plasma pistol because that was just asking for trouble in an area surrounded by civilians, so I had to hit Adams somewhere fleshy.

Like his face.

Imogen was far enough back that I had a clear shot. I brought up my pistol and squeezed the trigger. Adams must've caught my movement because he jerked back at the last moment and the pulse punched through his visor rather than his skull. That was twice that I'd missed the asshole, and I didn't plan to let it happen a third time.

I adjusted, but before I could shoot again, he twisted and shoved Imogen at me. On her way down, she yanked his gun away from him and then tucked, trying to avoid me. I didn't reach for her. A fall wouldn't kill her, but Adams might.

His armor shimmered, but he didn't disappear. I must've damaged the active camouflage when I hit his visor. He raised an armored arm, shielding his face. "Cover me!" he shouted.

I might not be able to punch through his armor with a single shot, but I'd get through eventually if I kept hitting the same spot. I ignored the plasma pulses winging through the air and squeezed the trigger as fast as I could aim, hitting him in the side under his arm. He was *not* going to walk away from this.

"We have to go!" Imogen shouted from next to me. She leaned around the column, shooting at the advancing soldiers in the courtyard. "There are too many."

"You go!"

I caught a glimpse of Adams's head and adjusted my aim. The pulse hit the top of his helmet and he ducked, bringing his arm up more.

"Kill them both!" he shouted. Then, before I could do anything else, he turned and ran.

I growled out a curse. If I left the relative safety of the column, I'd be shot before I made it a meter. And while my central mass was protected by the armor, my head was *not*.

The soldiers without armor had retreated behind the columns on the far side, and two of them were down. One soldier in armor was still down, but the rest were getting close based on their shots.

There was no option. "Fall back!" I shouted. I hoped the rest of my team could hear me.

Imogen turned and kicked open the door behind us. I followed her inside, then barred the door. The apartment was as abandoned as it had been earlier. "Are you hit?" I asked her as we dashed to the tunnel that would take us to the next building.

"Grazed," she said. "I'm okay. I tagged the armor Adams had on. Once we get outside of the net dead zone we'll be able to track him, assuming he doesn't dump the armor."

I laughed. "Excellent work."

We raced through the second building until we came to the door leading out. I pulled up my hood and peered through the window. I didn't see anyone, but that wasn't exactly comforting. My next set of contacts would definitely include thermal imaging.

I opened the door and stepped out before Imogen could stop me.

No one shot at me.

Adams had three options: return to his house, head to his ship, or hunker down and wait for his team to catch up with him. They each seemed equally likely, and I wouldn't know which he'd chosen until I could connect to the net and track him, which meant I needed to get out of the dead zone.

The nearest airlock led to Block 18. I headed for it, Imogen on my heels. Both Adams's building and ship were on the other side of the station, so if he picked a direct route to one of them, he would use the 18-19 airlock.

We ran, keeping to the shadows as much as possible. We crossed two sectors before the net connection spluttered back to life. The group link came back, too, but I didn't have time to respond.

"Where is Adams?" I asked Imogen.

She frowned and sent me the tracker link.

I pulled it up and cursed again. He was heading for the *other* airlock, the one that led into Block 20. Did he know about the team waiting at his house? I changed direction and then asked the group, *Where are you?*

We're in Block 18, almost to 19, Valentin responded, his tone relieved.

They were going to be too slow.

Head to the courtyard, I said. *My team could use help with Adams's soldiers. There are still at least three in Kos armor, and they may have found a way to defeat thermal imaging, so be careful. Adams is on the move, heading to the 19-20 airlock. His armor is damaged. Imogen and I will follow him.*

We should follow you, Valentin argued.

I agree, Ari chimed in.

I blew out a breath. My team in the courtyard had cover and exits on their side. I had to trust that they were capable of taking care of themselves. *Fine, do what you will, but we're not slowing down.* I sent the group the link to the tracker.

Be careful, Valentin said.

We will be. You, too.

I sent the group link to the background and focused on running. We were slowly closing the gap, but we wouldn't catch Adams before he made it into Block 20. Without the tracker, he would've disappeared completely. Finally, one thing was going right today.

The people who were out at this hour pretended not to see us when we ran past. We returned the favor. We were still several minutes behind Adams when he approached the 19-20 airlock. As soon as he crossed into Block 20, an alarm began to sound overhead, deep and reverberating.

"What is that?" Imogen shouted over the noise.

The people around us started running for the airlock, panic on their faces.

"An emergency has been detected," a calm, pleasant voice announced, "please proceed in an orderly fashion to the nearest airlock or emergency shelter."

Oh, fuck me. That's what I got for thinking the universe was on my side for once.

The timing was too close for it to be a coincidence. I didn't know how he'd managed it, but Adams had initiated a block lockdown, and if we didn't make it to the airlock before the outer door closed, we would be trapped until they determined that there wasn't really a disaster happening inside.

I ran faster.

15

I sprinted as fast as I could while dodging people in the growing crowd. Imogen shouted something from behind me, but I was too focused on not plowing into anyone to pay attention. The group link was also blowing up, but I ignored it, too.

According to the tracker, Adams had stopped just on the other side of the airlock. The distance between us shrank with each step. The doors wouldn't close instantly. I still had time. I could make it.

The crowd got thicker and thicker as I approached the airlock. Many people were in pajamas, carrying whatever they could grab in thirty seconds. Frantic parents clung to their wailing children as they tried to get them to the safety of the airlock.

My heart twisted, but it would be far worse for everyone if Adams escaped. I shoved my way through the growing crowd, trying not to injure anyone.

I rounded the corner and finally caught sight of the airlock and the sea of people trying to escape. The heavy door on the Block 20 side was nearly closed. A few people still slipped through, but the gap would be far too narrow by the time I fought my way closer. The outer door had no safety shutoff—to prevent people from holding it open during a true emergency—and it would crush anyone caught between it and the frame.

I scanned the faces beyond the door. Commander Adams stood a few meters back, his pistol held loosely. He scanned each person coming through the airlock, presumably looking for me or Imogen. There were far too many people between us for me to get a clean shot, and I clenched my jaw in frustration.

Adams couldn't possibly see me in the crowd, but his smirk grew wider and wider as the door closed and I didn't appear. Just as I considered risking a shot anyway, a little girl's head jerked into my line of fire. The crowd was too unpredictable. I would never forgive myself if I killed an innocent.

The outer airlock door sealed closed with a loud *thunk*. The inner door started to close but immediately halted due to all of the bodies in the way. The feel of the crowd shifted as people shoved and shouted and tried to cram inside the airlock. Those already in the airlock pushed back against the encroaching crowd.

People could theoretically escape through the airlock, but trapped, panicked people had to let the inner door of the airlock close with nothing more than the hope that it would open again after those inside made it through. And in any crowd, there was always that special asshole who refused to wait their turn and so ended up killing everyone.

Today, that asshole was a dark-haired young man. He threw the first punch and then the fight was on.

Someone grabbed my shoulder and I spun, ready to defend myself, but it was only Imogen. The crowd jostled around us, growing by the second. Imogen grabbed my wrist and towed me back the way we'd come.

I let her pull me. There was no way we'd clear the area enough for the inner door to close, not even with the number of weapons we had. And the situation was volatile enough without us adding fuel to the fire. Hopefully, once people realized there wasn't an emergency—or didn't appear to be, at least—they would calm down.

We're on our way, Imogen said over the group link.

The others must also be trapped with us. Fantastic.

Adams's tracker started moving again, away from the airlock and deeper into Block 20. If there was ever a time for the universe to strike someone dead, it would be now.

The tracker kept moving.

Of course.

The emergency announcement repeated every thirty seconds, but now people emerged from their buildings and looked around instead of immediately running for an airlock. There was no obvious sign of an emergency, but it also didn't appear to be a drill, so everyone was confused.

A quick check of the net confirmed that messages were flying fast and furious. No one knew what was happening, but rumors ran rampant. Apparently, Block 19 had suffered a fire, an explosion, a hull breach, and a terrorist attack—or possibly all of them at once.

Cooler heads were starting to prevail due to the total lack of evidence, but it would take a while before the airlocks were reopened.

I checked in with the team I'd left behind in the courtyard. Adams's remaining soldiers had escaped, but everyone on my team had survived—so far. Two were down with life-threatening injuries, but some of the others were rushing them to the nearest doctor. I prayed they would both recover. The whole team's bravery ensured that Imogen and I had survived, and so, as far as I was concerned, they had all earned a very nice bonus.

I told the remaining team to quickly search the casualties for clues about their identities and then clear the area. I didn't know if the remaining soldiers had made it out of the block before the lockdown, but Adams would absolutely trap his own people if it served his interests. We needed to be careful. I updated both attack groups and told them to watch their backs.

Rather than heading back to the courtyard, Imogen led me closer to the edge of the block. I was happy to follow her lead as I kept an eye on the net. The few people we passed were too busy trying to figure out what was going on to pay any attention to us.

Imogen ducked down an alley and then knocked on a nondescript door. Luka swung it open, and relief briefly crossed his face before he wiped it away. He waved us in and then shut and locked the door behind us.

Valentin still wore his Kos combat armor, but his visor was open. He carefully pulled me into a hug against his chest. "We have to stop meeting like this," he murmured. "It's bad for my blood pressure."

I squeezed him tight, though I doubted he could feel it. "I totally agree."

Once he let me go, I pulled back and looked around. Unlike our rooms in Block 48, this was just one large space with a few chairs and tables scattered around.

Stella and Ari, both in armor with their visors open, stood next to Eddie, who had declined to wear the Kos armor, preferring the same lightweight, flexible armor that Imogen and I wore. They were all gathered around the largest table, along with a few others who must be from the team the council had sent. Imogen and Luka had silently left us alone and joined the others.

"What's this?" I asked.

"Backup plan," Valentin said.

I raised an eyebrow. "*Whose* backup plan? Because I distinctly remember discussing various fallback plans, and this wasn't one of them."

A grin tugged on the corner of his mouth. "Mine, naturally. I didn't mention it because I hoped we wouldn't need it, and if you didn't know, you couldn't fuss at me for spending unnecessary money."

My eyes narrowed. "I dare you to say that again."

He cupped my jaw as his eyes traced over my face. "I'm so glad you're okay," he whispered. "When your message about the armor cut off halfway, I nearly lost my mind."

I laughed bitterly. "It certainly was an unwelcome surprise for me, too. How did they get past the thermal cameras?"

Valentin straightened reluctantly. "We discussed it on the way over. The current theory is that they came from a different building than the one we were watching. Sawya's information indicated there was a backup team but not a separate location, so we assumed they would be in the main building. But perhaps they slipped through the cracks or maybe they were staying on the ship."

"You don't think they figured out how to defeat the thermal imaging?"

Valentin shook his head. "The best Kos scientists have been working on it for *years* and haven't figured it out. It's not *impossible* that Adams figured it out in a matter of months, but it's not very likely."

"That still doesn't explain why my spotters didn't see them."

"Maybe they took a different path. A lot of the buildings around here are connected internally."

"It's possible," I allowed with a grimace. I hated having so many unknowns, but I let it go and changed the subject. "Do you know how long we'll be locked in?"

"No. I suppose it depends on how Adams managed to trigger the lockdown in the first place. If a sensor is giving the station authorities bad data, it could be a while until they confirm it's a glitch. If someone hacked into the system, it could be even longer."

"How *did* Adams manage it? The station controls are behind

layers and layers of security. My guess is that he had someone purposefully trip a sensor."

Valentin looked thoughtful. "Any chance Sawya is playing both sides?"

"There's always a chance," I said slowly, "but I don't think so. Sawya wants Adams dead. That wasn't faked. It doesn't make sense to help the person you want dead."

Valentin sighed. "I suppose you're right. Do you think there's a way out other than the airlocks?"

"I am not hopeful, but if anyone would know, it'll be Eddie. Let's see what he thinks."

Valentin agreed, and we joined the others standing around the table. Ari and Stella looked me over with identical worried expressions.

I waved them off. "I'm not hurt, but Imogen was grazed. Stella, can you take a look at her?"

Imogen rolled her eyes. "It's barely a scratch."

She shouldn't have wasted her breath because Stella already had her first aid kit in hand. "Sit," she said to Imogen, pointing at a nearby chair. "I can patch you up while you listen."

Imogen knew a losing battle when she saw one. "Grazed my side," she said as she sank into a chair facing us.

Stella moved behind her and pulled up the hem of her shirt. "If this is 'a scratch' then I'd hate to see what happens when you actually get shot," Stella said drily.

I glared at Imogen, but she just shrugged. "It didn't feel that bad."

I looked around, checking the rest of the group for injuries. "Does anyone else need to be patched up?" When they shook their heads, I blew out a relieved breath. "I'm glad you're okay."

"Same to you, boss," Eddie said.

I inclined my head. "Do you know a way to get us out of the block without going through the airlock?"

Eddie grimaced. "It might be possible, but from what I can

tell, station security tends to quickly crack down on all illegal modifications outside the single-digit blocks, so I wouldn't count on it. I don't suppose you could ask your friend?"

"That's maybe not the best idea until we figure out if they're still on our side."

Eddie's eyes widened and he nodded. "Ah, in that case, I'll keep digging."

Imogen muttered a curse under her breath. "Adams's tracker just died. He must've found it."

When I checked the link, the last reported location was more than two minutes ago in Block 7. At the time, Adams *seemed* to be heading straight across to Block 8, but that may have changed after he found the tracker.

"That's not the fastest way back to his building," I said. "Where's he going?"

"He could be heading for his ship," Luka said. "It's not the most direct path, but if I were trying to avoid the blocks around 14, that's how I would go."

"You think he's running?" I asked, dubious.

"Or planning something else," Valentin said.

That sounded more like Adams. I clenched my fists against the urge to pace. I was trapped in this fucking block until the airlocks opened or we found a way out while Adams waltzed off to do whatever he wanted. "I want everyone searching for a way out."

They all nodded in agreement and we started reaching out to contacts and scouring the net for information. If there was a way out, we'd find out. We just had to keep looking.

NEARLY AN HOUR LATER, we still hadn't found anything. The airlocks hadn't opened, but at least the emergency broadcast had stopped playing. I paced, striving for patience and failing.

Adams was escaping, *again*. I went over the encounter in the courtyard, thinking through all of the things I should've done differently.

I paused when an unknown neural link with a local address requested a connection. I had enabled unknown connections in case someone needed to get in touch with me through an intermediary, so I accepted, unsure what to expect.

What, Sawya's clipped, angry voice demanded, *have you done?*

It was the angriest I'd ever heard them, and that was never a good thing. I went straight into damage control.

The lockdown happened right after Adams cleared the 19-20 airlock, so blame him. We tracked him into Block 7 before we lost him, but we think he's heading for his ship. There's no emergency in Block 19. Can you get us out?

Your little lockdown is the least of my concerns, Sawya growled. *There is a fucking Quint armada outside, and they are demanding that we turn you and Valentin over.*

16

I froze even as my heart raced. *What did you say?* I demanded, certain that I'd heard them wrong. Adams didn't have the ships or support to summon an armada. Right?

Which part of 'fucking Quint armada' is giving you trouble?

"What's wrong?" Valentin asked.

"Sawya says a Quint armada just showed up. Check the news."

The group all started asking questions, but I waved them away and returned to my conversation with Sawya. *Has Chairwoman Soteras been in contact? Are they truly backed by the Quint Confederacy?*

Regretfully, I've been a little too busy dealing with a fucking Quint armada *to make any social calls,* Sawya shouted across the link. There was a long pause, then they continued, their tone calm and deadly, *Friends we may be, but I will not risk the station for you. Turn yourself in, and I will do what I can for you. If you make me find you... don't make me find you.*

Open the airlocks and I will turn myself in.

You are in no position to make demands.

I closed my eyes and took a deep breath before I snapped out something that would get us all killed. *I am making a request. There is no emergency in Block 19. The people here don't deserve to be trapped, and it was already devolving into violence right after the lockdown. People will die if it continues.*

"I left a message for Soteras because she was unavailable," Valentin said. "I would like to believe she's not behind it, but if Adams doesn't have her support, then he is attempting a coup."

"Sawya wants me to turn myself in."

"No," Valentin said, his voice hard.

"I'm with Valentin," Ari said. "We're not turning you over." Stella, Imogen, and Eddie also nodded. Even Luka looked like he was on my side for once.

I appreciated their loyalty, but my mind was made up. "I've already agreed, assuming they open the airlocks."

"I won't let Sawya hand you over to Adams," Valentin said. His hands clenched into fists. "I refuse."

I laughed without humor. "Adams is demanding you, too, so maybe you'll get to join me."

"I can have my fleet here before Sawya lays a finger on you, and I will give the order without regret."

I considered it, then shook my head. "Having a battle so close to the station is not a good idea. I'm sure CP57 is already readying their own ships. We don't need to add to the chaos quite yet. But maybe send your advisors a heads-up."

"Already done."

I held up a hand as Sawya resumed the linked conversation. I could technically handle both conversations at once, but it would be better if I could give Sawya my full attention.

The airlocks will open in ten minutes, Sawya said. They sent me an address in Block 6. *Meet me there once they do. Bring your entourage.*

I will turn myself in, but I won't lead the others to their deaths.

Sawya snorted. *Don't be so dramatic. No one will die. Yet. Don't give me a reason to change my mind.*

They cut the link before I could demand more information.

I debated not telling the others, but I wouldn't be able to slip away with nearly a dozen people watching my every move. "The airlocks are opening in ten minutes, and then I'm supposed to meet Sawya in Block 6."

"If you insist on going, then we're going with you," Ari said. Everyone nodded.

I sighed and rubbed my forehead. "Well, that's convenient because you were explicitly invited." At her frown, I clarified, "I was told to bring my entourage."

———

As PROMISED, the airlocks opened. Despite the announcements that the block was safe, a massive crowd still waited to exit. Imogen, Luka, Eddie, and I joined them, cloaked and hooded, with Ari, Stella, and Valentin camouflaged in their Kos armor in between us.

Our extra teams had left and headed for another exit. It was a thin hope that Sawya didn't already know about them, but I didn't need to drag *all* of my citizens on CP57 into the fire— taking the people I cared about most was bad enough.

The address Sawya had given me turned out to be a very posh private building. The door opened as I approached, despite the fact that I hadn't lowered my hood. Point to Sawya. A thickly muscled man in a dark suit held the door open. The empty foyer beyond didn't give me much insight into what kind of situation I should expect.

I stepped through the door with Valentin right behind me. The guard did not try to stop him, even though he still wore combat armor with the visor open. Valentin would be monitoring the local neural links for signs of betrayal. Using the ability drained him, so I needed to keep this meeting short.

The foyer was huge and tastefully decorated with marble and stone that must've cost a fortune to ship. A discreet security desk was tucked away on the left side, but the security guard was missing. Straight ahead, past a bank of elevators, a wide door stood open with another of Sawya's guards standing next to it. He gestured us inside.

I crossed the foyer, my boots whisper-quiet on the beautiful floor. I lowered my hood, but the guard at the door did not ask me to remove my weapons. Valentin, Stella, and Ari were also admitted in their armor. At least Sawya's boundless confidence hadn't changed.

The room inside was clearly a waiting room, albeit a very nice one. Plush carpet, ornate furniture, and soft lighting gave a sense of cozy luxury. Two long sofas faced each other across a low glass coffee table. Other small groupings of chairs and tables were scattered around the room.

At least a dozen guards lined the walls, half in dark suits and half in fatigues. All bristled with visible weapons.

Sawya rose from their seat on the far sofa. Even though it was stupidly late, they looked perfectly put together in a finely tailored navy suit with a crisp white shirt and striped tie. Their curly blond hair was slicked back into a severe style and their expression was cool and guarded.

"Sit," Sawya said, pointing at the opposite sofa. It was not a request, and they did not smile.

Valentin, with me, I said across the group link. *The rest of you, spread out behind us.*

I perched on the edge of the sofa, and Valentin stood beside me. I had coached everyone on the way over, so we all waited in silence for Sawya to make the first move.

Sawya sat with deliberate carelessness, sprawling back on the sofa and taking up space. If they were bothered by Valentin looming over them, they didn't show it. "I wasn't sure you would come," Sawya said at last.

"I told you I would."

Their chin dipped. "So you did." They studied Valentin with casual intensity. "And you, why did you come?"

"I go where Samara goes."

"What if I told you that you could walk away with your life, and the lives of your friends, right now, but only if you leave her behind?"

Valentin's smile was quick and sharp. "I would politely decline. And then I would caution you against making threats that serve neither of us."

I held my breath until Sawya laughed.

They met my eyes. "I wasn't sure the little emperor had a spine. I'm glad to know that I was wrong." Sawya's expression turned serious. "He's going to need it."

"Have you been able to contact Quint?" Valentin asked.

"No. I've sent urgent messages, but I haven't received any response."

"Same," Valentin said. "But my battle fleet is ready to tunnel in whenever they are needed."

I had to give it to Valentin, the threat was delicately delivered. A smirk touched Sawya's mouth. "And if the net unexpectedly goes down?"

Sawya snapped their fingers, and my net connection died.

One of the guards made a low sound, and Sawya frowned at him. The poor guy must be new, but he wouldn't last long if he kept drawing Sawya's attention.

Valentin remained outwardly relaxed. "Then I hope it is fixed promptly or the fleet will arrive earlier than expected," he said with a smile that didn't reach his eyes.

Sawya watched Valentin for a long second before grinning. "Touché." They waved a hand and the connection came back.

The tech to selectively and surgically take down neural

connections was hideously expensive and *ridiculously* illegal. It hadn't surprised me that Sawya had it in their office, but to be able to set it up here on such short notice was impressive.

"What does Adams want?" I asked.

"He says that he wants you two delivered to his ship."

"What does he actually want?" Valentin asked.

"Oh, I'm sure he wants you two—that wasn't a lie. But he didn't need to bring two battle cruisers, a quartet of destroyers, and a half dozen corvettes for that."

That was a lot of firepower, considering Valentin's fleet had downed Adams's destroyer and supporting ships during the battle in Arx. Where did Adams find so many new ships, especially in such a short time? "You think he's planning to take over the station?"

Sawya's eyes narrowed. "He's welcome to try."

"He's staging for an attack on either Arx or Koan," Valentin said. "After he's done with CP57."

"Arx doesn't have anything worth the time," I said.

They both looked at me, and I rolled my eyes. "If he makes it to Arx, it'll be because I'm dead, so that won't be his motivation."

"I'm so glad you offered your life," Sawya said. "It saves us so much time."

"Don't get ahead of yourself," I said. "If I'm going down, I'm going down fighting. Can you get me to Adams's ship without being noticed?"

A whole chorus of muttered curses came from behind me as the rest of the group tried to follow my advice and stay silent, but they clearly weren't happy about it.

Sawya considered it, then shook their head. "He's on *Implacable,* one of the destroyers. They will spot anything we have. And while I would offer to escort you in a transport shuttle, I don't think my presence would make Adams *less* likely to blow it up."

I glanced at Valentin. "Could *Ardia* do it?"

A muscle in his jaw flexed. He didn't want to answer, but I waited him out. "It's possible," he finally ground out. "But even if you get there, what are you going to do? Take out a whole destroyer by yourself?"

"I won't have to if I'm *stealthy*," I said, giving him a significant look.

"If you're talking about this *delightful* new armor," Sawya said with a wave at Valentin, "then do go on. I'm all ears." Their eyes flickered over my shoulder to Stella and Ari.

I huffed out a half laugh. "I thought you *weren't* all-knowing."

Sawya's smile was thin and self-satisfied. "I'm not, but I *do* know quite a lot. And the Kos Empire hasn't exactly been leakproof lately, has it?"

Valentin cursed under his breath. "I don't suppose you know how Adams got his hands on our proprietary armor?"

One corner of Sawya's mouth tipped up, but they said nothing.

"Figures," Valentin muttered. He turned back to me. "Even in armor, we can't hope to take on the entire crew of a destroyer, and they'll know as soon as we try to dock."

I noticed he'd switched to including himself in the attack, but I didn't bother arguing yet. "I just have to be faster than they are, and that should be easy enough because they won't be expecting me. Then I will hold long enough for you to get some soldiers to me."

"It's suicide," Valentin snarled.

"You two are a delight, but time is wasting," Sawya said. "Adams was quite adamant about having you found and delivered. And he doesn't seem like the type of person who would be too torn up about civilian casualties."

"If time is so critical, you could *help*," I said pointedly.

Sawya heaved a long-suffering sigh. "Must I do *everything*?"

I rubbed my temples and fought for patience. "Unless you

want a battle on your doorstep, yes, you should do everything you can to prevent it."

Sawya's expression iced over. "If I recall correctly, *you* promised to take care of this problem for me. Instead of a dead commander, I now have an enemy fleet outside, threatening my station. Tread carefully, darling."

"I'm sorry," I said, dipping my head in apology.

Their expression thawed slightly. "If you have a ship that can get to Adams's destroyer, then I can assist you in taking control of it."

"How?" Valentin asked.

"Soldiers. Information. Distraction. Take your pick."

Valentin's eyes narrowed, and I jumped in before he could say something rude. "How many soldiers can you spare?"

Sawya spread their arms. "How many can you haul?"

"How will we get past the airlock?" Valentin asked. "We can force the outer hatch, but the inner door won't open without authorization as long as the bridge remains active. If we blow it, the ship will go into emergency lockdown and we'll never make the bridge."

"Leave that to me," Sawya said.

"I thought you're weren't going with us," Valentin said.

"Oh, I'm definitely not," Sawya said with a shark-like smile. "But I don't have to be there in person to finesse a door open, not when I have such a capable thief available to help, isn't that right, Mr. Tarlowski?"

Eddie swallowed when Sawya's gaze landed on him. "Ships were not my specialty."

Sawya waved him off. "Not to worry, I have faith in you. I have the tools and the codes you'll need. I just need you to have a delicate touch and the ability to follow directions."

Eddie glanced at me out of the corner of his eye, and I nodded. "I can do that," he said. "What will I need to do?"

I listened with half an ear as Sawya explained. Eddie kept

nodding, so apparently it made sense to one of us. While they were busy, I linked Ari. *Have the teams move all of our supplies from your ship to* Ardia.

This is a bad idea.

Do you have a better one?

Let Valentin's fleet deal with him. Or CP57's.

Because that worked so well last time. Move the supplies. I disconnected the link before she could argue.

"Adams will retaliate as soon as he realizes we're breaching his ship," Valentin said. "Is your fleet capable of defending the station?"

"The station can defend itself," Sawya said, "but our fleet will draw his attention."

"If the station can defend itself, then why do you need us?" Valentin asked. "Blow him up and be done with it."

"Or I could hand you over and be done with it," Sawya drawled. "And that option would be less risky, too."

They let that sink in for a moment before continuing. "As I'm sure you're aware, defenses have weaknesses, no matter how well they are designed. And weaknesses mean innocent people die. If you attack from inside while I attack from outside, perhaps we can keep those deaths to a minimum."

17

Despite their threats and grumbling, Sawya did start helping and a plan took shape. My team would head to *Implacable,* Adams's destroyer, and forcibly board it while Sawya distracted Adams with negotiations. Then CP57's fleet would protect the station and draw fire from the other ships while we worked our way to the bridge.

The big question was what the rest of the Quint fleet would do once we captured or killed Adams. We hoped they would surrender, but it was entirely likely that they would turn on us, in which case Valentin's ships would tunnel in to assist, chaos be damned.

Sawya loaned us three platoons of elite armored soldiers. Fitting an extra seventy-five soldiers on *Ardia* was going to be a stretch, but we weren't going very far, so we would make it work.

Plan set, we stood. Sawya rose with liquid grace and held out a hand for a handshake. "Do not betray me."

I slid my hand into theirs and met their eyes. "Same to you."

Sawya agreed with a grin, then added, "Also, do not die."

They shot a sly glance Valentin's way. "I am looking forward to my invitation."

What invitation? Valentin asked.

I could feel the color creeping into my cheeks, but there wasn't a damn thing I could do about it. *I'll tell you later.*

"My soldiers are already on their way to your dock," Sawya said. "They will meet you there. I've arranged a transport for you. It's waiting outside. It will stop by your quarters before taking you to the dock. Be quick."

"We will be. You have my link if something comes up. Otherwise, we'll see you in a few hours."

"Good hunting."

I bowed and ushered everyone out of the room. Ari, Imogen, and Luka were all stone-faced, but Stella didn't try to hide her worry. Eddie grinned like he didn't have a care in the world.

We had barely settled into the small autonomous transport when Ari rounded on me. "Are you out of your fucking mind?"

"Not as far as I know," I said as the transport began moving, my voice bone dry.

Sadly, she did not appreciate my tone. Her brows drew together into a truly ferocious scowl, and she jabbed a finger at me. "Sawya is using you."

"And I'm using them—and seventy-five of their soldiers."

"You are taking all of the risks while they sit here in safety and move you around like a pawn."

"Arietta," I warned.

She threw her hands up. "You know it's true!"

"I would go after Adams without their help," I said sharply. "And then I would probably die because no matter how good I am, I *can't* take on the entire crew of a destroyer by myself, not even if I took all of you to die with me. When we attacked Adams's ship outside Arx, the coward escaped and then *blew up my fucking home*. I will not risk a repeat. You don't have to help, but you *do* have to stop talking shit about our allies. I know exactly what Sawya is doing, and I am fine with it."

Ari looked stricken. "You think I won't help?"

I blew out a slow breath. "No, of course I think you're going to help—and I *need* your help. But I also need you to stop focusing on what is done and start focusing on what's left to do. This won't be easy, even with the extra help, and I need you to come up with a strategy that gives us the best chance of success."

Ari's posture changed as she fell back on her military training. "First priority will be keeping you safe," she said, a challenge clear in her expression. When I didn't object, she said, "Second priority will be disabling or defending the emergency shuttles, both so we have an exit and so Adams does *not*. I need a map of the ship."

"I'm working on it," Valentin said.

Ari nodded gratefully. "We'll need explosives to breach the bridge."

"We have shaped charges in our supplies. If we need something else, I'm sure Sawya can procure it for us."

"Do we have more Kos armor than I know about?"

I shook my head. "We just have the four sets. Eddie decided not to wear one, so we have an extra, and Sawya is going to include a few sets of regular armor with their troops."

Luckily, the transport stopped outside our building before I had to explain who I thought should be in the Kos armor—and deal with the resulting fight. We piled out of the vehicle. "Grab everything you can in five minutes." I drew a pistol. "And clear the rooms as you go."

We didn't find anyone inside, so everyone retreated to their rooms to pack up. Valentin followed me into our bedroom, and we packed in silence. Neither of us had much, so we were done well ahead of the deadline.

Valentin stopped me when I would've joined the others. "Why are you avoiding me?"

"Because I'm going to ask you to do something you're not going to like, and I'm avoiding it as long as possible."

His mouth flattened. "You want me to stay behind."

"Yes and no. I want you to stay on *Ardia*. But if it looks like the ship's stealth won't be enough to protect you, then I want you to tunnel to safety."

He raked a hand through his hair, frustration etched into every line of his face. "You want me to *leave* while you're fighting for your life?"

"I told you that you weren't going to like it," I said softly.

A wry, bitter grin twisted his mouth. "You weren't wrong. Why do you want me to stay on *Ardia*?"

"Honestly, I would like for you to stay on the station, but I figured that would be a no-go. And, selfishly, I don't want to lose another ship, so someone has to stay behind to fly it to safety once we're clear. You helped design it. You know it better than anyone. I trust you to get it—and yourself—to safety. And finally, I need to be utterly focused. If you're with me, I will worry about you."

"You won't worry about the others?"

"Of course I will. But Adams is gunning for you specifically. And if you fall, the Kos Empire will fall with you."

He shook his head. "It wouldn't."

"Would Nikolas end the war? Or would he bow to whoever threatened to expose his parentage? Billions of lives hang in the balance."

Valentin's eyes slid away from mine. "You are playing dirty."

"I will do whatever it takes to keep you safe."

"The great irony is that you don't seem to realize that we all feel the same way about *you*. It's all I can do to prevent myself from locking you in a closet and barring the door until Adams is dead. How am I supposed to fly away and leave you trapped on an enemy ship? Could you? Could you deliver me and then leave?"

I swallowed and dropped my gaze to his chest. I knew with absolute certainty that I could not.

He pulled me into a hug, wrapping me in a cocoon of strength and care. "Please don't ask me to do this," he whispered into my hair.

Pain sliced through me. I could hear it in his voice. He would do it if I asked, but it would break the fragile thing between us, perhaps irrevocably. But there were no good options.

I drew a shaky breath. "What would you have me do instead?"

"Take me with you. Let me watch your back. Let me help with Adams. The asshole kidnapped me and attacked my home. I have just as many reasons as you do to want him dead. And I am the only one who can listen in to what they are planning, but I have to be close."

His arms tightened around me. "Do you know why I named your ship *Ardia*?"

I silently shook my head.

"It's derived from an ancient word meaning heart," he said, his voice whisper soft. "Because no matter where you go, you'll take my heart with you. Please don't ask me to stay behind."

Tears pressed against my eyes. "You're killing me," I whispered. "If anything happens to you..." I trailed off, unwilling to contemplate a future without Valentin in it.

Valentin smoothed a hand over my hair. "That's exactly how I feel about you. Take me with you, and we can watch each other's backs."

I knew he was right, that I should take him, but the thought of him on Adams's ship made my blood run cold. Valentin could take care of himself, but every fiber of my being demanded that I keep him safe. I fought against the urge.

"If you can come up with a better option—truly better, not just one you like more—by the time we leave, we will go with it."

He pressed his lips to my forehead. "Thank you," he murmured.

"Please don't make me regret it. I can't lose you."

"You won't," he promised.

I hoped it was a promise he could keep.

———

THE TRANSPORT MOVED SWIFTLY through the station, carrying us back to Block 83 in under five minutes. I didn't see the madam who had stopped me originally, so I hoped she was having a pleasant—and lucrative—night. I vowed to keep her and the rest of CP57 safe.

The hallway to our docking tunnel had been temporarily restricted, but it was late enough that only a handful of people milled around, waiting for it to reopen. The guards at the airlock waved our transport through.

As promised, seventy-five soldiers wearing heavy armor waited for us. Each soldier was equipped with a plasma rifle, a pistol, and a shield. Two sleds stacked with the crates of supplies from Ari's ship sat farther down the hallway, and two additional sleds with CP57 logos on them sat next to them.

The three platoon commanders waited by the door to the docking tunnel, and they saluted as we approached.

I turned to Ari. "I'll let you deal with the commanders. Get them briefed on the high-level plan. Everyone else, grab a sled and help me get this stuff into *Ardia*."

The sleds were a tight fit through the docking tunnel, but we managed to get everything aboard. We delayed loading the soldiers until we were ready to go because they were going to be standing shoulder to shoulder, but Ari brought the commanders into the cargo bay to discuss strategy.

Major Morley was in her early thirties with pale skin and blond hair. She had a petite, slender build. She was clearly the senior officer of the three, both in age and rank, and the other two deferred to her without a second thought. She looked around with raised eyebrows but didn't comment on the obvious opulence.

Lieutenant Osborne was in his mid-twenties, with dark hair and light brown skin. He was an average height and build, but the hard look in his eye told me that he'd already seen more than his fair share of war and death.

Captain Howe rounded out the trio. He was in his late twenties. He had tan skin and black hair, cut short. He towered over the rest of the group—except for Luka—and looked like he could run straight through a wall and keep going.

After the introductions were over, Valentin sent everyone a blueprint and spec sheet. "This is the default layout of the type of ship Adams is on. There may be minor differences, but it should be similar enough to *Implacable* for planning. The ship has a standard complement of 150 soldiers and officers."

I did not ask him where he got the information, but I was desperately curious if he'd asked Copley Heavy Industries for a favor.

We all studied it for a few minutes, aware that we'd be outnumbered by at least two to one. Major Morley turned to me. "You are aiming to take the bridge?" When I nodded, she continued, "How many soldiers will you need?"

"At least two squads. The bridge usually isn't heavily guarded, but it will be the first place extra soldiers are deployed. If we don't get there first, then we'll need the extra firepower."

"A full platoon should go with Queen Rani," Ari said. A platoon would give me three squads rather than two. She continued, "Once the bridge is secure, we might be able to send teams elsewhere, but the bridge is our highest priority target."

Morley nodded. "I agree. Captain Howe, you are with Queen

Rani and her people. Lieutenant Osborne and I will secure the emergency shuttles. We'll be in the open, so we're counting on you to take the bridge and put the ship in lockdown."

I looked at the ship's map. Valentin had highlighted the closest exterior hatch to the bridge, but it wasn't exactly *close*. "How many doors will we have to clear if Adams locks down the ship before we get to the bridge?"

"Three," Valentin said. "Maybe four if we have to take the longer route. Plus the bridge door itself."

"Adams won't lock the ship down unless he has no other option," Ari said. "We're entering in the same zone as the emergency shuttles, which is one of the most reinforced sections of the ship. If he locks it down, he won't have an escape path, and his soldiers won't be able to reach us."

"Can he depressurize that section?" I asked.

Morely shook her head. "It's not easy on a military vessel. Destroyers are designed to withstand hull breaches with the smallest possible internal damage. We will anchor just in case, and our suits have a limited supply of oxygen, but it's far more likely that he'll send soldiers after us since we'll already be outnumbered."

"Okay. I want my team carrying enough explosives to clear ten doors," I said. "Adams absolutely will try to fuck us over, and he won't care who he hurts to do it. We do not want to be stuck on the ship when the stardrive recharges because I don't think he will take us to a nice tropical beach. And I don't want to sit in an emergency shuttle for a month while we hop back to populated space."

"How long until the drive is ready?" Morley asked.

"Probably around two hours."

She sucked in a breath. "Then we need to move. I'll requisition more explosives. The extra armor is in the boxes you brought in. You should put it on to ensure everything fits."

"Give us a second," Ari said.

Morley nodded and she and the other two stepped away to the other side of the cargo bay.

"Who should wear the Kos combat armor?" Ari asked.

Valentin responded before I could. "Samara, Imogen, Stella, and me." Valentin cut me off before I could utter a word. "I'm going with you. Eddie will fly the ship to safety after he opens the airlock."

Not one person in the group looked surprised, and I realized why the trip from our temporary quarters had been so quiet—Valentin had been busy plotting behind my back.

"What about Luka and Ari?" I asked as Ari started stripping off her armor without complaint.

"He and Ari will wear the armor Morley brought. The standard Kos armor doesn't fit Luka well, and it's better to keep Stella hidden since she'll be the one patching us up. Ari and Stella will stay with the two platoons near the emergency shuttles. Imogen, Luka, and I will accompany you to the bridge."

Ari's mouth pinched into an unhappy line, but she didn't contradict him.

They'd decided without me. Pain stabbed deep, but I boxed it up for later. I buried everything under a layer of emotionless determination. "Let's get ready, then."

Valentin frowned and drew me aside as the others moved to don their armor. "Are you okay?"

I ruthlessly smothered the panic that tried to rise at the thought of him on Adams's ship. "Yes."

"Are you sure?"

"I already shared my concerns, but I also agreed that if you came up with a better plan, we'd do it. You apparently did." I couldn't quite keep the bitterness out of my voice.

"Samara..."

"No," I said, slashing a hand through the air. "I need to be utterly focused, and dealing with this right now isn't that. We'll go, kick Adams's ass, and then come back and celebrate our victory." *Assuming we both survived.* Panic slithered through me again, and I took a deep breath. "Let's get ready."

Valentin looked like he wanted to say more, but finally he swallowed and nodded without speaking.

I silently donned my armor and loaded up on weapons and gear. I disliked combat armor, but I understood how important it was to my survival, so I dealt with it.

But I would leave my visor up until the last possible moment.

My standard gear consisted of a compact rifle, a pair of pistols, a combat knife, and a few grenades, both explosive and smoke. I also carried a trio of shaped explosive charges used to breach doors. Imogen had an additional two. If we were separated from Captain Howe's soldiers, we wouldn't be entirely trapped. The others had different gear, including a few of the active camouflage pucks that Adams had used when he'd attacked Arx.

Imogen, Luka, Ari, Stella, Valentin, and I retreated to the bridge while Sawya's soldiers loaded into the cargo bay. Eddie stayed near the airlock because he would have to work fast once we attached to Adams's ship.

Once everyone was loaded, I sent a message to Sawya. *We are ready when you are.*

While I waited for the response, I mentally went through every plan and contingency. I firmed my resolve. Adams would die and my people would live—no matter what I had to do to make that happen.

Sawya's response, when it came, was a single word. *Go.*

18

The combat armor was too bulky to let me comfortably sit in the captain's chair, but I didn't need to manually fly *Ardia*. I was directly linked to the ship and could fly it from anywhere, though it was safest and easiest from the bridge. If I didn't need to focus on killing Adams, I could even fly the ship to safety after we'd disembarked—at least until it got out of range.

I spun up the engines and dropped us into stealth as Valentin whispered directions across a private link. I hadn't gotten a chance to test the Kos tech yet, but I hoped it was as good as he thought, or this was going to be a very short, very explosive trip.

When all of the stealth checks came back clear, I disengaged the docking port and it retracted. Then I released the berthing clamps, and *Ardia* floated free of the station. I eased us away from the dock. According to Valentin, I would have to be very, very careful about the ships around us because neither their sensors nor visual scans would pick us up.

Luckily, traffic was basically zero thanks to the Quint armada hovering in the distance.

I kept our speed relatively low. The less we had to use the

engines, the harder we would be to detect. Even so, *Implacable* loomed in front of us in less than five minutes. We hadn't been fired upon yet, so either this was an elaborate double-cross on Sawya's part or the plan was actually working.

I eased *Ardia* up and around the bow of the destroyer, aiming for the forward hatch in the starboard side. We slid past the main guns, close enough that a direct shot would punch straight through all of our hull shielding and come out the other side.

The guns remained silent and still.

I drew a quiet breath. One obstacle down. *We're coming up on the hatch,* I sent across the main group link. It included my team, the three platoon commanders, and Sawya. I got back a chorus of acknowledgments.

On *Ardia's* exterior cameras, the fleet from CP57 rose from the camouflage of the station's many hidden flight paths. Our distraction had arrived.

With no help from the systems on *Implacable, Ardia's* autopilot would only kick in once we were within a few meters of the hatch. I kept an eye on every sensor and camera as I slowly maneuvered us closer and closer. When the docking sensor turned green, I handed off control to the ship, but I held my breath until a gentle *thunk* and a green light from the airlock signaled the connection was successful.

We are docked, I told the group. *Eddie, go.*

On it, he said.

I led my group from the bridge to the cargo bay. Rows of soldiers were packed in, but a narrow path from the stairs to the airlock remained clear. I headed to the door, where Eddie worked on *Implacable's* hatch.

If I could keep all of the people I loved here in safety, I would, in a heartbeat. But they had made their own decisions, and I would respect them, even if I hated it.

I just hoped they would respect mine.

The hatch swung open and two soldiers wedged a thick

metal bar against it to prevent it from closing again. Eddie moved on to work on the inner airlock door. We were on the clock because there would be all kinds of alarms going off on the bridge.

It felt like forever, but it was probably less than a minute later when the inner door opened. Once again, a pair of soldiers wedged the door open. We'd cleared the second obstacle.

Eddie moved back into *Ardia,* and Captain Howe's platoon moved forward to secure the hallway.

After everyone had transferred to *Implacable,* Eddie would remove the first brace and close the hatch between the airlock and *Ardia.* Then the final two soldiers in the airlock would remove the inner door brace and use it to wedge the airlock *closed,* ensuring that Adams couldn't send us all jettisoning into space.

I snapped down my helmet's visor and shimmered out of view of the cargo bay camera. Good to know the active camouflage still worked. Imogen, Valentin, and Stella showed up on the visor's screen with a faint green outline. None of the rest of the soldiers had an outline, but I could see them overlaid with the faint red blobs of the thermal image.

Alpha Team is go, Morley said.

That was all I needed to hear. I bolted into the airlock tunnel. Ari cursed, but the others followed me with only a moment's hesitation.

Bravo Team is go, Morley said.

Behind us, the rest of the troops began streaming out of *Ardia* as Morley and Osborne issued orders. I let go of the cameras I'd been watching with the exception of the cargo bay camera.

Howe's soldiers had spread out on both sides of the airlock tunnel, wedging themselves into the sparse cover the hallway provided. *Implacable* was eerily quiet. It had been less than five minutes since we'd docked, but that should've been enough time for Adams to rally *some* defense.

Where was everyone?

I turned right, following the map I'd memorized. Imogen, Luka, and Valentin were directly behind me, and the Alpha Team soldiers fell in behind them. The soldiers had thermal imaging overlays turned on, but they couldn't tag Valentin, Imogen, or me as friendlies. We would have to stick close or risk getting accidentally shot if more soldiers in Kos armor showed up.

We moved quickly through corridors that were suspiciously empty. Adams was planning something, I just hadn't figured out what.

In the video from *Ardia,* the last soldiers left the cargo bay. Eddie removed the brace and slammed *Implacable*'s hatch closed, then closed the airlock on *Ardia*. He waved at the camera and then disappeared toward the bridge.

The Quint armada likely wouldn't attack *Ardia* while it was attached to *Implacable,* but as soon as Eddie moved away, he would become a target. I hoped the Kos stealth tech held up or he was about to have a very stressful few minutes.

I sped up. We needed to distract Adams to keep him off of Eddie. I rounded the next corner just as Valentin shouted over our team group link, *Wait!*

The others stopped, but Imogen and I were already in the open.

A dozen Quint soldiers with pistols waited in front of the first lockdown door. They were arrayed in two lines stretching across the corridor, and none of them wore combat armor. These soldiers were sacrifices sent to slow us down long enough for the others to get ready, and I didn't have any nonlethal weapons.

Fuck.

I snapped my rifle up, but the soldiers didn't shoot. They remained focused on the corner.

The soldiers couldn't see us because Imogen and I were hidden by our armor's active camouflage. Adams had tossed their lives away for nothing. I might be able to edge around them without killing them, but Howe's soldiers couldn't.

My stomach twisted. We had to go through them. It would be a slaughter.

Before I could pull the trigger, an alarm blared and the heavy door behind them began to close. I moved on instinct, plowing past the Quint soldiers and knocking a few down. The rest spun to shoot at me, but without being able to see me, their shots went wide.

The hallway devolved into chaos as Howe's soldiers rounded the corner. *Don't shoot Samara and Imogen!* Valentin shouted over the link.

The door was more than half closed when I dashed through. Luka would keep Valentin safe and Howe's soldiers could take care of themselves. I kept running.

Samara! Valentin shouted over a private link.

Be careful and catch up when you can, I said.

Done, he said, his tone wry.

I stopped and whirled around. My visor screen showed a green outline around the red blob of a camouflaged soldier. I scanned the rest of the hallway, but no one else was visible and the door was fully closed. *Valentin?*

Surprise, he said, and his outline waved at me.

I wished I could see his face. I wished he was on the other side of the door, or better yet, safe on CP57. *Where is Luka?* I demanded.

He's shouting at me over a private link, Valentin said.

I knew exactly what he meant because Imogen was doing the same to me. *Why did you follow me? How?*

Valentin closed the distance between us. *Imogen got held up by the soldiers. I was the only one close enough to slide through the door before it closed.*

I clenched my jaw against the urge to shout. *Did it ever occur to you,* I said coldly, *that I left you behind for a reason?*

And I followed you for the same reason, he said, his tone gentle but firm.

I raised my hand to rub my face, only to be stopped by the armor. Valentin had made his choice, and I didn't have time to wait for the others to blast through the door, not if I wanted to catch Adams off guard.

Are you eavesdropping on the local neural links? I asked.

Yes, but everyone is staying very quiet. Either Adams suspects I'm here or there aren't many soldiers in this part of the ship.

Let me know if anything changes. Shoot anything that moves and don't fall behind.

I will follow your lead, he promised.

———

CUT OFF FROM OUR BACKUP, our strategy became speed and stealth. We narrowly avoided the next group of soldiers because Valentin heard them just before we saw them. We flattened ourselves to the wall, guns ready, but the group came around the corner and passed us by without stopping.

Adams's soldiers still weren't in combat armor. Destroyers were nigh impregnable at a distance and weren't meant to deploy ground troops, but they should still have *some* combat armor aboard. If I had to guess, Adams had surrounded himself with armored troops and left the rest to fend for themselves.

Maybe we could use that against him and persuade some soldiers to give up the fight. *Can you tap into the ship's intercom system?* I asked Valentin.

No.

I sighed. So much for that idea.

Eddie linked me. *Boss, the Quints* really *didn't appreciate our little stunt. I'm tunneling to Koan. Stay safe.*

You, too. I'll see you soon.

The link cut off and so did my connection to the cargo bay camera. *Eddie tunneled,* I told the main group. We'd agreed to keep communication to a minimum once we were on the ship, but they needed to know that Eddie hadn't been blown up.

Morley acknowledged the message and let us know that soldiers had started attacking her position at the emergency shuttles as expected. Hopefully, with Adams's people divided, we'd run into fewer on the way to the bridge.

A distant explosion rang through the corridor. Captain Howe's troops had blown the first door. We needed to move if we were going to stay ahead of them.

I sent Imogen a warning about the soldiers between us and then sprinted for the next door. Adams seemed to be locking down the ship as little as possible, but with the first door breached, he'd lock this section soon.

Valentin kept pace a step behind me. I relied on him to tell me if we were running face first into a trap, but he remained quiet.

I could see the second door when the alarms started. The door was unguarded, but it had begun closing already. Was the timing a coincidence or a trap?

With no time to hesitate, I sprinted faster, pushing myself and the armor to the limit. I slid through with centimeters to spare. I heard armor scrape against metal and spun around, my heart in my throat. If Valentin had missed the timing, the door would crush him.

Valentin jerked to a stop just before he plowed into me. *What's wrong?* he asked.

I let out a shaky breath. He was okay. He wasn't crushed. Anger roared in after the relief, whiting everything out. *What were you* thinking? *You could've died!*

It wasn't that close, he said, his tone infuriatingly calm.

I bit my tongue before I said something unforgivable. *This was why I hadn't wanted him on the ship.* I should still be sprinting for the next door, but I'd stopped to check on him. He was a distraction that I couldn't ignore, and my failure would cost us our lives.

As if he could read my mind, he said, *Samara, trust me to take care of myself. I may not be as good as you, but I've been a soldier for most of my life. I will follow your lead. I won't take unnecessary risks. Stop worrying about me and start* using *me. We are on the same team.*

If only it was that easy, I grumbled. But I turned and started for the next door.

Valentin fell in behind me. *Trust me, I know,* he murmured.

Rather than heading straight for the bridge, I turned off and took the longer route. It was a risk, but if Adams was locking down the ship one zone at a time, he might not expect us to take a detour. We passed two more groups of unarmored soldiers and made it through the third door before our luck ran out.

Soldiers, Valentin warned. *At least six.*

Before I could ask for more details, a side door farther down the corridor slid open, and the first soldier stepped out. They were in Quint combat armor. Turning on thermal overlays wasn't standard procedure, but Adams had to suspect that we were in Kos armor. It could go either way on whether the soldier would see us or not.

The question was answered when they started to bring their gun up. I beat them to it and put two rounds into their visor. Today I *had* equipped armor-piercing rounds, though using them on a spaceship carried some risk. The rounds punched through the visor and the soldier fell, dead.

I didn't have time for regret because the remaining five soldiers poured out of the room. They were too close for a grenade, and the corridor we were in offered minimal cover, but a cross corridor between us and them at least gave us a place to hide, if we could get there.

Go left. Get to the corner, I told Valentin as I dashed to the right. I kept moving forward, shooting as I went. It was clear the soldiers hadn't expected to be attacked here. By the time they rallied, we had taken out half of their number and made it to the corner.

Alarms started blaring. If Adams hadn't known we were in Kos armor, he did now.

I squatted down and quickly peeked around the corner. Across the hall, Valentin did the same. The three remaining soldiers had retreated back into the room, but the door remained open. If they were smart, they would stay put until backup arrived.

I waited a moment, but none of them appeared in the doorway. Maybe they *were* smart, which was bad for us. I could toss a grenade inside, but I'd rather see exactly what I was blowing up before I made a mistake that ejected us all into space.

"Drop your weapons and come out with your hands up, and I won't kill you," I shouted, my voice amplified by my armor. I wasn't sure *what* I would do with them since I didn't have an electroshock pistol, but I'd cross that bridge when I came to it.

The soldiers remained silent.

If they were relying on thermal imaging, then they would see me as a red blob and aim for center mass, where my armor was thickest. Of course, if they had armor-piercing rounds, then taking shots to center mass was a good way to get dead.

Decisions, decisions.

I had almost decided to move forward and take the risk when the tip of a pistol appeared around the corner, followed by a soldier's head. So much for surrendering. Valentin and I both landed shots, and the soldier collapsed.

I moved forward, my rifle up. Valentin shadowed me.

A pair of empty hands appeared around the edge of the doorway. "Don't shoot!" a male voice shouted.

"Keep your hands up and come out. What about the other soldier?"

"She's surrendering, too."

The first soldier edged around the door only to freeze when he realized how close we were. I kept my rifle trained on him even though he probably couldn't see it in his thermal view. "Come out and keep your hands up."

He stepped over his fallen teammate and moved to the middle of the hall.

"Next, the same way," I called.

Two more empty hands appeared and then another soldier crept into the hall.

Well, now what the fuck was I supposed to do?

"Take off your helmets, slowly." When they hesitated, I said, "My rounds will punch straight through your armor. If I wanted you dead, you'd be dead. Don't do anything stupid and you'll live."

But I still needed this to be quick. I linked Valentin. *Watch them.*

After he acknowledged the order, I peeked into the room. There were no remaining soldiers inside, so perhaps these two really were trying to surrender. The room had been converted into an auxiliary armory, likely for the soldiers working around the bridge.

A quick scan didn't turn up any explosives, but I found an electroshock pistol on the wall. It would hurt like hell, but they would survive it, and it would put them down long enough for us to escape.

I returned to the hallway. A blond man and dark-haired woman waited, their expressions nervous. Without their helmets, they couldn't track us.

"Back up," I said. "There are more behind us, and we need

you away from the dead. You also want to be away from the door."

They gulped but backed up.

"I will tell the others to restrain you. You won't be hurt as long as you don't attack. But they will expect a trap, so be very careful how you act. Understand?"

Imogen and the others weren't actually coming this way because they were taking the faster route, but I needed these soldiers to be concerned about getting up and moving around once the stun rounds wore off.

When the soldiers nodded, I shot them. The stun rounds shorted out their armor in addition to locking their muscles, and they fell with grunts of pain.

I tossed all of the fallen weapons into the room and then pulled out a small grenade designed for use on ships. It *shouldn't* do much more than make the armory unusable, assuming *Implacable* had decent automatic fire suppression tech and there wasn't a fuel line on the other side of the wall.

If not, then I hoped these two knew where the closest manual extinguishers were. I activated the grenade and tossed it into the room so the explosion would be focused away from the doorway. Then I attached the electroshock pistol to my armor and sprinted for the next door.

A few seconds later, the grenade went off and another host of alarms started, but we hadn't been hurtled into space, so I chalked it up as a win.

As expected, the next heavy lockdown door was closed. This was the last door between us and the bridge. We still had a few hallways to go, but after this door, Adams couldn't lock us out except for the bridge door itself.

Imogen, how close are you to the last door?

Two minutes.

We couldn't afford to wait that long. Adams might not have had this route protected because the visible soldiers were taking the other route, but with our little stunt a few minutes ago, he'd be working to fix that.

And if the soldiers we'd just left had linked out before they'd surrendered, then Adams would know there were only two of us—the perfect number to use as hostages.

We didn't have time to circle all the way back to the other group. The only way was forward. *We're going now. Good luck.*

You, too. See you at the bridge. Stay alive so I can yell at you.

Will do, I said with a smile.

I slung my small pack around to the front of my body and carefully retrieved one of the shaped charges I carried. The explosive was incredibly stable and wouldn't detonate accidentally, but I always took extra care—I liked all of my fingers exactly where they were, thanks.

Valentin watched the corridor while I applied the charge to the door. I set the timer for ten seconds and then activated it.

It was time to see if the gods of luck were on our side.

19

Valentin and I retreated a few meters in the precious seconds before the charge exploded. The shape of the explosion was designed to send all potential shrapnel in the direction of the blast, but the extra distance would help our armor protect us just in case something went wrong.

My helmet automatically muffled the sound of the explosion, but I still felt the vibration. The heavy door wasn't completely gone, but it had a large gap in the middle, big enough for us to fit through even in armor.

If there was any sort of hull breech in the zones we'd crossed, then *Implacable* would be fucked without these doors, but that was the risk Adams had taken when he'd used them to slow us down.

The other group is a couple of minutes behind us at the other door, I told Valentin. *We need to move quickly.*

The local links have gone completely silent. Be careful.

I will be.

I hugged the wall as I approached the door. The heat and smoke from the explosion made it difficult to see what—or who

—waited on the other side. At the door, I crouched down and peeked around the edge of the gap.

And very nearly got a plasma pulse to the face for my effort.

I jerked back with a curse.

My quick glance had revealed at least four soldiers in Kos armor, but it could easily be more thanks to the overlapping red thermals barely visible behind some kind of cover.

"Samara Rani, surrender or we will destroy the station," a female voice called. "You have five seconds to decide."

They are threatening the station, I sent across the main group link.

I will handle it, Sawya said. *But hurry.*

"Why don't *you* surrender and then I won't have to kill you?" I shouted back.

I didn't expect a response, and I didn't get one. They had the superior position and they knew it. I had two explosive grenades left. I'd hoped to save them for closer to the bridge, but we wouldn't get to the bridge if I didn't make a path through the soldiers.

Blowing up something I couldn't see wasn't my favorite option, but I would have to take the risk.

I activated a grenade and sent it sailing through the door in a high arc. The armor covering my forearm deflected a glancing plasma pulse, proving that these soldiers were of a higher caliber than those we'd been fighting so far. Maybe we were closing in on Adams's personal troops.

The soldiers shouted as they caught sight of the grenade, but it was too late. As soon as the flash from the explosion faded, I ducked through the door, Valentin behind me.

The grenade had flown true. Five soldiers were on the ground behind a barrier of composite shields. The blast had punched through their armor, disabling the active camouflage and taking them out of the fight. One red blob remained, but it wasn't moving. I couldn't risk them sneaking up behind us, so I aimed for center mass and put three rounds in a small grouping.

The soldier flickered into view, slumped on the floor.

I was no stranger to death, but it never got any easier, especially not when these soldiers were dying for an asshole like Adams who thought nothing of throwing their lives away.

Over the link, Imogen warned me that they were blowing their door. I swapped in a fresh magazine and edged down the hallway toward the bridge. Once Imogen and the rest made it through the door, we'd be in the same zone, but we were both closer to *Implacable*'s bridge than to each other.

I heard the explosion in the distance, and over the link, Imogen cursed. *It feels like half the ship is waiting for us.*

Do you need help?

No, stay back. We're going to have to blast our way through.

We'll head to the bridge. Meet us there when you're free.

She either agreed or was too busy to respond. Ari's group was also taking heavy fire near the evacuation ships, which meant Adams was attempting to secure a way out. If he'd already abandoned the bridge then all of this was going to be for nothing, but at least he wouldn't get past Ari.

Our path to the bridge was eerily empty. We could hear distant explosions and rifle fire from where Imogen's team still fought, but there were no soldiers on this side of the ship. Adams was practically rolling out a red carpet for us. It *had* to be a trap, but one I would be happy to turn back on him.

The bridge could be approached from three directions. The bridge doorway was in the middle a long corridor that stretched across the ship from port to starboard. If Imogen and the rest of the team took the most direct route, they would be coming down that hallway from the starboard side. The port side led to parts of the ship that hadn't been locked down yet, so enemy soldiers would likely approach from that direction.

A second corridor led straight out from the bridge, allowing a head-on approach. That was the closest option for us. It was also potentially the riskiest, but wasting time going around brought its own risk.

I stopped at the last intersection before I had to commit to a direction. *Do you hear anything?* I asked Valentin.

No. Adams has to know we're close, and he's inviting us to come closer. Any idea what he has planned?

No. I still wished I could see Valentin's face. This would be so much easier if I could read his expression. *I don't suppose you'll wait here?*

Not unless you do. His tone told me that he wouldn't budge.

Fine. We're taking the main hallway. If we get to the bridge door, I'll set up one of your active camouflage pucks before we blow it open. If we run into trouble, we'll fall back and wait for Imogen and Luka to catch up to us. Sound good?

Yes. Be careful. I've got your back.

You, too. Let me know if you sense anyone.

I will try, he promised.

I crept forward, and turned down the main hall leading to *Implacable*'s bridge. This corridor wasn't divided into sections, so I could see the bridge door in the distance.

The passageway looked clear all the way to the bridge, but a half-dozen side doors were closed. Based on the blueprint, these were likely quarters and amenities for the ship's officers. That didn't mean that they couldn't be full of soldiers right now, though.

But despite my worries, no one jumped us as we moved through the hall. I would actually feel better if someone tried it, because the closer we got to the bridge, the worse my sense of foreboding became. Adams wouldn't let us get this close without some sort of last-ditch plan.

I don't like this, I told Valentin.

I agree. He should be throwing the entire ship at us.

Valentin was right. Destroyers usually carried enough crew

for three full shifts, which meant that two-thirds of the soldiers should be available to fight our invasion—and that was before pulling any soldiers from their duty assignment, which Adams would absolutely do to save his own sorry ass.

So where was everyone?

The bridge was the likely answer, at least for some of them. Adams's personal troops would certainly be nearby, and he would want as many bodies as possible between him and danger.

I kept moving forward, my senses on high alert. I slid up beside the next side door. It refused to open, but I wasn't sure if that was because it was locked or because the sensor couldn't detect me while I was camouflaged in Kos armor. These doors weren't reinforced, so I could *probably* kick one down if we needed emergency cover, but it would take a few seconds and then we'd be trapped.

We're finally clear of the last door, Imogen said. *But we're down four people.*

Luka?

He's okay, Imogen said. *He's too stubborn to get shot. We're approximately five minutes out.*

When I relayed the information to Valentin, he asked, *Are we going to wait for them?*

That was the question. Waiting would be the safer option, but if Adams *wasn't* on the bridge, then it gave him another five minutes to escape.

Let's get into position and then we'll wait before we blow the door, I said at last. Once we could see down the other corridor, we could at least warn Imogen and the rest if they were walking into an ambush.

I kept my rifle up as I swept down the passageway, but we made it to the corner without any resistance. I took the right side while Valentin moved to the left. A quick peek revealed the other hallway was empty in both directions, but I could only see for a few meters. Unlike the main passageway, this hall was divided with section doors. They weren't as heavy as the lockdown doors, so even if they were locked shut, they wouldn't stop Imogen's group.

I can't sense anything past the bridge door, Valentin said. *They may be blocking links.*

If they were blocking links, then as soon as we stepped inside, we'd be cut off from the rest of our teams. That solidified my decision to wait for Imogen to arrive before blowing the door.

Give me a camouflage puck, I said. *We're too exposed here.*

Valentin handed me one of the small devices, and I activated it before setting it on the floor facing back the way we'd come. If anyone came down the main hallway, they would see themselves reflected rather than us. It wouldn't stop plasma pulses, but it would make us harder to hit.

If Adams didn't know we were here, he would as soon as I moved away. Our armor might not show up on the ship's cameras, but the puck certainly would once it was outside of the armor's camouflage radius. And it wouldn't exactly take a genius to figure out that the puck hadn't placed itself.

I was still standing over the puck when a distant explosion rocked the ship hard enough that I felt the vibration through my boots. It seemed to come from our right, on the starboard side of the ship. *Imogen, was that you?*

She did not respond. The link seemed to be connected, but only silence came from her end. Was she unconscious?

Alpha Team, what is going on? I asked over the team group link.

Ambush! I didn't recognize the voice over the staticky link. The connection cut out for a few seconds, then came back. — *need help!*

On our private link, Valentin said, *Luka's link is down.* His tone was perfectly flat, and I knew exactly what it had cost him because worry for Imogen twisted my stomach into knots. It was all I could do to prevent myself from dashing down the hall to them.

But getting myself killed in an ambush wouldn't stop Adams. And if I didn't stop him, he would continue to attack CP57 before moving on to Koan. Thousands more would die.

I closed my eyes against the tears of rage and worry. I could either save the people I cared about or I could save the universe. It wasn't fair and it wasn't right, but I knew what I had to do.

Staying put was the hardest decision I'd ever made.

I buried my rage and pain under a mountain of icy determination. Adams would die today, no matter what I had to do to see it done.

Alpha Team needs backup, I told the main group. *They were ambushed somewhere after the final door. I'm pushing into the bridge.*

I'm on it, Ari said. She didn't even try to argue, which meant my tone must've been worse than I thought.

If you want to go find Luka, you should, I told Valentin. *I have to deal with Adams.*

I'm staying with you, he said quietly.

Valentin moved to the left side of the bridge door while I attached the breaching charge. I activated it and then pressed myself to the right wall. A few seconds later, the charge did its job and blew a hole through the door.

I peeked through the gap while the smoke and heat would disguise my thermal signature. There were nearly twenty soldiers, half in camouflaged Kos armor. Adams, surprisingly, was not.

He was farthest away from the door, with two lines of soldiers acting as a shield.

I pulled out a grenade. Blowing up the bridge wasn't the *smartest* idea, but if we needed to, we could control the ship from the backup console in maintenance.

I paused as Commander Adams's voice boomed through the

gap in the door. "Samara Rani, I presume. I believe I have something of yours. Drop your weapons and come in before I decide to break it."

A familiar groan echoed from the bridge and I froze. There was *no way* they'd snuck Imogen past me, but I had to check. I peeked again. Two of the screens behind Adams were streaming video from what looked like a combat armor camera, and Imogen's bruised and bloody face stared back at me.

She was missing her helmet, but the rest of her combat armor appeared to be on, if not entirely intact. Her face was bloody and her eyes were fuzzy and distant—a concussion, at best. I couldn't see anything else, but the sounds of rifle fire came through the speakers.

Someone was still alive and fighting.

I pulled back before one of the soldiers in the bridge could take a shot at me.

Adams is on the bridge with fifteen to twenty soldiers. Imogen has been captured, I said on the main group link.

"I'm tired of waiting," Adams said. "Kill—"

"Don't be so hasty," I called. "Kill her and you won't live long enough to draw another breath."

Adams laughed. "You really didn't think I'd let you get all the way to the bridge without some sort of insurance, did you? It's in your best interest to keep me alive." His voice hardened. "Step inside, *now,* or your little guard dies."

Stay here, I told Valentin. Then, before he could argue, I unstrapped my rifle, turned off my armor's camouflage, and activated the grenade I still held. I kept the grenade's safety lever held down—the countdown timer wouldn't start until I released it.

If Adams shot me when I stepped through the door, at least I'd take his smug ass with me to hell.

I eased through the door, grenade first. "Watch your soldiers, Adams, or we'll all go down in a blaze of glory."

Once I was fully in the room, my connection to the net wavered. It didn't die completely, but that could be because I was close to the door. If they really were blocking links, then Adams was communicating with his people by some other method.

My connection isn't stable, I told Valentin. *I might lose it if I move deeper into the room. There are eight soldiers in Kos armor and eight more without armor.*

I will keep our connection active as long as possible, Valentin said, *and I'll relay your updates to the others.*

I added my camera's view to the link I shared with him. It was quite a bit of data to transfer over an unstable connection, but it would let Valentin see what was happening in the room, if not in full video, then at least in still frames.

Adams wore a standard Quint officer's uniform, but I couldn't get a shot at him. "Welcome to *Implacable,* Scoundrel Queen," he said. "As you can see, I've shut down your net connection, so any help you were hoping for isn't coming, but I have to admit, the grenade is a nice touch."

He didn't know that I could still connect out, at least as long as I stayed close to the door. I might be able to use that to my advantage.

"Unfortunately for you, it looks like we both had the same idea." Adams smirked, then lifted his right hand, revealing a cylindrical detonator. "Except my bomb won't just blow up a room—it'll take out the station."

20

My breath caught, and I made and discarded plans at lightning speed. The detonator in Adams's hand had to be constantly depressed or it would activate —much like my grenade. If he died, his grip would relax, and the explosives would go off. I would have to get close before I killed him.

Assuming there were any explosives in the first place.

"It seems that we are at an impasse," Adams said when I remained silent. "Of course, if *you* let go, then you die with me. If *I* let go, then several Blocks of the station will cease to exist, along with all of the people inside. So why don't you tell me where the emperor is hiding and deactivate your little grenade before I kill your guard."

I'm alerting Sawya, Valentin said.

See if they can shut down all signals to the station, I said. At the same time, I responded to Adams. "You don't really expect me to believe that you snuck enough explosives past Sawya to actually do any damage to the station, do you?" I scoffed. "You would've been better off telling me that you'd wired Arx to blow."

Adams laughed again. "If you think there aren't powerful

people on CP57 who are eager for a change of leadership, then you haven't been paying attention."

"It'll be hard to lead a station that is in pieces. Your new friends are powerful all right—powerfully shortsighted," I taunted.

I needed more information about the location of the explosives. Isolating the station from all signals would be incredibly difficult. And while I doubted I could stall long enough for the explosives to be found and disabled, I had to try.

Adams ignored my taunts. "Where is the emperor? I know he was on the station with you, and I suspect he's here now. Turn him over and I'll let your guard go."

"I haven't seen him since I left the station," I lied. "He's probably back in Koan by now."

Sawya needs five minutes, Valentin whispered in my head.

Five minutes was an eternity.

I started a timer. The numbers counted down in the corner of my visor's screen.

On the video behind Adams, the rifle fire moved closer. I had to hope that help was coming for Imogen because if I had to watch her die, I wasn't sure what I would do.

"Why do you want Valentin anyway?" I asked. "Your support in Koan is gone. The war is all but over. What do you get by killing Valentin?"

Before Adams could answer, the video behind him shifted as the soldier with the camera slumped to the side and a hulking shape lurched into view just before the camera cut out. I only caught a glimpse and couldn't see his face, but the silhouette was unmistakable.

Luka is injured but alive, I told Valentin. *He made it to Imogen.*

Adams hissed something low and furious at one of the soldiers next to him. The soldier touched his earpiece and demanded, "Status report."

They were communicating with low-tech two-way radio

transceivers rather than neural links. Links operated on a completely difference frequency and tech stack, so there was no way for us to intercept their communication without recovering a transceiver.

The soldier must not have gotten good news because his face paled. He whispered something to Adams and the commander casually backhanded him, sending him staggering back a step.

"That's no way to treat your people," I said with an exaggerated shake of my head. "The Rogue Coalition offers sanctuary to anyone who wants to join us."

One soldier shifted. "Move and die," Adams threatened. The soldier stilled, and Adams turned to me. "Enough stalling. I know Valentin was with you, and I bet he's outside the door right now. Maybe I should send some soldiers to flush him out."

I swept an arm toward the door. "By all means." Valentin could handle himself, and I would happily take out anyone who was stupid enough to approach.

"You have no power here. You're going to give me Valentin, or I'm going to let this go." Adams waved the detonator around with a carelessness that made my blood freeze. One slip and thousands of people would die.

"Dropping that detonator will be the last thing you do," I promised. Seconds trickled through the timer, each seemingly slower than the last. There were still more than two minutes remaining.

Adams smirked. "Your little grenade doesn't scare me. I have two squads of people who will throw themselves on it for the cause."

I looked around at the soldiers. The ones I could see remained stone-faced. "I don't see anyone volunteering to die in your place. But suppose I *could* produce Valentin. What would you give me?"

"I will trade you the detonator for Valentin."

I snorted. "Even I'm not stupid enough to believe that."

At some unknown signal, two armored soldiers rushed at me from opposite sides of the room. I drew my pistol with my free hand and put rounds through both of their visors before they'd taken more than four steps.

Retreat and find Ari, I told Valentin.

The rest of the soldiers raised their weapons, and I dived behind the closest console. My connection to the net died.

"I figured you'd be too spineless to actually use the grenade," Adams shouted smugly. "That's why I'm going to walk away and you are not. Kill her and find Valentin!"

I deactivated the grenade and pulled my second pistol. Adams was right—I *wouldn't* use the grenade until I was sure it wouldn't destroy part of CP57. I activated the camouflage on my armor. There were over a dozen guards between me and Adams and at least half of them would be able to see me.

I had no illusions about my chance of success.

"If you wanted to find me, you only had to ask," Valentin called from outside the door.

Adams held up a hand and the soldiers in the room froze.

I silently cursed Valentin. My whole gambit had been designed to keep him *safe* and now he was offering himself up on a silver platter.

"Does Chairwoman Soteras know you are here?" Valentin asked. "Or are you betraying the Quint Confederacy along with everyone else?"

"I'm doing what's *best* for the Confederacy," Adams said with all the zeal of a true believer. "Why should we settle for a compromised peace when we can wipe you out and take everything for ourselves? The current Chairwoman doesn't have her father's vision, but she will thank me when I'm done."

"You're just another puppet on a string," Valentin taunted. "When you fail and your backers cut you free, what will you have? Nothing."

Adams shook his head. "I won't fail. And Hannah Perkins

already paid me more than enough for me to live comfortably for the rest of my life. The stupid bitch thought she was using me, but she never understood that I was using her, too."

"Why didn't you kill me when you captured me?" Valentin asked. He was far better at stalling than I was. The five-minute timer was nearly up, but without a link, I didn't know if Sawya had managed to find the explosives or shut down the signals. Attacking would still be risky.

Take off your armor, now, Valentin said, his mental voice faint.

I hesitated. Was he *trying* to get me killed? There were still more than a dozen soldiers in the room and the armor was the only protection I had. After a heartbeat, I sighed and started quietly stripping off the pieces. I trusted Valentin—and if this didn't prove I was in love with the man, then nothing would.

"I had a feeling that Perkins didn't want to make the second part of my payment," Adams said, his tone smugly superior. "Your life was my insurance. And I was right—she sent the soldiers after me the night the Scoundrel Queen showed up. In fact, I thought they were working together. And maybe they were, have you considered that?"

Sixty-second window in ten seconds, Valentin said. *Secure the detonator. I'll cover you.* Aloud, he said, "Samara wasn't working with Hannah. She planned to ransom me back to my advisors."

Seconds that had crawled by before now drained away too quickly.

"I would've loved to see your face when you figured that out," Adams said with a laugh. "The great Valentin Kos, outsmarted by—"

Adams bit off the rest of what he was going to say as all of the lights, screens, and terminals went dark. Muffled shouts came from the soldiers weighed down by their unresponsive armor.

I didn't know how Sawya had managed it, but they had shut down every electrical system on a ship that had been specifically hardened to withstand such attacks. Now Valentin's warning to remove my armor finally made sense because I could move while the armored Quint soldiers were trapped.

I silently started counting the passing seconds. I had sixty of them, and I needed every one because I couldn't see a fucking thing.

I attempted to link Valentin but got nothing but silence in return.

"Get the lights on!" Adams snarled. It sounded like he had remained in place.

I hadn't worn my night-vision contacts and even if I had, I wasn't sure if they would've survived the shutdown. Luckily, our weapons still worked, and plasma pulses came from the door as Valentin shot into the room. His eyes were biologically augmented and allowed him to see in total darkness. Hopefully he was taking out anyone else with the same augments or I'd be very dead, very quickly.

The armored soldiers hadn't moved, and I had a map in my head. I shot blind while I moved toward Adams's last known location. From the shouting, at least some of my shots landed.

Ten seconds.

I'd mentally broken the minute into ten-second intervals and the first one was gone already.

A green glow stick flared bright in the darkness, its chemical reaction unaffected by the outage. I squashed the instinctive urge to look at it. I needed my eyes to stay adjusted for the places where the glow stick's light didn't reach.

"Protect the Commander!" a male voice shouted. He must be the squad commander.

Shadows flickered as the unarmored soldiers moved in the soft green light of the glow stick. With the light, they could see well enough to return fire, but it took them a critical moment to find my new location. I shot two before I had to duck behind cover. Adams had vanished behind a wall of bodies.

The stretchy base layer I wore wouldn't protect me from even a grazing shot, so I needed to be fast and careful—two things that didn't go well together. I darted to the next console while Valentin leaned around the door and shot into the room. His face gleamed in the low light. He'd also dumped his armor, which meant we were both unprotected.

I'd left my grenades and other weapons behind with my armor, so I only had the two pistols I carried. If I needed more ammo, I'd have to steal a gun from one of the other soldiers.

Twenty seconds.

I moved again during a lull in the shooting. I took down another soldier before a plasma pulse clipped the outside of my left arm, deep enough to burn like the fucking sun. I ducked behind the console with a low hiss.

I flexed my left arm. White hot pain flashed down to my elbow, and my hand trembled, but the arm moved, so good enough.

"Secure the exit!" the squad commander yelled. He still had enough soldiers to be problematic, but Adams could not be allowed to escape with the detonator.

While the soldiers concentrated their fire on the door, I dashed to the next console. I wounded two more soldiers, sending them to the ground. Valentin and I had thinned the soldiers enough that I finally caught a glimpse of Adams—and his empty hands.

He no longer held the detonator. Had he dropped it or tucked it into a pocket?

Whatever Sawya had done to suppress the electronics had an expiration date or Valentin wouldn't have told me that we had a sixty-second window. That meant I had just over half a minute to kill Adams and find the detonator.

A pained groan from the hallway almost netted me a plasma pulse to the face. I jerked back at the last second, and the heat seared my cheek. My worry for Valentin would get me killed. I had to trust that he could look after himself, at least for a little while.

Thirty seconds.

I was nearly to where Adams had been standing when I first entered the bridge. Shadows turned the floor into an impenetrable black hole. If he'd dropped the detonator here, I'd have to crawl around until I felt it, leaving Valentin completely on his own. The remaining soldiers would overwhelm him, and Adams would escape while I searched.

The soldiers advanced on the door. A couple of them faced me, trying to keep me pinned down, but the majority focused on Valentin. I had to decide: go after Adams, assuming he still had the detonator, or search here, assuming he'd dropped it?

My gut told me to go after Adams, but I hesitated, torn. Was revenge clouding my judgment?

From everything I knew about Adams, he wouldn't let go of something that might prove useful later. Decision made, I started picking off the soldiers guarding Adams's back from the deep shadow of the console I was using as cover.

The pistol in my right hand was nearly out of ammo and the left wasn't much better. I dropped them both and swiped a compact rifle from one of the Quint soldiers on the ground, then took a deep breath.

I was about to do something stupid, but time wasn't on my side.

Forty seconds.

I broke cover, shooting as I went. Four guards remained. I counted on speed and shock—plus a little help from Valentin— to tilt the odds in my favor.

The next round of shots from the doorway came from both sides of the opening. Since they were hitting Adams's soldiers rather than me, I figured Valentin must've gotten some backup. Trapped between us, the remaining soldiers didn't stand a chance.

In the soft green light from the glow stick, Adams saw his death in my face. He backed away with a sneer. "If you kill me, the other ships will destroy the station. Their deaths will be on your head."

"Where is the detonator?" I demanded.

Luka and Valentin eased into the room, keeping an eye on the soldiers who were injured but alive. Luka looked like he'd survived a bomb blast—and maybe he had. Imogen was not with him.

Adams's eyes narrowed and a sly smile replaced the sneer. "Let me go and I'll tell you."

As much as I wanted him dead, we might need him alive to force the other ships to stand down, so I shot him in the thigh. The round punched straight through the bone, and he fell with a scream.

Fifty seconds.

"Search over there!" I yelled at Valentin. I pointed to where Adams had been when the electronics had died. With his vision augments, Valentin would have a better chance of spotting the detonator in the shadows, anyway.

Mad laughter echoed around the room. "You're going to fail after all of this," Adams taunted from the floor.

I dropped my gun and lunged for him, but even injured, he was strong, likely augmented, and he fought like his life was on the line. I punched him at full strength, snapping his head back. While he was dazed, I patted down his legs. His uniform didn't offer too many hiding places, but the detonator wasn't very big. It would easily slip in a pocket.

I reached for his jacket. The inner pocket was my last hope. A twitch of movement was all the warning I got before his arm flashed up, aiming to slide a blade between my ribs. I deflected the blow at the last second, and he changed direction, burying the knife in my left thigh.

White spots danced in my vision and the world froze for a breathless second.

I slammed the pain aside. The wound wasn't fatal and with his hand occupied, I had free access to his inner coat pocket. My left hand closed on the cylindrical detonator just as my mental timer ran out.

Sixty seconds.

Agony blossomed burning and bright as Adams twisted the knife deeper. I clenched the detonator with grim determination and wrenched it free, though the movement caused fiery pain all down my injured arm.

I confirmed the detonator's safety lever was depressed, but before I could figure out how to disable it entirely, the lights came on, blindingly bright after the soft light from the glow stick.

Valentin shouted something that I couldn't parse. All of my focus centered on keeping the detonator safe, even as shots echoed around the room.

Adams made a triumphant noise and pulled the knife free. A wave of pain threatened to pull me under, but then all of this really would be for nothing. Adams would kill me, and I would let go of the safety lever. I refused to let that happen.

I reacted on instinct, grabbing for his wrist. With only one hand, I was at a disadvantage, but I'd been in far more fights like this than Adams had. When he jerked his arm out of reach, I jabbed his thigh wound. He howled but didn't drop the knife.

He slashed blindly at me. A knife fight was a good way to bleed to death and I was already losing blood at an alarming rate. I needed to end this before he got lucky and hit something that I wouldn't recover from.

I scrambled back on a wave of pain, reaching for the gun I'd dropped. Adams twisted, stretching for a pistol I hadn't seen in the shadows.

Time slowed.

My hand closed on the rifle. It was meant to be fired with a supporting grip, but I lifted it one-handed, my aim steady despite the pain. All of the choices in my life, both terrible and wonderful, had led me to this moment, and I knew, even as Adams lifted the pistol, that he wasn't going to be fast enough.

He was good, but I was better.

With the detonator secure, I squeezed the trigger. Adams slumped back, a round through his head. A heartbeat later, two more rounds followed mine, both in his chest, and I blinked at the gun in my hand.

Had I shot more than once?

It took me far longer than it should've to remember Valentin and Luka. I blinked and Valentin was carefully trying to pry the detonator out of my clenched fingers. Blood smudged his upper lip.

"What are you doing?" I asked.

"I'm worried you're going to pass out. I need to secure this before I can help you."

"Is the station okay?" I asked. My tongue felt heavy in my mouth and it took time to shape the words. "Did I get it in time?"

Valentin nodded, but his mouth compressed into a hard line.

"What aren't you telling me?" I demanded.

"More Quint ships just arrived."

21

I stared at Valentin for a long moment while the words worked their way through my fuzzy brain. "What?" I finally asked, sure I'd misheard. My arm hurt; my thigh hurt. I didn't think I was up for fighting off yet more Quint soldiers. Hell, I wasn't even sure I was up for dragging myself back to an emergency shuttle.

Before Valentin could answer, all of the screens at the front of the ship flickered to life and the intercom squawked as it came on. After a moment, Chairwoman Soteras appeared on screen, dressed in a dark navy suit and pale blue shirt that complemented her light brown skin and dark hair. She looked cool and collected even though she must've been awoken in the middle of the night.

She calmly stared into the camera. "All Quint troops receiving this message are hereby ordered to immediately stand down and prepare to be boarded," she said, her words broadcast over the intercom as well as the speakers. "Those who refuse will be executed as traitors to the Confederacy. Resist or run and my fleet will destroy you. Any further attacks will result in immediate eradication."

"Do you think she knows we're in here?" I asked.

"Sawya is communicating with her. And I also sent her a message, in case Sawya conveniently forgets us."

"You can link from in here?"

Valentin grimaced. "Not very well. I overdid it earlier. We need to move so I can figure out what's happening."

He carefully peeled the detonator from my hand and disabled it. Then he tightly wrapped several layers of tape around the whole thing to keep the safety lever depressed, just in case.

His hands were bloody, and I didn't know if it was his or mine. Neither of us came out unscathed.

Luka reappeared with a first aid kit in hand. He looked like he needed the entire contents for himself. He'd also lost his armor, so he only wore the stretchy base layer, and it was shredded. I could see at least three holes caused by plasma pulses, each of them leaking blood. Blood had also dried on his face and in his hair. I wasn't sure how he was still moving.

"Imogen?" I asked him, my heart in my throat.

"Stella is with her." He swallowed. "Last I heard, she was badly hurt but alive."

Anything that caused Luka to worry had to be bad indeed. I tried to link to Stella, but the room blocked my attempts. How long had it been since Luka had talked to her? Was Imogen still alive?

Bitter worry churned in my stomach. I tried to stand, but Valentin put a hand on my shoulder.

"Stella said to stay put until she gets here. Imogen is in a trauma-doc but stable."

Any injury that needed a trauma-doc was grave, but Stella would do everything in her power to ensure Imogen survived. Imogen was in good hands and bleeding out because I tried to get up and go see her wouldn't help her at all.

The message from Chairwoman Soteras repeated, and I

glanced at the screen. I hadn't realized that it was a recording. "Is Soteras here?"

"Not as far as I can tell," Valentin said. "That looks like her office in Iona."

Valentin carefully sliced away the fabric around the hole in my thigh. The knife had gone in cleanly, but then Adams had wrenched it around, so the wound was deep and ragged. Valentin irrigated it with a sterile solution, then slathered it in renewal gel.

I hissed as he gently stretched an elastomer bandage over the whole thing. The first aid kit was sadly lacking in painkillers, and now that the adrenaline was wearing off, I felt every ache.

"Sorry," he murmured.

I couldn't force any words past my clenched jaw, so I merely nodded.

The sound of booted feet in the hall pulled me from my stupor. We were too exposed here, but I didn't think I'd be able to stand long enough to get my armor on. Still, I could shoot from the ground.

I raised my weapon as Stella shimmered into view, still in her Kos armor. "Samara!"

I lowered the rifle on a wave of relief.

Ari stepped into the doorway and said, "You're supposed to let me clear the room *before* you turn off the camouflage."

Stella waved a hand. "The room is clear."

I could *hear* Ari's eyes rolling, but she didn't argue, she just directed the three soldiers with her to watch the outside corridors. The she swept inside and started checking to see if any of the enemy soldiers still lived. I vaguely remembered shots during my tussle with Adams, so I doubted that she would find any alive, even the ones in armor.

"How is Imogen?" I asked.

Stella opened her visor. "She's stable. A team is evacuating her and the others to the emergency shuttles. Sawya got us clearance to head back to the station, we just had to come get you, first."

"How many did we lose?"

Stella's lips pressed flat and her jaw clenched. "Nine."

Both too many and surprisingly few. "Are the Quint troops still fighting?"

"No," Ari said. "Most of them fell back during the power outage. The rest fled when the announcement started, so whoever Soteras sends in to clean this mess up will have their work cut out for them. They'll have to sweep the ships room by room to find everyone."

Ari finally made it to where Adams had fallen and toed his body. "I think you got him."

I understood the need for gallows humor in this room full of carnage. I still felt disconnected, and I found it hard to believe that he was really dead, even with his body as proof.

Stella apparently decided Valentin was doing a good enough job patching me up, because she turned and started on Luka. He tried to wave her off, but whatever she lacked in height, she made up for in sheer force of will.

"It's easier for everyone if you just give in," I advised him.

He scowled at me. While he was distracted, Stella pulled out her supplies and started cleaning his wounds. He finally sank into a chair with a grumble and let her work.

While Stella worked on Luka, Valentin cleaned and bandaged the wound on my arm and several cuts I hadn't realized I'd gotten. By the time he was done, I felt like I was more bandage than person.

Valentin helped me to my feet. My thigh burned like fire and barely held my weight, but I gritted my teeth against the pain.

"I don't think I can carry my armor," I admitted.

"Leave it," Valentin said.

"But—"

"It's not worth it. I'm sure Soteras already knows about it, and I'll give you a new set."

"What should we do about Adams?" Ari asked.

"Leave him, too," Valentin said. "Let Soteras worry about how we boarded a Quint ship and made it all the way to the bridge to kill the Commander."

"She needs to clean her house," Ari grumbled. "Adams showed up with a dozen ships. Their commanders had to know they were operating off the books, but they all went along with it. Someone high up in Quint had to be helping him."

I nodded. If peace was going to have any chance of success, then both sides needed to stop harboring warmongering traitors. Valentin had put a dent in the ones in his court. It was time Soteras did the same.

With that sobering thought, we left the bloody bridge behind and limped toward the emergency shuttles.

———

DESPITE SOME VALID concerns about our safety, we left *Implacable* on a pair of emergency shuttles and headed back to CP57. Captain Howe was amongst those who hadn't survived, so Major Morley directed his troops as well as her own.

A squadron of Quint fighters escorted us back to the station. Having so many ships around made me nervous, but no one attacked so perhaps our shield worked. Or maybe the traitors were just pretending to comply and biding their time until they could tunnel again.

The ride was somber. We had over a dozen injured soldiers, some of them critical, and a hastily opened emergency blanket covered the bodies of the fallen. It was only thanks to luck that none of my loved ones were under that blanket, but Imogen was gravely injured. She'd taken an explosive blast at close range. The two soldiers in front of her had died instantly.

I stared at her still form. Her chest was encased in the trauma-doc and her face was wrapped in bloody gauze. I willed her to hang on. Stella assured me that she would pull through, but I wouldn't believe it until Imogen opened her eyes and griped at me for leaving her behind.

We docked at Sawya's private berth, and they met us in the hallway outside. The cool perfection of earlier was gone. Sawya's suit was rumpled and their hair looked like they'd run their hands through it nonstop since we'd left.

Sawya greeted Morley first. The two of them spoke softly. I couldn't overhear what was said, but Sawya appeared to be comforting Morley. The major hadn't spoken at all on the flight from *Implacable*. She felt the loss of each of her soldiers, but Captain Howe's death had hit her particularly hard. Morely remained dry-eyed and stone-faced, but anguish was carved into the lines of her body.

Stella left to accompany Imogen to medical. On her way by, she stopped to point at me and Luka. "I expect to see you both within the hour. Don't make me come find you."

I nodded. She'd given me a shot of painkiller, but even so, I doubted I'd be up and moving for more than an hour. I desperately wanted to sit down, but if I did, I might not be able to get back up again.

Luka said nothing, but he stared after the cargo sled carrying Imogen, his jaw clenched. He had vowed to stick with Valentin, but I could see that the decision was costing him.

Sawya broke away from Morley and headed our way. I wasn't anywhere near sharp enough to deal with them right now, but it couldn't be helped.

"Welcome back," they said. "What of Adams?"

"He's dead."

"How?"

"I shot him in the head after he jabbed a knife in my thigh. Did you find the explosives?"

Sawya's mouth turned down at the corners. "Yes. I have teams searching the rest of the station, but I believe we've found them all. They are being disabled as we speak."

"How did someone sneak explosives past you?"

Their expression blanked into an impenetrable mask. "That's something I intend to find out. While I'm not *delighted* that you brought this trouble to my door, I am glad for the chance to clean my house. I knew Adams had some sort of plan for the station, but I didn't realize that I had quite so many rats scurrying around in the dark."

"What about the station? Did it take damage?"

"There were a few minor hits but nothing breached the hull. We lost a few ships, but overall, it could've been far worse."

I blew out a relieved breath, and then raised a questioning eyebrow. "Care to share how you shut down a destroyer?"

Sawya smiled and remained silent.

I chuckled. "Fair enough. However you managed it, I'm grateful. Adams would've absolutely used the detonator, and my soul is bloody enough without thousands more deaths on my head."

"Thank you for stopping him," Sawya said. "I knew he was threatening the station from outside, but I didn't expect an attack from inside as well. If you ever need anything, you know where to find me. Now get to medical before you fall over."

A favor from Sawya was no small thing. I inclined my head in gratitude. "Does it look like Soteras is serious about rounding up the traitors? She wasn't behind Adams's attack?"

"As far as I can tell, she's serious." Sawya sighed. "She knows CP57 isn't big enough to bring the war to her, but we can make life very difficult for her citizens. She preemptively offered recompense and wants to strengthen our peace treaty."

"Will you accept?"

"Eventually," Sawya said with a grin.

I silently wished them luck. Soteras wouldn't be the first

Quint leader to promise peace and then fail to deliver, but so far, she seemed to be sincere. Only time would tell if that trend would hold—and for how long.

"Are the original Quint ships surrendering?" Valentin asked.

"For now," Sawya said. "They are outgunned by the new fleet, and the news of Adams's death is spreading. We'll see what happens when their stardrives recharge."

"I can't fight a fleet of Quint warships," I said, "so I'm going to go spend a few hours in a med chamber. While I'm gone, try to keep the number of emergencies to a minimum, okay? Taking out one megalomaniac a day is my limit."

Sawya's eyes softened. "Rest well. I promise to keep the drama to a minimum for the remainder of the day."

———

LUKA TRIED to fight going into a med chamber, but fighting Stella in medical was like fighting the sea—impossible and exhausting. She was two seconds from sedating him when Ari vowed to watch Valentin until Luka was healed.

Luka finally agreed and all but collapsed into his chamber.

Despite knowing it was futile, I tried to get Stella to slather some more renewal gel on me and call it good. She cocked her head and pointed at the next med chamber, injector brandished like a weapon. The doctor that usually ran this medical unit had given up on helping and just watched her with open-mouthed shock.

I held up my hands. "Fine, fine. Just get me minimally healed, you don't need to worry about the scarring."

"Do I tell you how to do your job?" she growled.

"Yes, as a matter of fact. All the time."

"Get in the med chamber before I forget that I like you," she said with a scowl. "You have until I'm done here, then I'm sedating *you*." She turned to Valentin. "If you want to help, cut off the base layer she's wearing." She handed him a pair of scissors, then closed the privacy curtain around Luka's chamber and disappeared from view.

Valentin helped me up onto the med chamber's bed, then wrapped his arms around me. "I'm so glad you're okay," he murmured. "For a while there…"

He trailed off, but I knew exactly what he meant. There for a while, our survival was pretty iffy.

I hugged him back, even though it made my arm burn. "Same to you. Don't do anything stupid while I'm out. I already made Ari promise to sit on you if you try anything dangerous."

He pulled back. "Does that sound like me?"

"Yes."

He pressed a kiss to my forehead. "I'm going to be here until you're okay, so don't worry about me."

"I will always worry about you," I whispered. "I love you."

A tender smile touched his mouth. "I love you, too." He waggled his eyebrows and held up the scissors. "Now let's get you naked."

22

The next couple of days passed in a blur. Soteras's troops had captured all of the traitor's ships, and then the entire Quint fleet had disappeared as quickly as they'd appeared. Imogen had been released from medical after a day and a half in a med chamber. And true to form, she'd spent ten minutes berating me for leaving her behind. Eddie had returned from Koan with *Ardia*.

And through it all, I barely saw Valentin because he was in constant meetings, both with the leadership of CP57 and with his advisors back home. Even Chairwoman Soteras had reached out for a meeting. I hoped Valentin planned to grill her on how Adams had gotten access to so many Quint ships.

Valentin and I both needed to return home soon, but I kept putting off the conversation because I didn't know when I'd get to see him again. The peace talks were accelerating, which was good news, but it meant he was buried in work.

And sometimes, in the quiet moments, I wondered if Adams truly was dead, or if I'd just tricked myself into believing it. I'd never had this worry after a kill contract, but I'd also never had so much riding on the outcome. When I'd confessed my worry to Ari, she'd sent me a photo she'd taken with her armor's camera.

Adams was completely and irrevocably dead.

I was celebrating that fact with a glass of Valentin's whisky when he surprised me by arriving early. We'd returned to the rooms I'd rented, even though Sawya had offered to put us up in their tower in Block 1.

We'd politely declined. At least here we had *some* illusion of privacy.

"Everything okay?" I asked when Valentin sank onto the sofa next to me.

He sighed and poured himself a splash of whisky. "I have to return to Koan."

I knew it was bound to happen soon, but hearing it still stole my breath. I sipped my drink and gathered my thoughts.

He turned and met my eyes. Quietly, he said, "Come with me."

I wanted to. I wanted to *so much*. But I had my own responsibilities. And while they were not as vast as his, they were no less important. I shook my head. "I can't. I've been away from Arx for too long already. I need to check in, especially because the most trusted members of my advisory council are here with me."

He sighed again, deeply. "I was afraid you'd say that, but I selfishly hoped I was wrong."

"Before, you said you'd be willing to discuss splitting our time between Arx and Koan. Is that still something you'd consider?"

"Yes, but with the treaty negotiations starting in earnest, I need to spend the majority of my time in Koan, and that's not fair to you. Maybe we could spend our weekends together and swap cities every weekend until things quiet down. I know it's not ideal, but—"

I set my glass aside and pressed my lips to his. He groaned

and pulled me closer. The slide of his tongue against mine sent shivers all the way to my toes. I lost myself in the simple pleasure of kissing.

By the time he pulled back, we were both breathing hard.

"We will make it work," I said. "We each have things that need to be taken care of, so weekends are a good place to start. And it's only a single tunnel transit between the two cities. If we spend a night together here or there, no one will be the wiser."

His eyes lit, and he wrapped an arm around me and pulled me close. "I do enjoy the way your brain works."

"And then, once the war is over, we can make some more permanent decisions, if I'm still queen."

"What do you mean?" he demanded. "Why wouldn't you be?"

I smiled softly at his outrage. "While I'll always try to put the Rogue Coalition first, I'm no longer impartial. My people made me queen, and they deserve to know what's going on. I'm going to hold a vote to see if they want to appoint a new leader."

He looked at me in shock. "You would step aside?"

"I would. It would hurt, and I would feel a little lost afterwards, but my people have been through enough. I don't want to add to their hurt. I would do my best to steer them toward a good successor, but ultimately, the decision is up to them."

"What do you think they'll do?"

I shook my head. "I don't know." I dropped my eyes and asked the question I secretly worried about. "Will you be disappointed if I'm no longer a queen?"

Valentin thought about his answer for a long moment. "I would be disappointed for you," he said at last, "because you enjoy it and you're good at it. Otherwise, I could not care less. I love *you,* not your title. And, selfishly, it would be far easier for us to be together if you *weren't* queen, but I will never ask you to give up something you love just to make my life easier."

His expression turned wistful and haunted. "Sometimes I wish that Father hadn't altered the succession," he admitted. "I know it's awful of me, because the war would likely continue under Nikolas's rule, but part of me still wishes I could walk away. So, no, I won't mind if you aren't a queen."

"You wouldn't walk away if you people still needed you," I murmured.

He sighed. "No, I wouldn't, which is why I'd never ask you to give up being queen."

"You say the nicest things," I murmured. "When do you need to leave?"

"Soon. The ship arrived this morning, so it's ready to go."

"Then you probably need to pack. I'll help. Let's start in our bedroom."

"I already—" He bit off the rest of what he was going to say when he caught my significant look. "Yes," he amended hastily, "that is an excellent idea."

I laughed. "I thought you'd see it that way."

———

VALENTIN STOOD at the door of his ship's docking tunnel. It wasn't his personal ship because he didn't trust anyone else to fly *Korax*. This ship was small and sleek, designed to ferry passengers with limited cargo between systems. It was berthed next to *Ardia*.

Luka stood next to the hatch, conversing quietly with Imogen.

Valentin lingered, and I let him because I didn't want him to go any more than he did. Once he disappeared into the ship, I likely wouldn't see him in person for almost a week. Maybe more if some new disaster befell either of us—which, with the way things had gone recently, wasn't beyond the realm of possibility.

"I'm going to miss you," he whispered. "I'll visit you this weekend."

My heart twisted. I'd expected it to be difficult, but I hadn't expected it to be *this* difficult. Every cell shouted that I shouldn't let him go. "I'll look forward to it. Get the treaty hammered out while Soteras is willing to talk because I'll be a wreck if we have to keep doing this for a year."

Valentin chuckled without humor. "You and me both."

I kissed him, slow and deep, focusing on the pleasure and not the coming pain. When I reluctantly drew away, Valentin's hands clenched against my back before he released me. "I'll see you soon," I vowed.

He swallowed and nodded wordlessly, then turned and entered the docking tunnel with Luka without a backward glance. I understood. I pivoted away before I had to watch him disappear. It wasn't forever, but it still hurt.

Ari watched me with a sympathetic expression. "Ready to go?"

"No," I admitted, "but I suppose it's time anyway." We'd already packed everything on our ships, and Ari had sent her Rogue Coalition ship back to Arx ahead of us. She, Stella, and Imogen would ride along with me in *Ardia*. Eddie was waiting for us to launch, then he, too, would return to Arx in his ship.

I hadn't told any of them that I planned to let the people vote on my future. I needed to let at least Ari and Stella know before I approached the entire council. Their reaction would guide my path forward.

Imogen bumped her shoulder against mine. "The weekend isn't so far away," she said gently.

Ari's mouth curved into a teasing grin. "Are you hoping that a scowling, ice-capped mountain shows up along with the emperor?"

Imogen didn't even try to hide her smile as she dipped her chin in agreement.

"How do you handle it?" I asked her.

She shrugged. "My family is in the transport business, and

then I joined the military, so I'm used to people I care about coming and going. You make the most of your time together, and while the partings are painful, they make the homecomings sweeter. And Koan and Arx aren't exactly that far apart. If you get lonely, you can just pop over for dinner."

Ari narrowed her eyes. "And why do I get the feeling that you'll happily volunteer to accompany our queen on these hypothetical little jaunts?"

Imogen gave an exaggerated sigh. "If I must, then I must."

We all broke into laughter and some of my sadness melted away. It was likely their plan all along, but I didn't begrudge them. I was lucky to have such good friends.

"Thank you," I murmured. Then I turned toward *Ardia's* docking tunnel. "Let's go before Stella decides to rearrange medical on my brand-new ship."

Ari laughed. "It might be too late."

We boarded the ship—with medical still in one piece, thankfully—and headed to the bridge. Ari and Stella, who'd only caught a glimpse while on our way to *Implacable,* whistled in appreciation. "You weren't kidding about this ship being nice," Ari said. "You need to lock the emperor *down.*"

"About that," I said, then stalled out.

Stella raised her eyebrows. "Do you have something to share with the class?"

"Valentin and I are going to try to make a relationship work."

All three of them rolled their eyes. "I hate to break it to you," Stella said drily, "but that's not exactly news."

"I'm going to hold a referendum to see if the people want to appoint a new leader."

Stunned silence fell.

Imogen recovered first. "What?"

"The Rogue Coalition doesn't get a say in my relationship, but they *do* get a say in who leads them. I will understand if my relationship with a foreign sovereign makes people uneasy."

"You'll be wasting your time," Ari said. "No one will ask you to leave."

"You're hardly an impartial judge," I said with a gentle smile.

"Are you going to sell us out to Kos or Quint?" she persisted. When I shook my head, she nodded. "Hold the vote, if it'll make you feel better, but don't be surprised when the outcome is wildly in your favor."

"Once the war is over, Valentin and I plan to split time between Koan and Arx. The people deserve someone who can devote all of their time to the job." I looked at the three of them. "I don't suppose..."

"Not even for all of the chocolate in the universe," Stella muttered. Ari and Imogen silently agreed.

That was the problem. Most of the people who wanted the job shouldn't have it, and the perfect candidates didn't want it at all. I hadn't really wanted it, either, but my rusty conscience had groaned to life, and the responsibility slowly fell on my shoulders. Still, I'd fucked it up plenty in the early days.

"Think about it," I said as I slid into the captain's chair. "I'd feel better about stepping aside if I knew that I was leaving our people in good hands."

"You will be," Ari said. "Yours."

23

Arx had weathered my absence with barely a ripple. My entire council, including the three elected officials, had agreed with Ari that a vote was unnecessary, but I pushed for one anyway. I wanted the people to have their voices heard.

The referendum was just to see if people wanted a new leader—selecting that leader would come later. Because it was a single-issue vote and all of my citizens could vote remotely from wherever they were, the date was set for two weeks after we returned from CP57.

I recorded a video stating my case: I was in a relationship with Valentin Kos, which impacted my impartiality. Once the war was over, I planned to split time between Arx and Koan. I would always put the Rogue Coalition first, but I would understand if people wanted new leadership. If a simple majority passed the referendum, then I would start the process of electing a new leader.

Never mind that the Rogue Coalition was young enough that electing someone new had never been done before.

I asked Valentin's permission before making our relationship public, and he enthusiastically agreed. That should've made me suspicious, but I was just glad to be able to release the video and call it done.

For two weeks, I was headline news in both the Rogue Coalition *and* the Kos Empire, much to my embarrassment and Valentin's eternal delight.

He and I were starting to get the hang of a long-distance relationship. The first weekend, he came to Arx, and then I joined him in Koan for the second. It wasn't ideal, but we made it work—especially because we'd each snuck over for a mid-week dinner and sleepover during the week.

But today was election day, and it wasn't anywhere near a weekend. I missed Valentin. We'd chatted earlier, and I'd assured him that I was fine.

I'd lied.

I had blocked myself from checking the results, which were tallied in real-time but weren't released to the public until after the voting day closed. Instead, I stalked through Arx, trying to keep my mind off the vote—and thinking about nothing else. Everyone gave me a wide berth, and I couldn't decide if it was because they were guilty about voting me out or because I couldn't stop scowling. Maybe both.

Ari found me prowling through the dark half of the market. The market had grown on the former base's parade grounds, and it was the largest gathering space we had. Panels overhead mimicked the sky, but we only kept the front half on because we didn't need the whole space.

In the lit half, a few solid buildings—like the bakery—had sprung up, but most of the smaller stalls leaned against one another, built with whatever materials the builder could scavenge. The narrow pathways in the unlit half let me prowl around without feeling like I was under a microscope.

"Hiding?" Ari asked with a smile.

My scowl bounced right off her, so I kept walking.

She fell into step beside me. "Do you want to know how you're doing?"

I sighed. "Do you think I'd be hiding if I wanted to know?"

"You're worrying for nothing. Election day is half over and nearly three-quarters of people have already voted. Unless every future vote is in favor of changing leadership, you're easily in the clear."

That didn't bring the relief I thought it would. My feelings were a jumble, but I couldn't help but ask, "Is it close?"

"No. If the current ratio continues, you'll coast through with over 80 percent approval. People are happy, and it's thanks to you. They trust you to look out for them."

My brain, being how it was, immediately jumped to the 20 percent who were *un*happy.

Ari glanced at me. "Nope," she said with a pointed look. "You're not going to focus on negatives. You're winning by a landslide."

She knew me too well.

"I thought I'd be relieved, and I am, but I'm also…" I trailed off. I wasn't sure *what* I was, exactly.

"Disappointed?" Ari asked gently.

I stopped walking and sighed. "Something like that. And worried. Being queen makes it harder for Valentin and me to be together, but I care about all of the Rogue Coalition's citizens, and don't want to leave. It's a mess."

"You'll figure it out." She waved a hand. "And if worse comes to worst, make some imperial proclamations or something."

I grinned. "I see. You just want me to be murdered in my sleep by Valentin's angry citizens."

"A few assassination attempts will only spice things up," she said with an exaggerated wink.

I broke into laughter, as she'd intended, and it was exactly what I'd needed. "Thank you," I said when I could talk again.

Her smile was kind. "Someone has to look after you. Speaking of, where's Valentin?"

"He had a lot of important meetings today. It seems like now that Adams is out of the picture, Chairwoman Soteras is moving forward with negotiations. Or maybe she captured more traitors than I thought at CP57. Either way, I assured Valentin that I was fine and told him not to come."

"He believed you?" she asked, her eyebrows high.

I shrugged and started walking again. "He didn't *not* believe me."

"You're a terrible liar," Valentin said from behind me. "I definitely did not believe you."

I whirled around. He was wearing a dark suit that complemented his coloring. I wanted nothing more than to throw myself into his arms. Instead, I demanded, "How do you *do* that? I should've been able to hear you."

He grinned. "I'm sneaky. And I had a little help to keep you distracted."

I pivoted back and pointed at Ari accusingly. "I thought you didn't like it when he just showed up."

Valentin wrapped his arms around me from behind and pressed a kiss to my hair. "I went through all the proper channels this time, and Ari was kind enough to allow me to land in the main hangar."

Ari smiled. "I figured you could use the company today. Now stop scowling at everyone." With that parting shot, she raised her arm in farewell and disappeared into the maze of walkways.

I turned to face Valentin, still within the circle of his arms. "How did you even find me in here, anyway?"

"Ari, of course." He made a vague gesture. "Luka and Imogen are lurking around somewhere, too."

I wrapped my arms around him and squeezed him tight. "Thank you for coming."

"You're welcome," he said softly. He stroked his fingers over my jaw. "But next time, just tell me the truth. Meetings can be rescheduled, or I can take them remotely. I want to be here for you when you need me." He pressed his fingers against my lips when I would've argued. "Just as I hope you'll be there for me when I need *you*."

"I will be," I promised. "Now kiss me and tell me you're happy to see me."

His eyes sparkled as he slowly lowered his head toward mine. "I'm happy to see you, Samara." He kissed the very tip of my nose and pulled back with a playful grin.

I sniffed. "I suppose if that's the best you can do, I'll accept it."

He tipped my chin up and his lips covered mine, slowly, thoroughly. Desire blazed bright and fierce, and I forgot about the election. I forgot about Luka and Imogen. I very nearly forgot my own name.

The kisses blended into each other so that I didn't know how long we'd been locked together, but I wasn't complaining. He gave me one last, lingering kiss, then pulled back and rested his head against mine. "I am delighted to see you, my love," he whispered.

I shivered as the endearment washed over me.

"You, too," I murmured.

Valentin squeezed me one last time, then stepped back and linked his fingers through mine. "What do you want to do today? My afternoon is clear." He looked around with interest, like he hadn't just kissed the hell out of me. "Did you build this?"

I ordered my rioting pulse under control and attempted to string two thoughts together.

"No, this part of the market was here before us," I said. "We don't have enough people to need it. But I like to come here when I need to walk and don't want to be bothered." I glanced down at his shiny shoes. "Are you okay to walk in those?"

When he nodded, I started walking and pulled him along with me, hand in hand. I was heading for my suite, but I planned to take the long way. Anticipation made the payoff sweeter.

"How are the negotiations going?" I asked.

"Soteras has agreed to an in-person meeting on CP57 early next month."

I turned to him, mouth open. "That's huge! Why didn't you tell me?"

"Because we only got all of the details confirmed this morning. It's been something of a nightmare to get everyone on the same schedule."

"Why do you think she's so friendly all of a sudden?" I asked. "Is it a trick?"

Valentin shrugged. "Maybe. But killing Adams also sent a pretty clear message. Now that all of my advisors actually want peace and Quint has lost a host of traitors of their own, maybe we'll make true progress."

I hoped so. I wasn't sure I could get to someone as protected as Soteras, but if she hurt Valentin, I'd do my damnedest to make her life miserable.

VALENTIN and I spent a delightful afternoon in my suite until hunger drove us to the mess hall. Eddie took one look at Valentin's suit and whistled. He slanted a sly glance at me. "You should've told me you had big plans tonight, boss. Are you celebrating your win?"

"How do you know I'm winning? Maybe I'm celebrating my upcoming freedom from you lot."

Eddie grinned. "In that case, take me with you. I could be a fancy palace chef."

"I'm afraid you might be stuck here with me," I said. "I

blocked myself from checking the results before the end of the day, but Ari is a blabbermouth."

"She probably didn't want you to worry," Eddie said. "You're the only one who thought you might lose." He shook his head, but it didn't take long for his grin to reappear. "You want dinner to go?"

"Yes, please. And servings for Imogen and Luka, too."

Eddie dished up four servings in reusable to-go containers. "As much as it pains me to admit it," he said, "you might want to visit Zita later. She was cooking up something special for your victory celebration. She'll be hurt if you disappear for the night."

"I'll have Ari spread the word that I'm planning to emerge after the results are public. Until then, I'm going to go back and hide in my suite. Don't burn the place down."

Eddie sent us off with a wave. Imogen and Luka stayed in the public rooms on the ground floor while Valentin and I retreated back upstairs. We still had three hours until the voting window closed, and restless energy pulsed under my skin.

I led Valentin to the small table near the kitchenette. He set out the food while I poured us drinks, and I was reminded of our dinner in the guest suite. So much had happened since then that it was hard to remember that it was only a month ago.

"What's on your mind?" Valentin asked.

"I'm just thinking about how much has changed in the past month and wondering where we'll be a month from now."

Valentin pulled out my chair, and I slid into the seat. He sat across from me and smiled. "I did promise you a vacation in a remote fortress, and I intend to make good on it. After I meet with Soteras, I'd like to have you to myself for a week or two."

"I'd like that, too," I agreed. "And the timing should work for me."

We turned our attention to the food. Eddie had prepared a creamy chicken and vegetable pasta that was delicious. He really would make a fine palace chef, and I dreaded the day he decided his skills were wasted here.

After dinner, Valentin and I snuggled on the sofa and watched a vid. While my desire for him hadn't waned, it was nice to just spend time together and hang out, especially when I was already wound.

Cuddling had loosened some of my tension but as the hour grew later, it came back with a vengeance. At a quarter to nine, I climbed to my feet and pulled Valentin up with me.

"Results come out in fifteen minutes. I need to head to the market."

"Have you checked on how it's going?"

I sighed. "Not yet." But I couldn't hide any longer. I went through the authentication process and accessed the real-time results.

The referendum had failed. I was still queen.

I blew out a slow breath.

"Is that a good sound or a bad one?" Valentin asked, his tone uncertain.

"I will remain queen. The margin is wide enough that I can't lose at this point."

"That's... good, right?" he asked with a frown.

I gave him a hug. I was confusing him, but I was confused myself.

"Yeah, it's good," I said. "I *want* to remain queen. I want to help my people. But not having the responsibility would've made our relationship easier."

"Since when do we like easy?" He pulled me close. "First and foremost, I want you to be happy. And looking after your people makes you happy. We'll make the rest of it work."

I brushed my lips against his. "Thank you."

———

THE MARKET WAS full of people by the time we arrived. Luka cleared a path while Imogen watched our back. I didn't really think the precautions were necessary, but neither had budged. I had a feeling that this was going to be my new normal.

Worse, I was going to have to get *another* guard just so Imogen and Luka could spend some time together off the clock. Imogen had refused to even consider my offer to find another primary bodyguard, but she couldn't complain about me adding an additional guard.

I made a mental note to talk to Valentin because he would need another guard, too. Then we really would have an entourage. My days of slipping through crowds unnoticed were behind me now that my face had been plastered all over the news in two systems.

At least no one had figured out my past, yet. Only a handful of people knew my face from my days as the Golden Dahlia, and they were smart enough not to blab about it.

We finally made it to the bakery and Zita beamed at us. Her smile was infectious. Even Luka unbent enough to put his scowl away and dip his head at her.

"You're just in time," she said. She waved us to a large table draped with a white tablecloth. Stella and Ari waited nearby, and two covered objects rested on the table, one flat and rectangular, one tall and cylindrical. I guessed the flat one was a cake or other dessert, but I wasn't sure about the cylinder.

Overhead, the ceiling panels twinkled with stars. There were no vid screens for the news, but we really didn't need them. Everyone was linked into the net and could get the results as soon as they were public.

The space quieted as the clock ticked over the hour. It took a few seconds, then a cheer started as the results became available. Zita, who always had a flair for the dramatic, whisked the covers off the objects on the table.

As expected, the flat one was a cake, exquisitely decorated

and with *Congratulations Queen Rani!* written in a beautiful script. The cylinder was a cupcake tower, with each cupcake decorated with a tiny, delicate crown.

Another cheer rose at the sight.

"Long live Queen Rani!" Zita shouted.

"Love live the Queen!" the crowd shouted back.

Zita's assistants moved through the crowd with additional trays of cupcakes, each one perfectly decorated. Even with help, this had to have taken Zita *hours*. Tears stung my eyes at her confidence in me.

I pulled her into a tight hug, and she fondly patted my back. "Thank you for this," I said.

She leaned back and smiled at me. "Thank you for looking out for us and keeping all of these rascals in line. Now, do you want to cut the cake?"

"And ruin your beautiful creation?" I shook my head. "No way."

Her smile grew. "It was meant to be eaten. And it has a layer of strawberry jam in the middle."

"Give me the knife," I demanded.

She handed it over with a laugh. I sliced the cake into generous servings and handed the first piece to Valentin. He dipped his head and kissed me, much to the crowd's delight. I also cut pieces for Zita, Ari, Stella, and the rest of my council. When Eddie sidled up, I slipped him a piece, too.

After his first bite, Eddie growled, "How is this so good? What is her secret?"

Zita heard him and laughed. "It's experience. When you get to be my age, you'll be even better than this."

I picked up my piece and took a bite. The frosting was sweet without being overpowering, the cake was light and moist, and the jam layer was a bright burst of sweet and tart. It combined into a whole that was even better than the parts.

"If there's cake better than this, I've never had it," I told her honestly.

Zita waved a modest hand, but her smile glowed like the sun.

When the cupcakes were consumed, people started breaking out instruments and drinks. The celebration turned into a party. Stella led Ari to the dance floor. Malcolm Peters—a soldier in his fifties with ebony skin, close-cropped gray hair, and a gorgeous smile—coaxed a blushing Zita into a dance.

Valentin turned and offered his hand. "May I have this dance, my queen?"

I slipped my hand into his. "You may, your majesty."

Valentin led me to the dance floor and pulled me close. I wrapped my arms around him and we swayed to the music.

"Thank you for coming," I whispered.

"You are welcome. I'll always be there when you need me," he vowed.

It was no wonder I fell in love with him when he said such sweet things. I pulled his lips down to mine. I ignored the delighted hoots around us and focused on showing him just how much I appreciated his care.

His hands tensed against my back and he groaned low in his throat. When I pulled back, he touched his forehead to mine. "I love you," he whispered.

I couldn't help the smile that curved my mouth. I would never get tired of hearing the words. "I love you, too."

We stayed on the edge of the crowd to make our guards' jobs easier, but we danced and laughed and pretended the rest of the world didn't exist for a few hours.

On the way back to my suite, I checked the final results. The referendum had failed by 80.1 percent. The people had resoundingly spoken.

And I remained Queen Samara Rani.

24

Just over four weeks after the election that had secured my future, I met Valentin on CP57. He had three days of meetings with the Quint Confederacy Chairwoman planned, but I wanted to be around just in case anything went wrong. And afterwards, he'd promised me a vacation.

We docked close to Block 1 because Sawya had insisted that their tower was the perfect meeting location. All objections were neatly resolved, sidestepped, or ignored. Sawya wanted the universe's two most powerful leaders close at hand and was willing to go to some lengths to make it happen.

Valentin's suite took up half a floor in Sawya's tower. The imperial advisors and security detail took up the other half of the floor, but I was not surprised when Luka opened Valentin's door.

Luka's eyes flickered over me, rested briefly on Imogen, and then stayed locked on the second guard I'd brought.

"Luka, meet Marian Sola," I said with a wave. "Marian, meet Luka Fox, Valentin's bodyguard."

Marian was a fit woman in her late twenties with tan skin,

hazel eyes, and light brown hair. She had been a mercenary for almost a decade before ending up in Arx. Despite their different backgrounds, she and Imogen got along well, and when I'd asked Imogen for her opinion, she'd enthusiastically agreed that Marian would make an excellent guard.

Luka didn't move. Marian held his stare without flinching, but the longer he stared, the higher one of her eyebrows climbed.

After a long moment, she turned to Imogen, completely dismissing Luka. "*This* is who you were talking about?" she asked, her skepticism clear.

Luka's eyes narrowed.

If I didn't head off this pissing contest, we'd be stuck in the hall all day. "I know she's approved, Luka, because I gave her information to Valentin a week ago. Let us in."

He begrudgingly stepped back and waved us in. Marian had a silent conversation with Imogen then swept in ahead of us. Imogen smiled at Luka, and, much to my amazement, he returned the gesture.

I stepped past him to give them a few moments of privacy.

Valentin and another man waited in the expansive living room. Valentin crossed the room and pulled me into an embrace. "I've missed you," he growled softly.

"I saw you two days ago," I said with a smile. "But I've missed you, too."

We went through the introductions again, this time including Valentin's second guard, Charles Reade.

Where Luka was huge and solid, Charles was lithe and flexible, with golden tan skin, dark eyes, and black hair. And, unlike Luka, he knew how to smile and charm. But his eyes remained alert and serious even as he laughed and teased. I had a feeling that, like Imogen, his facade hid just how capable he was.

"What is your plan for the evening?" I asked Valentin.

"I'm all yours until tomorrow morning."

"Cook me dinner?" I asked. "I'll keep you company then do the dishes."

A soft, lovely smile bloomed on his face. "I would love that."

———

THE TALKS WENT AS WELL AS COULD be expected for initial talks, which is to say that everyone left frustrated and feeling cheated. Despite that, Valentin assured me that some true progress had been made. Now both sides would return to their respective territories and continue to hash out the agreement.

Valentin assured me that his advisors had plenty to do and could survive without him for a week, so we sent off his envoy and headed to *Ardia* to start our week-long vacation—with all four shadows in tow. Valentin hadn't told me where his remote fortress was, but he'd cleared it with Ari and assured me that we'd only be a single tunnel transit from both Koan and Arx.

I slid into the captain's chair. "Where are we headed?"

Valentin slid into the navigator's chair with a smile. "Get us away from CP57, and I'll plot the course, if you don't mind."

"You know I'm going to peek as soon as you lock it in, right?"

His smile edged into a grin. "I had no doubt," he assured me.

By the time I'd maneuvered *Ardia* away from CP57, Valentin had locked in our route. True to my word, I checked where we were headed. It didn't surprise me that it was in the Kos Empire, but it *did* surprise me that we appeared to be heading to Achentsev Prime. "You're taking me to Koan? Your palace is nice, and I'll even give you fortress, but it's not exactly *remote*."

He laughed. "It's a big planet. Have a little faith." His expression turned serious. "It's also the best-protected planet in the system," he said. "Just in case Quint gets any ideas about negotiating a different way."

"Do you think it's a concern?" I asked with a frown.

"No, but I'd like to have an ironclad peace agreement in place before I take you somewhere truly remote. This will do for now."

Honestly, I didn't care *where* we went, I was just happy that I would get to spend a week with Valentin. "Works for me."

I confirmed the jump and *Ardia* slid through space with barely a shiver. Achentsev Prime appeared on screen, but rather than heading for Koan, we headed for the other side of the planet. *Ardia* dropped through the atmosphere toward what at first glance appeared to be open ocean covered in wispy clouds.

As we got closer, an island surrounded by sparkling blue-green seas came into view. Valentin communicated with ground control and the roof of a camouflaged hangar slid open. A minute later, *Ardia* settled into the hangar with a gentle *thump*. A pair of small, suborbital ships used to move around on-planet were already inside.

I turned to Valentin. "Do you own *an island?*"

He rubbed the back of his neck. "Kind of. It belongs to the emperor."

"Is anyone else here?"

"I dismissed the house staff for the week, but a security detail will remain. They have their own quarters." He stood and helped me up. He kept me close as he murmured, "And we're almost two thousand kilometers from anyone else. Is that remote enough for you, my queen?"

I pretended to think about it. "I suppose it will do."

Valentin smiled and led me out of the ship. Our shadows fell in behind us. I hoped they figured out their shifts soon because I felt ridiculous with four people following us around. Hell, I felt ridiculous with just *one* person, but at least I'd had a little while to get used to it.

The plain hangar door did not prepare me for the tropical paradise waiting on the other side. Tall palm trees, white sand, and water as blue as the sky made quite the impression. A path led deeper into the vegetation, but I couldn't see the house from here.

All I could hear was birdsong and the crash of waves. Something tight inside me began to unclench.

"Welcome to Nova Island," Valentin said softly.

Everywhere I looked, some new delight waited. I couldn't remember the last time I'd been to a beach. "It's beautiful."

Valentin linked his fingers through mine. "Wait until you see the rest."

THE HOUSE WAS FAR MORE UNDERSTATED than I'd expected after seeing the palace. Long and low, it was built into the side of a natural rise and had incredible views of the ocean from three sides. The kitchen, dining room, and living room were all one space that stretched across the front of the house, and an expansive wall of glass made it feel like you could reach out and touch the sand and sky.

Despite some grumbles, we managed to persuade our guards to stay in bedrooms on the other side of the house, so Valentin and I were surrounded by nothing but quiet as we unpacked the few clothes we'd brought. Our bedroom was furnished with simple wooden furniture and painted a gentle blue that mimicked the sea.

"Do you like it?" Valentin asked, pulling me into his arms.

"I love it. It's perfect." I kissed him, then leaned back and raised a finger as Imogen linked me.

Marian and Charles are taking the first shift, she said. *But Luka and I will be nearby if you need anything.*

I agreed to bring more people specifically so you and Luka could spend some time together off the clock. Enjoy yourself.

I'm planning to. Luka is going to cook me dinner. But we'll still be nearby if you need us. She ended the link before I could argue, proving she knew me well.

I lowered my finger and tapped it against Valentin's chest. "Marian and Charles are taking the first shift," I told him. "And I don't know if Imogen and Luka can stop working long enough to enjoy themselves even with the extra help, but at least he's cooking her dinner."

"Give them a few days. The lure of the sea will work on them eventually. Speaking of… care for a swim?"

"You just want to see me in a swimsuit," I teased.

He pressed a quick kiss to my lips. "Guilty as charged," he murmured.

I slid open the top button of his shirt. We'd left CP57 directly after a day of meetings, so while he'd lost his jacket and tie, he was still deliciously buttoned up—and I wanted nothing more than to muss his perfection.

Desire blazed as I walked my fingers down to the next button and glanced up at him from under my lashes. "Swimming *does* sound nice," I agreed slowly. "But what if I had a different plan for this…" I trailed off when I realized I had no idea what the local time was, but the sun was high in the sky.

"This afternoon, I suppose," I finished with a laugh. "So much for my sexy seduction. My body has no idea what time it is." We'd left the station around six, which was midnight in Arx. But it was barely noon here. It would take a while to adjust.

Valentin captured my hand. "Tell me more about this seduction," he demanded with a wicked grin.

"Well, I intend to rumple you. *Thoroughly.*" I slid the button free with his hand still on mine. "And if you're very good, I might even let you see me naked."

He made a low sound deep in his chest and dipped his head. His lips covered mine with intent focus and proved that I wasn't the only one who could be thorough. I licked his lip and he opened with a groan.

I would never tire of kissing this man.

I buried my fingers in the soft hair at the back of his head as his tongue slid against mine. The world disappeared until it was just him and me and heat and desire. At some point his hand found its way under my shirt and he stroked his thumb over my nipple. I moaned and arched into the touch.

It took me longer than it should've to remember that *I* was supposed to be seducing *him*.

I pulled back enough to work the buttons of his shirt free. He wasn't wearing an undershirt, so each new button revealed a hint of golden tan skin stretched tight over solid muscle. Once his shirt was unbuttoned, he moved to shrug it off, but I stopped him. "Leave it."

I pressed a kiss to his chest and stroked my hand lower, cupping him through his pants. He was hot and hard in my hand. He rocked into my grip, and I held onto my control by a thread. Desire pulsed through my veins and my muscles clenched in expectation of the pleasure to come.

When I pushed him back toward the bed without removing any more clothes, his eyebrows rose, but he did as I asked. His shirt had parted, revealing a flat chest and defined abs, but he still wore his pants and even his shoes. Having him sprawled out for my pleasure was the stuff of dreams, but he wasn't rumpled enough. Not yet.

I crawled onto the bed and popped the button free on his waistband, then carefully lowered the zipper. I pushed his pants and underwear down just enough to free his length.

He watched me with predatory focus, his hands clenched in the bedding. When I did nothing but look at him, he groaned and lifted his hips. "Touch me," he demanded, voice rough.

"Oh, I will. I'm just admiring my work first." Then I took pity on him.

I licked up the underside of his length before pulling him deep into my mouth. He bit out a filthy curse as I applied myself to the task with enthusiasm. Every twitch and groan drove my desire higher, and I wanted nothing more than to shove him over the cliff half-dressed and crazed with lust.

He buried his hands in my hair, seemingly unable to help himself as he alternatively cursed and praised me. He tried to get me to stop—as if that was going to happen—and when I hummed my disagreement against his flesh, that's all it took. His back arched and he lost himself in pleasure.

It was the hottest thing I'd ever seen and my muscles clenched, so close.

I watched his awareness return through the haze of pleasure. His gaze pinned me in place. "Strip, now, unless you don't like those clothes," he demanded.

I quickly shed my clothes and by the time I was done, Valentin had lost the last of his clothes, too. "My turn," he said with a wicked grin.

He smacked my ass when I crawled onto the bed and I shivered. His thoughtful look promised all sorts of fun for later, but for now, he spread me out like dessert and licked every part of me starting from my neck. By the time he made it to where I pulsed and throbbed, I was a mass of raw nerves.

"Valentin," I demanded.

His smile was full of love and heat as his slowly, so slowly, lowered his face. I lifted my hips, offering myself. He reached his destination and thrust two fingers deep just as his clever tongue landed exactly where I needed it.

Pleasure exploded into a thousand sparkling stars.

I had barely caught my breath when he was there, hot and hard. At my nod, he sank home and we both cursed and groaned. I didn't know if someone could die from pleasure alone, but Valentin seemed determined to test the theory and I was an extremely willing subject.

He sat back, holding my hips and driving into me with long, leisurely thrusts. When I reached between us to touch myself, his hands clenched and he jerked sharply, his rhythm faltering.

A glance at his face revealed he'd closed his eyes.

"Is this okay?" I asked, concerned.

"Fuck, yes," he groaned. "More than okay. Just give me a second or I'm going to…"

I smiled as I realized what the problem was. I was already close. "If I keep doing this, you won't be the only one who's 'going to,'" I murmured. "Maybe we should help each other out."

His eyes met mine and blazed as bright as the sun. "Yes," he demanded. "Now."

The words, the touch, and the sharp thrust of his hips was enough. I detonated and took him with me. We fell into bliss together.

————

WE DID, eventually, make it to the beach. The water was warm and clear, full of colorful little fish. Valentin and I splashed and swam while Marian and Charles stayed on shore, protected from the sun by an open-sided cabana.

When we got tired of swimming, we napped in a hammock under the trees while the ocean breeze kept the heat tolerable.

Later, Valentin cooked me dinner while I kept him company. Then he kept me company while I cleaned the kitchen.

I could not have asked for a more perfect day.

Now we sat snuggled together on an outdoor loveseat, watching the ocean swallow the sun. "I wish we could stay here forever," I breathed.

"Someday we'll be able to," Valentin said. "Until then, we'll just have to hide away every now and then."

I smiled. "While I appreciate the thought, I don't think your advisors are going to be happy to commute to an island in the middle of nowhere."

Valentin remained quiet for a long beat. "I'm thinking about implementing an elected parliament," he said at last. "If I give more power to the people, they'll only need me for special occasions."

I turned to him in stunned disbelief. "Can you *do* that?"

His grin was quick and sly. "I don't see why not. I *am* the emperor, after all. What use is all this power if I can't shake things up?"

"It's a good thing you have me," I murmured, "because your advisors really are going to kill you." I patted his leg. "I promise I'll keep you safe."

"Will you still love me if I'm an emperor in name only?" he asked. His tone was light, but the question was serious.

"Will I still love you if I get even more of your time for myself?" I tapped a finger on my chin, as if I really had to give it some thought. "I suppose I can make that work." I paused, then met his eyes. "To be clear, I love *you,* not your title. And I think an elected parliament is an excellent idea."

"It will take time," he warned. "We'll still have to jump back and forth between Arx and Koan."

"That's fine," I said. "My people understand that I plan to split my time. I'm going to hire more advisors to help run things while I'm away. And once the peace treaty happens, I believe that many people will return to their old homes in Quint and Kos. Not everyone, so I'll still need to look out for those who remain, but it will be more manageable. Hell, maybe I'll implement a parliament of my own."

"Whatever happens, we'll face the future together," he murmured.

"Together," I agreed.

We sealed the promise with a kiss just as the sun slipped below the horizon. I didn't know exactly what the future would bring, but Valentin and I would find out together.

EPILOGUE

Seven months after the first meeting between Chairwoman Soteras and Emperor Kos, the universe's two superpowers met one final time on CP57 to sign a binding peace treaty amid a great deal of pomp and circumstance.

Behind the scenes, both sides had worked feverishly to get everything ready. And for the past seven months, the tentative peace had held, despite a few close calls. The Rogue Coalition benefited from the new stability as well, and my people were once again in demand for mercenary work and shipping items between territories—legally, this time.

Mostly.

I watched from the group of Valentin's advisors as he and Daniella Soteras exchanged documents to sign. Luka stood behind and to the left of Valentin, and Charles was hidden nearby, out of the photos, but close enough to jump to his defense in an instant. Just like Imogen and Marian hovered somewhere behind me, twin shadows I was finally starting to get used to.

Once the papers were signed and the photos were taken,

Valentin and Daniella rose and shook hands. Valentin leaned in and murmured something to her and she nodded with a smile.

When Valentin's eyes immediately found mine, I was glad that Stella and Ari had convinced me to wear something nice.

Come meet the Chairwoman, Valentin linked to me.

You're lucky I like you, I grumbled. I had been perfectly happy remaining in the background, but if any photographers remained, I'd be news once again.

Something *else* I was starting to get used to.

I crossed the room, Imogen behind me. Daniella was in her early thirties and she'd been in charge of the Quint Confederacy for a few years. She was tall and curvy, with curly dark brown hair and deeply tanned skin. Whatever else she did, she spent a lot of time in the sun. Her dress was sapphire blue and tailored to emphasize her figure.

Valentin put a hand on my back and drew me close. "Chairwoman Daniella Soteras, meet Queen Samara Rani."

Daniella extended her hand with a smile. "It's lovely to meet you, Queen Rani. I've heard a lot about you."

I shook her hand. "It's nice to meet you, too, Chairwoman Soteras. I hope you intend to stick to the agreement."

Her eyebrows rose, then she inclined her head. "I am tired of the wars of our fathers. I am planning for a lasting peace." She slanted a fierce glance at Valentin. "Don't make me regret it."

He bowed slightly. "I am also tired of war. I look forward to a peaceful future."

She nodded, dipped her chin in a shallow nod, and made her farewells.

Once she was gone, I asked, "Do you think she means it?"

Valentin stared into the distance for a moment before nodding. "I think she does." He smiled at me. "I have a few more things to take care of here, then I need to pop back to Koan for a bit, but I'll meet you in Arx later."

I blinked at him in surprise. "I figured you're be busy all weekend. I could join you in Koan, if you want."

He shook his head. "It's your turn to get to stay home. And most everything can wait until Monday, but I want to check on Mother before I disappear. She had a cough this morning."

"Is she okay?" Marguerite Kos—Margie to her friends—had accepted my presence in her son's life with both warmth and joy. I'd expected the Dowager Empress to be cold and aloof, but Margie was exactly the opposite. If anything happened to her, Valentin would be devastated. I would be, too, honestly. She was the mom I'd never had.

"She let Junior examine her, after I talked her into it. It's just a cold. But I want to stop by and see her. And change out of this ridiculous getup."

Junior was Valentin's medical advisor. If he said she was fine, then she was fine. I let out a sigh of relief, then looked Valentin up and down. He *did* look a little silly in his full Kos regalia, with a braided rope on his shoulder, a chest full of medals, and a golden crown, but he also looked sexy. Of course, he looked sexy in about anything.

"Tell Margie I said hi, and I'll see you later," I said. "I love you."

Valentin pulled me close and kissed me. Flashes went off behind my eyelids. We'd be news once again. "I love you, too," he whispered.

———

As PROMISED, Valentin arrived at Arx late in the evening. I met him in the public hangar, where he had to land now because *Ardia* was in my private hangar. He was dressed in slacks and a gray sweater, as casual as he got outside of the bedroom.

Luka and Charles nodded at me from a distance.

"How's Margie?" I asked as soon as I was close enough.

"She's fine," he said. "I offered to stay and she all but pushed me out the door. It's just a mild cold. Junior gave her some medicine that will clear it up in a day or two."

Valentin lifted one of my hands and pressed a kiss to back of it. "I brought you a present," he murmured.

I glanced over his shoulder, confirming that *Korax*, his personal ship, sat on the landing pad. "It's not another ship, I hope."

He shook his head with a smile.

Nerves fluttered through my belly. "It's something small."

He nodded and sank to one knee, my left hand still clasped in his. "Samara, I love you. I want to spend my life with you, no matter what we have to do to make it happen. I want nothing more than your happiness, and I hope that I make you happy because you fill my life with joy. Will you marry me?"

He pulled a shiny ring out of his pocket and held it up, but it all became a blur as tears streamed down my face. "Yes!" I half-shouted, half-sobbed. "Of course I'll marry you. You're not getting away from me now." I futilely wiped at my face with my free hand. "I love you."

He handed me a handkerchief, then slid the ring on my finger. It fit perfectly. When I stared in awe, he grinned. "Ari and Stella might've helped with the sizing."

I dabbed at my eyes as he stood. "I had no idea they could be so sneaky." I laughed as another thought occurred to me. "And I suppose Sawya will get their invitation after all."

"How so?"

"Back when we were tracking Adams, Sawya told me that they wanted an invite to our wedding, even though we weren't even engaged at the time."

Understanding dawned on Valentin's face. "*That's* the invitation you wouldn't tell me about."

"I didn't want to scare you off."

Valentin pulled me close. "As if I would be so easily scared."

His lips covered mine. The kiss was a gentle exploration, an adoration, and a temptation, all rolled into one.

When he finally pulled away, happy tears shimmered on my lashes. I didn't know how I'd gotten so lucky, but I thanked the stars every day. I lifted my hand, admiring the ring once again. The deep red solitaire sparkled against the pale platinum band.

"If you don't like the stone, I'll get you something else."

"I love it," I told him honestly.

"Mom gave it to me. It's from her wedding set. She wanted you to have it."

My eyes widened. "You should've led with that."

"I didn't want to influence your decision."

I threw my arms around his neck and pressed my lips to his. "I love you," I murmured against his lips.

"I love you, too."

I was going to spend the rest of our lives showing him just how much.

EXCERPT FROM CHAOS REIGNING

**Read on for the first chapter in
Jessie Mihalik's latest romantic science fiction novel,
Chaos Reigning
Available now from Harper Voyager!**

CHAPTER ONE

The wineglass shattered in my hand, slicing deep into my palm and fingers. Red blood welled, but bitter disappointment overshadowed the physical pain.

Stupid, stupid girl. The silent words echoed in my father's voice.

I should not have checked my com at the party, but communication from my brother Benedict was scarce, and I couldn't resist. *Mistake.* Benedict's latest war update painted a bleak picture, and I'd stopped paying attention just long enough to break the glass.

I'd been doing *so well*, but there would be no hiding this, not with blood dripping down my arm. I glanced around. I'd stepped out into the garden, away from the rest of the party, but the twilight shadows were not deep enough for me to slip away entirely. Susan, my bodyguard, watched over me from the patio, and it was only thanks to the angle that she hadn't noticed the injury already.

There was nothing for it.

With a sigh, I tripped on the air and fell into the grass, landing with a yell. Glass shards sliced deeper and I didn't have to fake the next pained groan.

"Lady Catarina, are you all right?" Susan shouted, her voice full of concern. She was the first to notice, as expected, despite the distance between us. After Ferdinand's disappearance, House von Hasenberg family members were now assigned bodyguards at all times.

Footsteps approached, and I sat up, cradling my bloody hand. Susan gasped and called for a medic from the backup security vehicle outside. "I'm okay," I assured her, "but the wine-glass didn't survive."

She bent down to assess the injury. Her dark suit faded into the shadows, accentuating her pale skin and blond hair. Twenty-eight and happily married, she was one of my favorite bodyguards. She met my eyes, expression worried. "What happened?"

I gave her, and the growing crowd behind her, a bright, vapid smile. "I think I must've had too much of House Durand's excellent wine."

Twitters rose from the bystanders. No one was quite brave enough to insult me to my face—I was the daughter of a High House after all—but they weren't laughing *with* me, either.

Susan, who was used to my antics, didn't bat an eye, and that was somehow worse than the pitying looks from the crowd. I wanted to tell her that I wasn't this person, that I'd built this facade when I didn't know any better and now I was trapped.

But of course I couldn't.

So I smiled while the medic extracted the glass from my

hand and slathered it in regeneration gel. And I smiled as I moved through the crowd of vicious gossips who barely veiled their clever slights behind concerned looks and condescending advice.

At twenty-one, I was the youngest von Hasenberg heir. People thought that made me gullible, so I played into the narrative. I flitted from group to group, bubbly and shallow, more concerned with fashion and shopping than war and treachery. It was an exaggeration of my normal personality, but some days the mask was harder to wear than others.

Lately it had been harder still, especially when I could clearly hear the whispers that trailed in my wake.

None of them were kind.

It didn't help that I remained stuck here on Earth while all of my siblings went gallivanting off across the universe. They insisted on treating me like a child, never mind that I was an adult in my own right. I loved them to death, but they were smothering me.

Every day the thought of getting in my ship and pointing it at a distant planet grew more and more appealing. Only honor, duty, and love kept me earthbound. We'd all worried after Ada had left, and while her story had turned out for the best, I didn't want to put my brothers and sisters through another round of anxiety.

Not yet, not when everything was so unstable.

So I stayed at the party, because socializing was the one thing I was good at. I mingled, and laughed, and ignored the barbs. And if it all felt empty and hollow, I ignored that, too. House Durand was an ally, and we needed all the allies we could get while at war. I was here to strengthen that relationship.

It was all I could do.

For now.

———

Two days later, I felt like a spring that was wound too tight. My hand had healed, thanks to the regeneration gel, and I hadn't had any more accidents, but I couldn't settle. Enclosed in my private office, I paced and worried. I'd designed the space to be soothing, with pale green walls and antique wooden furniture, but right now it felt oppressive.

After months of careful planning, everything was finally coming together, with one tiny exception—I still had to tell my sister Bianca what I'd done. I'd scheduled breakfast with her, so at least I wouldn't have to carry this anxiety all day. Not that the rest of my schedule was any better. After Bianca, I had to face one of Mother's official House brunches.

One thing at a time.

I tucked away my restlessness and painted on the face I showed the outside world, then smoothed a hand down my pink-and-blue polka-dot dress. It flared around my knees and made me look young and carefree. My wardrobe tended toward bright colors as a distracting visual camouflage.

I checked my smile in the hallway mirror on my way out. There was too much tension around my eyes. I blinked and tried again. *Better.*

I didn't really look like a von Hasenberg. My four oldest siblings had all taken after our father, with strong features, ruddy skin, and light brown hair. Ada and I had taken after our mother, with more delicate features, golden skin, and dark brown hair. Ada had also inherited Mother's blue-gray eyes, but mine were a more common golden brown.

I joked that my five older siblings had used up all of the good genes, a joke that hit a little too close to home considering how sick I'd been as a child, but I liked the anonymity of not being immediately recognized as a member of my House.

My reflected smile turned wry. I was never anonymous, not really, but sometimes it was nice to pretend.

I continued down the short hallway to the living room. If my office was an oasis of calm, my living room was a riot of color. The walls were white, but large, colorful abstract prints adorned them. My furniture was all brightly hued. A lime green sofa, orange chair, and purple tables somehow formed a beautiful, cohesive design. The interior decorator I'd hired had earned every credit I'd paid her.

This was my public face, shown even to the few friends who were close enough to get to see the inside of my suite. We were all liars, to one degree or another.

Susan waited for me in the hallway outside, wearing her trademark dark suit, today paired with a pale pink shirt. "Going out, Lady Catarina?"

"I am heading to breakfast with Bianca, but I want to stop by a coffee shop on the way."

She inclined her head in agreement and silently fell in behind me. I liked her because she always instinctively seemed to know if I wanted to be left alone with my thoughts or if I wanted idle chatter to fill the silence.

We stepped outside and I let my gaze drift over the city. Serenity, the headquarters of the Royal Consortium and the only inhabited city on Earth, was just beginning to wake, bathed in the brilliant gold of early morning sunlight.

The city was laid out in a circle and each High House owned a quarter. The quarters were divided into sectors starting from the middle. The Royal Consortium government buildings were in the very center, colloquially called Sector Zero. The family residence for each quarter took up the entirety of Sector One. The other nine sectors contained shops, offices, residences, and all of the amenities found in a large city.

The closer the sector was to the center of the circle, the more expensive it was to live and work there. Also, the buildings closer to the middle tended to be shorter, driving up prices even more due to the lack of supply. It made for an interesting view as the city grew taller and taller in the distance. Sector Ten was almost entirely skyscrapers over a hundred stories tall.

I took a deep breath, closed my eyes, and let the warmth of the sun shrink my worries back into manageable sizes. There were *some* benefits to being stuck on a planet.

And being able to go outside was a major one. I spent a lot of time outdoors because my earliest memories were of the white walls and locked windows of a medical center. As a child, I'd spent hours staring wistfully out of the small window in my room. I'd been sickly, despite the nanobots in my blood that were supposed to keep me well, and I still carried side effects from my numerous treatments.

I masked the side effects, like I masked my true personality, but these secrets were much more important to keep.

I opened my eyes with a sigh. Secrets and lies seemed to be all I dealt in these days. It was exhausting.

Susan and I entered the House transport, and I set the destination for Bianca's favorite coffee shop. The transport lifted into the air with the familiar, soothing thrum of the engine.

My mind drifted and landed on the exact thing it shouldn't: the unknown man at the club last night. My best friend, Ying Yamado, had persuaded me to go out with her, and I'd caught sight of him as soon as we walked in the door.

A stranger was hardly unusual, but this man had been captivating. Powerfully built and radiating quiet confidence, he was likely a soldier on leave. He wasn't my usual type, but I'd been drawn to him like a moth to flame. I'd caught sight of him a few times, but before I'd worked up the courage to go say hello, he'd vanished.

And now my mind was stuck on him.

I acknowledged the attraction and then let the thought go. He wasn't for me, not even for a night. It took a while, but I let him drift from my thoughts and focused on centering myself for the day to come.

By the time we landed, I felt calmer. It wouldn't last, but I'd take what I could get.

———

The small coffee shop in Sector Eight of the von Hasenberg quarter bustled with customers, but the line moved quickly. I was meeting Bianca for breakfast at her apartment, but I wanted to bring her something she loved, and this shop served her favorite coffee. And if it helped to soften her up for the news to come, that wouldn't be a bad thing, either.

After securing our coffees, Susan and I returned to the transport and lifted off, trailed by an additional House von Hasenberg security transport—an unfortunately common sight now.

Ian Bishop was the director of House security, and between the attack on Ferdinand and his relationship with Bianca, he'd become even more overprotective, especially once Father kicked Bianca out of her suite in the main house. She and Ian shared a penthouse a block away from the main House von Hasenberg complex, but you'd think she lived deep in a war zone from the way Ian worried.

It was kind of adorable, unless you wanted to walk to see your older sister—then it was just annoying. In the past few weeks, Director Bishop had made a security team shadow me even for the short walk between the main house and their apartment, so I wasn't surprised that one followed us now.

Bianca's penthouse spanned the entire top floor and would have cost a fortune if our House didn't own the property.

Ten stories tall and situated on the corner of the block, the building was made of smooth gray stone. It had a view of the House von Hasenberg gardens as well as the ornate stone main house itself. Personally, I thought Father let her have the location because he wanted her to be able to see what she was missing.

I didn't think it had worked because in the last two months she'd been as happy as I'd ever seen her, even after the forced move.

The penthouse had its own private entrance from the street. I swiped the identity chip in my right arm over the reader and the entry door popped open. Bianca had always given her siblings free access to her suite, and that practice carried over here, too.

The entryway opened into a tiny lobby with a single elevator and a set of stairs behind a locked door. On the far side of the elevator, another door opened to an office and lounge for visiting bodyguards. While Bianca might not mind her siblings running roughshod over her privacy, that same attitude did not extend to our guards. Both the elevator and stairs opened only here and in the penthouse, so having the guard wait at ground level had been deemed acceptable.

It didn't hurt that the person making the rules was deeply in love with my sister and would do anything to make her happy.

The elevator required another identity check. I took the few seconds alone to check my smile in the reflective elevator doors. I didn't usually hide my true feelings from my siblings, but I didn't want Bianca to worry about me, not when there were so many other, more important, things to worry about.

Bianca's living room was a study in retro-industrial looks. Silver chain link curtains spanned the large windows and glittered in the sun. The furniture was sleek and black. Exposed ductwork in the high ceilings added additional visual interest, and a single vivid painting saved the room from being utterly colorless.

The air was rich with the smell of cinnamon and sugar, but my sister was conspicuously absent. "Bee?" I called.

"We're in the kitchen!" she yelled back.

My smile slipped at the *we*. I didn't know anyone else was joining us for breakfast, but if Bianca was yelling like that, then it couldn't be anyone too important. Maybe our oldest sister Hannah was back on Earth. She had taken some much-needed time away, but I hadn't expected her back for another month or two.

The living room and dining room were one large, open space, but the kitchen was tucked away out of sight. Bianca liked to cook and her vast kitchen reflected that. It had the full range of high-end appliances as well as two oversize synthesizers.

I took in the scene at a glance. An unknown man and woman sat at the bar while Bianca bustled around. My sister had on a casual outfit and *flats*. The only time Bianca went without towering heels was around close friends and family. So who were these two and why had I never met them before? They turned my way, and I froze.

It was the man from the club.

I blinked and switched into public mode, mind racing. *What was he doing here?* I had a feeling that the pause hadn't gone unnoticed by either of them as they tracked my progress into the room.

The woman had pale ivory skin, strawberry blond hair, and a lean build. Her eyes were sharp and neutral. Not unfriendly, more like undecided. The man had light brown skin, dark hair, and heavy musculature. His square jaw had a few days of dark stubble adorning it. His features were too strong for traditional beauty, but he was damn attractive all the same. His expression was even more guarded than the woman's.

He did not seem to recognize me. That should have brought relief, but I felt a vague sense of disappointment instead.

Both of them wore close-fitting black shirts. I'd bet utility pants and boots hid behind the bar. Not Consortium types, then. Were they Ada's friends from Sedition?

I realized I'd been staring for a beat too long and turned to my sister with a wide smile. "Bianca, you didn't tell me you had visitors," I admonished. "I would've rescheduled! And I apologize, but since I didn't know you had guests, I only brought coffee for you."

She accepted the coffee with a hug and a grateful smile. "These aren't guests, these are my friends Alexander Sterling and Aoife Delaney." She pronounced the woman's name *EE-fa*. "They helped me rescue Ferdinand. I wanted you to meet them."

I turned back to them. "Thank you so much for your help," I said sincerely. I'd gotten only the barest of details out of Bianca about how she'd found Ferdinand and gotten him out, but based on the introduction, I bet these two were a big part of it. We owed them a great deal.

The woman waved off my words. "Your sister more than paid us," she said. Her voice was pleasant, with just a hint of a lilt. She was likely lower to middle class from one of the more isolated planets where Universal Standard wasn't taught as rigidly.

Bianca put a tray of warm sticky buns on the small table in the kitchen's breakfast nook. "Shall we talk over food?" she asked a little too brightly.

I narrowed my eyes at her. What was she plotting?

While Bianca could have easily ordered food from the synthesizer, she preferred cooking. And, truth be told, synthesized food had nothing on Bianca's cooking, so I was always delighted to eat at her table. Today she didn't disappoint. The informal kitchen table was laden with four different kinds of pastries, all homemade, as well as bacon, eggs, and roasted potatoes.

The round table seated four. I sat next to Bianca. Alexander took the seat across from me and Aoife sat on my left. If anyone else noticed the tension in the air, they didn't show it. I was generally very good at reading people, but Alexander gave me nothing other than that he had good manners. I had to force myself not to stare at him.

"How goes the investigation?" Bianca asked.

My gaze cut to hers, but I couldn't tell what she was doing. "I don't want to bore your guests," I demurred. Why would she bring up House business in front of strangers? I was looking into Ferdinand's kidnapping. Both Hannah's husband, Pierre, and House James were involved, and that wasn't information we wanted shared.

"Not guests," she reminded me, "*friends*. And they are here to help."

I kept the shock and suspicion off my face. "Help how?"

"From what I've seen, you've wrapped up everything you can do here. What is your next step?"

While Bianca had been chasing after Ferdinand, I'd muscled my way into the investigation here on Earth, and I'd refused to give it up once she returned. Bianca had reluctantly agreed to let me help, but only if we worked together.

No one trusted me to be able to do anything on my own.

We had found the ties between Pierre and House James, but hadn't been able to tie House James to any of the other Houses or the Syndicate, despite Bianca's uncanny ability to gather intelligence. Either House James was acting alone or they were being very, very careful.

But so was I.

Over the last two months, I'd slowly expanded my circle of friends to include Lynn Segura and Chloe Patel, the two young women who had been caught talking shit about Bianca. Lynn was a genuine delight. Chloe was *not*. But both of them were friends with Stephanie James, youngest daughter of House James.

And every year, Stephanie James hosted a summer retreat at House James's estate outside Honorius. It was part vacation and part informal networking event, but mostly it was a chance to get out of Serenity and have some fun away from censorious eyes. It also coincided with the stunning annual Bouman meteor shower.

When guests weren't busy trying to steal kisses while watching space rocks burn up in the atmosphere, Honorius had some of the best haute couture shopping in the 'verse. House James also offered an assortment of entertainments on their sprawling estate, including an excellent hover bike rally-cross racecourse.

Invitations were highly coveted in Stephanie's circle of friends and acquaintances, and this year Chloe was finally old enough to help her best friend host—a task she had taken up with gusto.

Based solely on our brief friendship, Chloe had been cheeky enough to invite me, and through me, Ying Yamado, the daughter of High House Yamado. She was aiming high, which is exactly what I had expected. If even one of us accepted, it would be a major coup for her.

I had let her stew for two days before accepting, and then I'd talked Ying into accepting, too. But now I had to break the news to my overprotective older sister. In front of *friends*.

"I'm attending Stephanie James's house party in two days. I will be gone for at least two weeks."

Bianca smiled, which immediately put me on guard. That was not the reaction I'd expected. "That's perfect," she said.

Concern whispered through me—something odd was going on. "I thought you'd be against it," I said, fishing.

Bianca's smile softened just a tiny bit. "I don't love sending you into danger, Cat, you know that, but we need information, and right now, you're the one best positioned to get it."

I glanced at our silent dining companions. They were both pretending to focus on their food, but I caught Alexander's gaze. His eyes were a rich, warm brown. Despite his guarded expression, he had kind eyes, not what I would expect from a man with his build. Once again, I was struck by the fact that he looked like a soldier—or a bodyguard.

And then, like a light blinking on, suspicion hardened into certainty. I turned back to my sister. "Bianca," I said slowly, "why are Ms. Delaney and Mr. Sterling here?"

Bianca's smile never faltered. If anything, it got brighter. I was not going to like whatever came out of her mouth next.

She proved me right when she said, "Aoife is going to be your bodyguard while you're in Honorius."

"I already have a guard," I reminded her. "Several, actually."

"None like me," Aoife said without an ounce of humility *or* arrogance. It was less a boast and more a statement of fact, one I was inclined to believe based on nothing more than her attitude and confidence.

I might be the most sheltered of my siblings, but I was still a von Hasenberg. I'd grown up around—and trained with—all types of people until the side effects of my childhood became too difficult to hide. Aoife had the calm self-assurance of someone who knew that she could take anyone in the room and come out ahead.

I briefly wondered how she would fare against *me*.

It was a silly thought because I'd given up real fighting long ago—it was too dangerous for me. But that didn't mean I was going to roll over. "That may be true, but I've worked with my current guards for years. I know and trust them." I also understood how they thought and how they might be influenced.

Aoife's flawless composure was impossible to read, but I smiled apologetically at her. She inclined her head slightly, seemingly not offended.

My eyes snagged on Alexander. For such a big man, he had a way of fading into the background that was almost uncanny. If not for my humming awareness of him, I might've overlooked him completely.

"And you?" I asked him directly. "Why are you here? Are you Ms. Delaney's partner?" I glanced between them. "Or husband?"

A slow smile broke over his face and he chuckled quietly. My breath caught. He was utterly captivating when he smiled and for the first time I envied the beautiful woman next to me.

I felt his gaze like a physical weight and fought the prickling awareness trickling through my system. He focused on me intently, but I'd bet half my fortune that he also remained aware of everything else happening in the room and could react in a heartbeat.

What would it take to capture *all* of his attention?

I shoved the question away. He wasn't for me. Someday, I would marry for the good of the House, and until then, I preferred my men more manageable.

"We are partners," he said. His voice was low and delicious, a velvet rumble I felt in my chest. He had no discernible accent.

Partners could mean anything from business partners to romantic partners. Without knowing which, I had to stop mentally ogling him. I didn't pursue taken men.

I turned my attention back to Bianca. Mischief flittered through her expression before she smoothed it away. "Alex is here for you."

I forced myself not to react to the tiny thrill of pleasure I felt at the words. I frowned at her, not liking where this was going. "What do you mean?"

"He's going with you to Honorius as your plus one."

Buy *Chaos Reigning* today!

ABOUT THE AUTHOR

Jessie Mihalik has a degree in Computer Science and a love of all things geeky. A software engineer by trade, Jessie now writes full time from her home in Texas. When she's not writing, she can be found playing co-op video games with her husband, trying out new board games, or reading books pulled from her overflowing bookshelves.

CONNECT WITH JESSIE:

www.jessiemihalik.com
Twitter: @jessiemihalik
Facebook: /JessMihalik
Instagram: @jessmihalik
Want all of the latest book news, info, and snippets delivered straight to your inbox? Sign up for Jessie's newsletter! https://www.jessiemihalik.com/newsletter/